HAUNTED

Center Point
Large Print

Also by Kay Hooper and available from
Center Point Large Print:

Bishop/Special Crimes Unit Novels
  Haven
  Hostage
  Haunted

The Bishop Files
  The First Prophet

**This Large Print Book carries the
Seal of Approval of N.A.V.H.**

HAUNTED

KAY
HOOPER

CENTER POINT LARGE PRINT
THORNDIKE, MAINE

This Center Point Large Print edition is published
in the year 2014 by arrangement with
The Berkley Publishing Group,
a member of Penguin Group (USA) LLC,
a Penguin Random House Company.

The text of this Large Print edition is unabridged.
In other aspects, this book may vary from the original edition.
Printed in the United States of America on permanent paper.
Set in 16-point Times New Roman type.

ISBN: 978-1-62899-237-3

Library of Congress Cataloging-in-Publication Data

Hooper, Kay.
Haunted / Kay Hooper. — Center Point Large Print edition.
pages ; cm
Summary: "Trinity Nichols, Deacon James, and an odd band of FBI
agents must work together to solve a series of disturbances so incredible
that Trinity, and the town of Sociable, Georgia, will be changed
forever"—Provided by publisher.
ISBN 978-1-62899-237-3 (library binding : alk. paper)
1. Murder—Investigation—Georgia—Fiction.
2. Bishop, Noah (Fictitious character)—Fiction.
3. Government investigators—Fiction. 4. Large type books.
5. Paranormal fiction. I. Title.
PS3558.O587H34 2014b
813′.54—dc23
2014025777

This novel is dedicated to all the unsung
heroes who work tirelessly in animal rescue,
helping the homeless and helpless,
the injured, the neglected, abandoned,
and abused, giving voice to those who
cannot speak for themselves.

And in memory of all the
shelter animals who, unlike Braden,
never got their second chance.

AUTHOR'S NOTE

Once again, and at the request of many readers, I have chosen to place this note at the beginning of the book rather than after the story, so as to better inform you of the additional material I am providing for both new readers and those who have been with the series from the beginning. You'll find some brief character bios, as well as standard SCU definitions of various psychic abilities, at the end of the book, plus something new, a Special Crimes Unit timeline, information that will hopefully enhance your enjoyment of this story and of the series.

You'll also find a second Author's Note on a subject I care about deeply, which I hope you'll take the time to read. In the meantime, I hope you enjoy *Haunted*.

PROLOGUE

December 12

The face in the mirror was strange to him, and not only because it was streaked with blood. The blood was the least disconcerting thing he saw, and some deeply buried instinct told him he should have worried a lot more about both the blood and his acceptance of it.

But he didn't.

It was the strange face that worried him. It wasn't always strange, of course. Sometimes he looked in the mirror and saw familiar features, eyes he knew, a smile that was pleasant and crooked and his own, with no blood marring anything he saw. On those days, he was fine. On those days, he went about the business of living and felt normal.

But on days like this . . .

He stared for long minutes at that alien face, the blood streaking it . . . baffled and a little frightened.

More than a little. Because even though he didn't think much about the blood, it was *there*. And yet, the blood almost always disappeared when he closed his eyes and counted to ten and looked again.

Almost always.

But when it didn't disappear, when he had to splash water on his face and even use soap to scrub away the red stains, he had the gnawing certainty that he should be worried about the blood, because it was a sign that even though he couldn't remember what it was, he had done Something Bad.

Something Really Bad.

There were things he needed to remember, and every time he saw that face in the mirror, every time it was bloody and alien to him, he was aware of those unremembered things hovering in the shadows of his mind.

Desires. No . . . hungers. Needs.

Terrifying needs.

On those days, he called in sick and sat in his tiny apartment, furnished in Early Salvation Army, the worn shades drawn, the ancient TV that still had snowy channels on but muted, the sounds of traffic outside a sort of background noise that was unimportant.

On those days, he sat in the dark and listened to the voices telling him what he had to do. They were very clear, those voices. Very strong. Very sure.

And, gradually, without his even becoming aware of it, the fear faded away to nothing because he wasn't alone anymore. The voices were his friends. The voices understood him. The voices told him what he had to do.

As the days and weeks passed, he was eventually fired for calling in sick too many times so he could be alone in the dark listening to his voices, but by then it hardly mattered. He packed up his meager possessions in his worn duffle bag, left the old apartment building, and set out on foot because he didn't own a car.

There was a journey he had to make. And along the way, he had things to . . . understand. Things to . . . practice. And things to plan.

Still, he wasn't certain that he was doing the right thing. Not until his path took him higher into the mountains to one of the hiking trails along the Blue Ridge. Once he set foot upon those old, old trails, he felt at home.

And he knew where he was going.

South.

He stopped at one of those places that usually sprang up near the entrances to hiking trails and offered for sale just about anything one would need to hike the trails and paths woven all through the old mountains, and spent most of his money buying the few things he would need.

He wasn't worried about money. The Lord would provide.

There was a crowd of hikers about, stocking up for hikes or taking a break because their journey paused here, or began here. A number of people spoke to him, and he replied politely without making any effort to engage them in conversation.

Several invited him to join their groups, but virtually all of them were headed north, and that wasn't where he was being drawn. So he declined, politely, and went on his way before it got too late.

He was only a little surprised to realize there was a map in his head, that all this was familiar ground. Part of him remembered it very well—and yet to another part of him, it was an alien landscape.

He traveled only about half a mile before darkness began to fall, and he took the time to set up his little tent and make camp, the skills again both familiar and strange.

He thought about that as he lay in his sleeping bag in the darkness, listening to the night. He thought about the skills that felt familiar—and the names in his head.

There were, he knew, people who had to pay.

That was something he was certain he knew how to do.

Get justice.

Be the sword hand of God.

When he realized that, all his confusion and uncertainty melted away.

And the plan began to take shape.

ONE

January 23

Melanie James shook her head and said to one of her best friends, "See, I think you stack the deck when you're dealing out the cards."

"It's tarot, not poker," Toby Gilmore objected. "Why would I stack the cards?"

"To give me the future you want me to have, of course."

Toby sighed and looked at the other four people at their large table in the Friday-night-busy restaurant. "Help me out here, will you?"

Annabel Hunter shook her head solemnly. "Not me. I don't care if you stack the deck; last week you told me I'd find that ring I lost, and I did the very next day."

Xander Roth, dark eyes dancing, said to Melanie, "I'm with you. She cheats. I wasted my money on those lottery tickets."

"I *warned* you about that," Toby told him. "It's cheating, and the universe doesn't like that. Picking lottery tickets or winners in a horse race or anything like that is just not what tarot is for."

"Then what *is* it for?" Scott Abernathy asked. "If the point is to see the future—"

"That isn't the point. Always. And even when

11

it is, the future is always fluid, I keep telling you that. You don't plan your life with tarot, you just . . . let it guide you sometimes."

Caleb Lee, the only one at the table not drinking wine or beer, said, "Toby is right; the cards are only tools to help you focus. When you're centered and calm, then maybe the cards will tell you something helpful. Or maybe not."

Scott rolled his eyes. "Yeah, yeah. Meditate and concentrate and all good things will come to you. We've heard the spiel, Caleb. Again and again."

Caleb didn't appear at all dismayed by the sarcasm. Which didn't surprise anyone at the table, since he was virtually never dismayed. By anything.

Toby said, "Listen, I didn't mean to start a fight or anything. It's just that I thought reading for Melanie might be a good thing." She kept her gaze on her friend as she shuffled the cards, smiling. She didn't look at Scott at all.

Melanie said dryly, "You're about as subtle as neon, Toby. Stop trying to give me the happily-ever-after, especially with Scott." Even to her own ears, that last sentence had the air of flinty finality.

"Hey," Scott said, "I thought the group rule was no rehashing over relationships, especially at dinner."

Xander said, "Well, you *will* keep dating all our female friends, and then breaking up with them or pushing them to break up with you.

God knows why they keep accepting you, but—"

Annabel, ever the peacemaker, said, "Can we please not talk about this? Scott and Melanie had a little fight, and the fact that we *all* know about it just underlines one of the perils of living in a small town. They deserve their privacy, and besides, it really is none of our business."

Melanie sipped her wine, trying not to sigh out loud. They'd grown up together, her friends, and at times like this it really showed. She would have preferred her relationship with Scott—not exactly in the distant past—to remain between the two of them, but she had lived in Sociable for nearly three years now, and if she'd learned nothing else, it was that there weren't many secrets.

Especially among a group of friends who had played together in the sandbox thirty-odd years ago.

"It wasn't a *little* fight," Scott said, mildly enough but with a glitter Melanie recognized in his eyes. Despite his earlier words, he was perfectly willing to pick a fight in order to rehash not only that final battle but all the others in their brief but tempestuous relationship.

She spoke up before he could enlighten the others about whatever they might not already know, saying firmly, "But it was a *private* fight. Can we keep it that way, please?"

"Now, see," Xander said, "that's just going to make it worse. Because we'll all be imagining.

And whatever we're imagining is bound to be worse than the truth."

"Don't you have satellite TV to entertain you?" Melanie asked him, rather sharply this time.

"Yes, but it's not nearly as much fun." Xander was a good guy, most of the time, but he did have a streak of mischief in his nature that could be just this side of cruel, Melanie had decided. "I mean, usually it's Scott's conquests who get dumped; something he's generally not as obviously pissed off about as he is right now."

"You're a menace," Melanie told him.

"Just calling 'em as I see 'em," he retorted.

Scott said to Melanie, "Is that what you've been telling everybody, that you dumped me?"

"I," Melanie said evenly, "have not been discussing my private relationships. It's a preference I have. Not unlike the preference to avoid discussions like this one in crowded restaurants."

"Ouch," Xander murmured.

"I don't get dumped," Scott said, a bit louder than he'd intended.

Or not.

"Fine," Melanie said, "you dumped me. Happy?" The matter was clearly so unimportant to her that it caused Scott to flush a rather ugly shade of red.

"I don't think he's happy," Xander noted helpfully.

With uncharacteristic fierceness, Annabel said, "Scott, can you please pack away your ego and just let it go? You were no more serious about Melanie than you were about Toby—or about Trinity. Notches on your belt—"

"Speaking as one of the notches, I should probably resent that. But what the hell." Trinity Nichols joined the others, sliding in next to Annabel in the booth seating that enabled them all to fit around the big table. "Who knows—we all may hang in the Smithsonian one day, in the wing of Famous Conquests."

Toby noted Scott's lingering flush and wondered in satisfaction if he was finally catching on to the fact that the women who passed through his life and fleetingly shared his bed did so far more often on their terms than on his. Whatever he thought otherwise.

Xander laughed, but reached across the table to offer Trinity wine for the empty glass their attentive waiter had placed before her. "Off duty?" he asked.

"Yeah. And I could use a drink."

Xander poured her wine but was unusually serious when he asked, "Trouble?"

"Not local." She shook her head, as usual a bit hesitant to share the burdens of being sheriff of Crystal County with her childhood friends, even though the lifelong habit of sharing—even sharing Scott, as it turned out—was difficult to break. "It's just that usually this time of year, the dead of winter, we don't get reports of missing hikers along the Blue Ridge. That's rough country, and in winter fairly miserable even this far south. Hikers are usually spring to fall."

Toby lifted a brow at her friend. "You said not local?"

"No, it isn't. Or—they aren't, rather. Four young women reported missing from the general area of western North Carolina to just north of us. That's a fairly small span of the Blue Ridge, even though it's thousands of acres, and a little too close to home for my peace of mind."

"All hikers?" Caleb asked.

"In two cases, it seems certain they are—or were. Hiking with friends, supposedly just a day's outing during that warm spell we had around Christmas, so not that unusual; in a rough winter, people want to get out when the weather's unexpectedly good. Except that according to their friends, they were there one moment and gone the next."

"All four went missing, then?" Scott asked, making a clear effort to be casual.

"First two, just after Christmas, on the twenty-seventh. The latest two sometime between yesterday and today."

"Both today? I mean, were they together?"

Trinity sipped her wine and nodded. "Apparently together when they went missing, but no witnesses. Still far enough north that the search is being concentrated miles away, with some very

16

rough terrain between here and there. But these latest two . . . Not really hikers, or so it seems. They were together, on their way home from a ski trip, and stopped to pull their car off on one of the lookout points, apparently to take in the view. And the state police found the car today, this afternoon—two days after family members insisted they had left the ski lodge forty miles away and headed for home.

"They had no supplies except a couple of bottles of water and a few granola bars. Neither was even wearing hiking boots, and all the warm clothing they had taken to ski in was still packed in their luggage. According to the checkout desk at the lodge, when they left there, they weren't really dressed for overnight in the mountains."

"Dumb," Scott said.

"Maybe they found shelter," Annabel suggested, hope in her voice.

Sheriff Trinity Nichols swirled the wine in her glass and watched as it caught the light. "Maybe. Except they weren't supposed to be there to hike, so why get very far from the car at all? A report came in just as I was leaving the office. Search dogs found a shoe belonging to one of the girls. About five hundred yards from the lookout, and heading straight up a mountain. No footprints or other signs the girls were in the area. And as far as the dogs were concerned, the trail ended there."

Sociable, Georgia, was a small town by most any standards, boasting no more than five thousand or so permanent residents; during the tourist season a few thousand more passed through or even stayed awhile, drawn by spectacular scenery, friendly residents, and a number of shops offering stunning handwoven textiles and other locally handcrafted items.

Tourists passing through invariably left with a good opinion of the town and its residents.

Sheriff Trinity Nichols, on the other hand, not only had to deal with the usual practical and political irritants endemic even in small and friendly towns but had also grown up here— and knew the people better than many of them either liked or would have wanted to admit.

Such as Sociable's mayor, who suffered under the burden of having the surname of Fish. It had not made his childhood particularly happy and had proven bothersome to his adulthood as well.

There was just no way to make *Elect Dale Fish Mayor!* look good on a campaign poster, he had discovered. And he'd probably always wonder in his secret heart if he would have won if he hadn't run unopposed.

"It's *vandalism,* Trinity. And you're not going to do anything about it?"

She wanted to reply that she was in her office on a Saturday, her day off, in order to respond to his summons—in other words taking his concerns seriously—but instead kept her tone businesslike.

"What do you want me to do, Dale? I'll replace the sign, but if you believe taking away a NO TRESPASSING sign with a ghost drawn on it is going to keep the kids away from the church and parsonage, you can think again. I've already replaced that sign three times—just since Halloween."

"We need a fence around the place," he fretted.

"Well, that's more your bailiwick than mine," she reminded him. "Talk to the commissioners. But I'm betting they'll balk."

"Why?"

"A fence around a church. Think about it."

It was clear he hadn't until just then, and he slumped in the visitor's chair in front of her desk. "Dammit."

"Why worry about it at all, Dale? No actual damage has been done to the property. In fact, from what I'm hearing, the kids dare each other to touch the front door and then haul ass, running halfway down to Main Street before they stop. It's just to prove to each other how brave they are."

"I just don't like it. That might be what they're doing now, but no more than a year before you became sheriff, a team of those ghost hunters decided to stay the night in the parsonage, and even if nobody knows what happened, they were gone by daylight."

"Leaving the place undamaged, even if the front door was standing wide open. I read the report. And whatever did or didn't happen didn't end up on TV or YouTube, for which we can be grateful. So?"

"So how long will it be before some of the older kids dare each other to spend the night in the church or parsonage?"

"Don't hold your breath. It's just the younger kids trying to prove they aren't afraid of ghosts. The older ones are way too caught up in teenage stuff to worry about whether a local landmark is haunted. Though I imagine the preacher's story gets told around the occasional fireplace or campfire."

"I wish you wouldn't be so cavalier about it," the mayor complained. "It was a tragedy, what happened up there."

"Yes, I know. But it also happened a decade ago, and I'm being practical, or trying to. Dale, what is it you hope to accomplish? The Baylor sisters own the parsonage, and if they want to allow visitors—ghost hunting or otherwise—it's their business. As for the church, it's a respected historical landmark, kept in good repair, and hasn't been vandalized in my memory. So?"

Mayor Fish rubbed the back of his neck, clearly uncomfortable.

Trinity eyed him. "Come on, spit it out. What's really bugging you about the church?"

20

"I've just . . . heard things."

"For instance?"

"At least two people I know aren't imaginative have told me they saw the stained-glass windows of the church glowing in the middle of the night. A flickering glow, as if a fire burned inside."

"And they didn't call the fire department?"

"It wasn't that kind of light. I mean, they were sure the church wasn't on fire."

"And they were close enough to be sure?"

He sighed impatiently. "With binoculars, yeah, they were sure."

"And didn't see anything else suspicious? Through those binoculars?"

He flushed. "No. They didn't see anyone hanging around the place, or an unfamiliar vehicle, or anything like that. It was days ago, and, yes, the church is still standing. I drove up there yesterday to make sure there was no damage —which is when I saw the NO TRESPASSING sign defaced."

"Okay, okay." She frowned at him. It was sometimes difficult to take Mayor Fish seriously because he was a fretful man by nature and tended to fret about minor things, but Trinity had learned to read him well enough, she thought, to know that he was seriously bothered.

And not telling her everything.

"Look, I'll check it out," she told him. "I'll go up there and make sure all is well. Talk to the sisters and find out if anything odd has happened at the parsonage. Look for signs of trespassers past the age of twelve, and make sure the church is locked up tight. How's that?"

"All I can hope for, I guess." He clearly realized that hadn't been either the most gracious or the most professional response, and he cleared his throat as he rose to his feet. "Thanks, Trinity, I appreciate it."

"No problem."

She gazed after him for a long moment, then looked down at the black dog who had been lying silent and motionless on his bed behind her desk. "Come on, boy," she said, rising. "Let's go see if we can figure out what has Dale so worried."

"No trouble to speak of, Sheriff," Edith Baylor said, her round face placid as always. "Haven't seen anybody poking about the church or grave-yard, and no sign the parsonage has been disturbed."

"Are you and Lana in the parsonage much this time of year?" Trinity asked, referring to the other Baylor sister, now a widowed Lana Price; the two sisters did not live together, and Lana, according to her sister, was out at the mall near the highway, shopping.

"Oh, we go in with the cleaning crew every other week," Edith replied comfortably. "Janet and her girls don't really like being in the house without us. Same thing with the church, really. We don't mind, Lana and me. Even though the church belongs to the town, it was Baylor land for generations, so we feel a duty to make sure everything is kept as it should be."

"No more ghost-hunting crews asking to stay overnight?"

Edith smiled. "No, and only two groups came through back in the summer. I gathered from their disappointed faces that they didn't find anything of interest."

"Did you expect them to?" Trinity asked curiously.

"Not really," Edith confessed. "They keep coming back year after year, trying to find ghosts or some evidence of the supernatural, but all their little gadgets never show anything unusual."

Trinity had the odd notion that whatever the ghost hunter's "gadgets" had failed to show, Edith Baylor knew very well that the old parsonage was haunted—and was not the least bit disturbed by it.

And Trinity wasn't quite sure how *she* felt about that.

"Okay," she said finally. "I had a report that someone saw lights coming from inside the church the other night. Know anything about that?"

"Afraid not, Sheriff. I can't see either the church or the parsonage from here, obviously, and I seldom go out walking at night, especially this time of year."

They were standing on the front porch of Edith's small cottage-style house just a few streets back of Main, and Trinity knew without looking that neither the church nor the parsonage was visible from this point.

"Except for the steeple, of course," Edith added. "You can see that from just about anywhere in town."

That was true enough, and something that had always bothered Trinity just a bit. Her father had told her that they'd built the church up high, to watch over the town, but if they had expected any special protectiveness, that isn't what they'd gotten.

"Sheriff, would you like a cup of coffee? Tea?"

"Oh, no, thank you, Miss Edith." Trinity realized guiltily that she'd kept the older woman standing on her porch for some time now in the chilly January air and hastily apologized. "I'm sorry to keep you so long. Just wanted to check in and let you know I'm going to drive up to the church and parsonage and take a look around. Just to make sure everything's okay up there."

Edith Baylor nodded, still placid. "Probably just as well you're checking. I haven't been up there since the cleaning crew was, and that'll be two weeks on Monday. You know where the key is; if you want to go inside, feel free. I'll give Lana a call on her cell—if she remembered to take it with her—and tell her you'll be up there."

Trinity had been about to turn away. "You think she'll object?"

"Oh, no, of course not, Sheriff. She mentioned back last summer that we should probably invest in some kind of security system in the parsonage. But it didn't make any sense to me, not when we've never even had a window broken."

Which, now that Trinity thought about it, was a bit odd in and of itself, considering how the kids in town viewed both the church and the parsonage.

"Here you go, Sheriff." Miss Edith reached into the pocket of her apron—she wore one always except in church—and produced what looked like a bone-shaped cookie. "For Braden."

Trinity knew her dog was visible sitting in the front seat of her Jeep only a few yards away, but she wondered just when the elderly lady had acquired the dog treat to give to him. When she had seen the Jeep pull into her driveway? Then again, perhaps her capacious apron pockets held all kinds of treats.

"Thank you," she murmured.

"My pleasure. You have a good weekend, Sheriff."

"You, too." Trinity took a couple of steps back, then turned and retreated to her Jeep.

As soon as she was inside, she offered the treat

to her dog. "With Miss Edith's compliments. You want it now or later?"

Braden sniffed and made a soft huffing sound Trinity recognized. "Later, then," she said, dropping it into one of the cup holders in the Jeep's console.

Very shortly, she had backed out of the cottage driveway and was driving along one of what the locals referred to as cross streets that ran parallel to Main Street, the lowermost street in Sociable. The rest of the town proper climbed a mountain, literally; there were half a dozen streets that climbed straight up from Main, most reaching or nearly reaching the topmost cross street in front of the church, and a good dozen cross streets connecting most of them.

Trinity turned her Jeep and started up the mountain, catching a glimpse of the white steeple rising high above Sociable; it was indeed visible from nearly any vantage point in the town, though the church itself had long ago become hidden by overgrown shrubbery planted rather inexplicably all the way across its front and the graveyard beside it as well.

Her radio crackled suddenly. "Sheriff?"

She reached for the handset, using the one in the Jeep both because it was more reliable and because she hadn't bothered to wear any part of her normal uniform except for her gun.

"Yeah, Sadie?"

"You asked to be notified if any more information came out about those lost hikers?"

"There's news?"

"Not good, I'm afraid." Sadie wasn't really accustomed to dealing with violent subjects in a town like Sociable, so her shock was both obvious and entirely natural, even though she was clearly doing her best to sound professional. "Report is, a few hours ago they found the bodies of the first two girls miles south of where they disappeared. I thought they said more than seventy-five miles, but could that be right?"

Trinity said, "It would be an unusually large search area, even after weeks of searching. Unless they got a tip where to look."

"Maybe that was it. Anyway, they . . . thought at first a bear had gotten to them, but . . . They said it was a knife, and a sharp one. Cut them all up, those poor girls."

Trinity kept her own tone detached with an effort. "Raped?"

"No, and while I say that's at least one thing they didn't have to endure, it seems the FBI people they have on scene are saying it's significant there was no sexual assault."

"They say why?"

"Not that I've heard. You want me to call and ask?"

"No. No, I'll do that myself. Anything else, Sadie?"

"Just a general warning to law enforcement to be on the lookout—though for who or what they don't really say. Anybody suspicious, I guess. Asking that we spread the warning that nobody needs to be hiking the southern Blue Ridge right now. And that whoever murdered those girls might be heading south."

Toward Sociable.

Neither of them said it.

Neither of them had to.

TWO

Hollis Templeton accepted a hand up from her partner and tried not to show how winded she was. "Man, that's a hike."

Reese DeMarco, looking past her to the ravine they had just climbed out of, said, "If he was looking for an inaccessible place to leave them, he chose well."

"Not too far off one of the trails, though," she pointed out.

"Yeah, but in January, it's not likely to be very well traveled; we're fairly lucky there's no snow cover at this elevation. If we hadn't had a chopper up, we never would have spotted them. And if we hadn't, wildlife would have disposed of the remains in a matter of days no matter what the weather did."

Miranda Bishop left the ranger she'd been speaking to and joined them at the edge of the ravine. "We won't know until an ME gets a look," she said, "but rangers are pretty experienced at estimating how long . . . carrion . . . would last out here."

"I'm afraid to ask for details," Hollis confessed.

Miranda nodded understanding. "I know what you mean. But it may turn out to be important that if he's familiar with these mountains, and we have to assume he is, he would have been safe betting that a harsh winter has left a lot of hungry animals in the area. The rangers say wolves, coyotes, and even some big cats have come far enough down out of the mountains to trouble area ranchers."

"Then," DeMarco said, "these girls haven't been here long."

"Probably not even overnight. He doesn't profile as the type to stick around and watch law enforcement trying to figure him out, but we may be closer to him right now than we've been so far."

Hollis said, "Wait. If we're saying that the same killer took not only Sara Knotts and Jill Crandall back just after Christmas, but then Angela Fox and Megan Dorchester just a couple of days ago . . ."

"Then he probably didn't kill Sara and Jill until he had two more . . . replacements," Miranda said.

Hollis kept her voice level with an effort. "I don't see how he kept these two girls alive, not if he's been working on them for nearly a month. I don't have to be a doctor to know that the bruises on those girls vary from weeks old to only a day or two. *And* they both have broken bones, that's clear enough. Even if most of the slashes look . . . fresh."

DeMarco shook his head slightly. "I think that in addition to using them as punching bags he found some creative ways of mental and emotional torture to try out before he finished them with the knife or knives," he said. "The girls have clearly been starved and bound, and I'm sure he scared the hell out of them in a dozen different ways. Keeping them in total darkness, maybe locking them in coffin-like boxes; one of the girls has wood splinters in her hands and feet. Maybe he separated them so they felt totally alone. Or did whatever it took to make one scream to further terrify the other."

"Which," Hollis said, "begs the question of where he kept them. I somehow doubt he was herding them along in front of him for weeks, even way out here. Especially way out here. And yet we're at least—what?—eighty miles south of where these two disappeared?"

"About that," Miranda agreed. "The rangers didn't think he would have made it this far, but . . ." But they'd had inside information disguised as a hunch. And Miranda could be very persuasive.

Hollis was still thinking out loud. "And no signs of tire tracks anywhere in this area, except for the ATV tracks the rangers have already eliminated as their own vehicles. If he's been on foot all this time, how did he transport the girls this far?"

"He's had the time," DeMarco pointed out. "But only if he had wheels or horses part of the way. No way he hiked this far in less than a month, not in this terrain, and definitely not with hostages."

"Horses," Hollis said. "I hadn't thought of that. He could have transported the girls that way. Maybe drugged or gagged to keep them quiet, and slung across a pack horse."

"Not exactly a common sight in these mountains," Miranda said thoughtfully. "But if he knows the terrain, he could have kept well off the trails. With so many pine forests, he could have passed a hundred yards from a well-traveled road without being seen."

DeMarco nodded. "But we're still left with the question of where he did his torturing. Where, presumably, he's currently holding Angela Fox and Megan Dorchester. And if he has horses, you're talking additional supplies and/or pasture. This time of year, he'd have to be feeding grain and hay; there's no grass to speak of."

Hollis looked at him with interest. "I hadn't thought of that, either. Sounds like a lot more trouble than just carrying extra gas for a rugged Jeep or something."

He nodded immediately. "Agreed. I'd be surprised if he's on horseback. Which means he must have some very rugged vehicle, and must be familiar enough with this part of the Blue Ridge that he was able to travel with fair speed and yet still avoid the main roads and trails, including the ones the rangers patrol."

Hollis frowned. "Which doesn't give us much more information. We know he's come this far south because this is where he left Sara's and Jill's bodies. Assuming he has Angela and Megan, they were abducted from an overlook about twenty-five miles from here. *North* of here. But he must have brought them back this way because Sara's and Jill's bodies haven't been here very long. Which means he almost *had* to have all four girls for at least a brief period of time."

"Tough for one guy to control four hostages," DeMarco noted. "Even if two of them have been beaten and starved into submission."

"Are we sure this is one guy? I mean, we all know how rare it is for a serial to do doubles, taking two victims at the same time or on the same day; every serial I've ever read about built to something like that, when the challenge of taking just one victim wasn't enough. But this guy grabs two right off the bat?"

"It's one of the things that makes him unique," Miranda noted.

"Okay, but how likely is it that one man managed to abduct two young women, travel with them over miles of rough terrain, *and* torture them so badly that by the time he abducted Angela and Megan, Sara and Jill were—and I *really* hate to use the phrase—deadweight?"

Miranda shook her head slightly. "I think we have to consider the possibility that he has help, maybe even a partner. Just for the logistics of travel and holding captives. But I can tell you that one person tortured and killed those girls; I knew it the moment I saw them. So *if* he has a partner, that person is a complete submissive, as much a prisoner of his will as the girls are."

"New possibility," Hollis said. "Still, all this, and all we really know or believe we know is that he's moving south."

"We know more than that," Miranda said. But her gaze was on Hollis, and she didn't continue.

Hollis sighed. "I get to be profiler?"

"Try," Miranda said. "Experience is what teaches us."

Hollis glanced down into the ravine, and then averted her gaze from two terribly mutilated bodies that had once been pretty, vital young women being put into black body bags.

That part, this part, never got any easier.

She drew a breath and let it out, then began musing aloud. "Wherever he held Sara and Jill has to be close enough that he was confident he could get Angela and Megan there and still have time to dump the first girls." She frowned. "Unless he *does* have a partner, and that partner set up a second location for the second set of girls. Maybe as a safety precaution; if Sara and Jill were found, which was always possible even if unlikely, he wouldn't want them found anywhere near where he's holding Angela and Megan."

"A possibility we have to consider," Miranda acknowledged. "Now focus on what he did to his victims."

Hollis kept her voice as matter-of-fact as she could manage. "No rape, not even object penetration. He used his knife, but not to stab, not deep wounds, so probably not an indication he's impotent; he just wasn't sexually interested in them. At all. He didn't cut their faces, but he did hit them, that's clear from the bruises and small cuts, so he didn't place any value on their beauty. All the slicing was overkill—but not in rage. He was careful, methodical, controlled.

"Whether it was their terror, their blood, or their suffering, he got whatever he needed from them, and then he dumped them like garbage, trusting the animals to clean up behind him. Which is what likely would have happened if we hadn't come this far south."

"Not bad," Miranda said.

"Yeah, but the only conclusion I can draw from that is that he's a psychopath, and we already knew that. Partner or no partner, he's the one killing. He's too controlled to be on a spree, too deliberate. The victims seem more of opportunity than anything else, not stalked or watched beforehand, just grabbed because they were there and they were vulnerable. Not surrogates for somebody he needs to strike out at, at least if you consider that the only thing they have in common is race and rough age: two blondes, a brunette, and a redhead, all white and all in their early twenties. If that's his type, it's a broad one."

"Which tells us?"

Hollis brooded a moment. "It's not about a type. The victims don't matter to him except in how they suffer. He must have some kind of goal. A plan. An ultimate destination. I just have absolutely no idea what any of those things are."

"Hey, Agent Bishop?"

They all three looked around in surprise, all realizing in the moment that it was Miranda the ranger was addressing, and two of them at least thinking that there was, really, only one Agent Bishop—and he was on the other side of the country at the moment.

"Something?" Miranda asked the ranger.

"Beats the hell out of me." He handed over a small plastic bag. "One of the crime scene people pulled it out of a girl's mouth."

"Which girl?" Hollis asked.

"Uh—the brunette. Jill Crandall."

"Right question," Miranda murmured, frowning. "And probably another piece of the puzzle."

Something in the other woman's voice made Hollis frown. "What is it?" she asked, never one to hesitate asking a question.

"It's a silver cross. A pendant for a necklace."

"Hers?" DeMarco asked.

Without having to refer to a file or her tablet, Miranda shook her head. "According to family and friends, Jill Crandall never wore jewelry except for gold studs in her earlobes. And she was an atheist, so unlikely to even have a cross in her possession."

"Then," Hollis said, "this is for us?"

"A message of some kind. I doubt she put it in her own mouth."

"What message?" Hollis frowned again. "She was a good girl and I still did this to her?"

"Or she wasn't a good girl," DeMarco said slowly. "In his mind, at least. Especially if he knew she was an atheist."

Hollis was still frowning. "I dunno. It doesn't feel like . . . an insult or punishment to me. More like . . . consecration."

"He did that to her to make her sacred?"

"He did that to her . . . and she became sacred."

Trinity hadn't expected to find anything either surprising or suspicious at the church.

She found both.

The first surprise was that the double doors of the church—Trinity Church—were standing wide open. And from inside, even in the afternoon light, a glow was evident.

Trinity got out of the Jeep slowly. She adjusted her jacket so that the gun on her hip was clear and unsnapped the holster for good measure. She was about to call Braden but found he had already left the Jeep and was at her side, his gaze on the church.

His calm gaze.

It reassured her somewhat; Braden, she had discovered, was very alert to trouble or danger, and very protective of her.

Still . . . those doors shouldn't have been open, and there shouldn't be any light coming from inside.

She walked steadily up one of the paths that led to the entrance to the church. Other than the stained wooden doors with their leaded glass inserts, the entrance was plain. The wide porch was shallow, only three steps leading up to it, with simple corbels rather than posts supporting the slight overhang of the roof.

It had been built in a simpler time, her father had told Trinity. White clapboard and a brick foundation, the only ornamentation the stained-glass windows along each side depicting, of course, scenes from the Bible.

Trinity, her dog at her side, went up the steps

and into the church, moving slowly, her gaze roaming.

The simple wooden pews gleamed dully from years and years of being polished by church ladies. The plank floor had, at some point, been covered by a dull red carpet worn noticeably thin in spots.

There wasn't really an altar. There was a podium where the preacher stood and delivered his sermon, and behind him was the section for the choir. Off to the right was a rather impressive organ. And behind the podium and the choir section, a glass window—covered by a red velvet curtain—concealed the baptistery. Above that on the wall hung a simple cross.

Large. But simple.

Trinity stopped only a few steps into the church, aware of the low growl rumbling from Braden's throat. She had no way of knowing what his senses were telling him, but what hers were telling her was that something was very wrong here.

She kept her hand on her weapon but didn't draw it free of its holster.

There was nothing to be deterred by a gun.

From the organ, over the podium, and across to the other side of the church, there was a kind of rainbow arch of . . . light. It was like a sunbeam, except that there was, clearly, no source to call it that. It was light, and within the light was . . .

sparks. That's the only way Trinity could describe it to herself. Sparks, metallic sparks, inside that arch of light.

Even as she thought about that, Braden's growl grew louder, and she had the eerie feeling of pressure above her head, as if something hovered above her, just above her.

Her head began to hurt.

Trinity glanced down at Braden to see that his attention had shifted, that he was looking fixedly above her head, and now his growl showed the impressive teeth of a pit bull.

Not at all the type to whistle in the dark or otherwise spook easily, Trinity tipped her head back suddenly and looked up.

She had seen, in photographs, objects some people referred to as orbs, round outlines, sometimes fuzzy, almost . . . shadows of lights. Hovering above people, sometimes seeming to zip around the room, leaving a bright trail like the tail of a comet behind them. Many people believed they represented spiritual energy captured by cameras, the stark and unblinking lens seeing what the questioning human mind failed to see.

But Trinity saw one now, hovering above her head.

She saw it, and despite its gentle glow, despite its fuzzy whiteness, she knew without any doubt in her mind that what she was looking at was nothing good. Nothing positive. Nothing she could allow into her—mind.

Because that's where it wanted to be, she realized. It wanted in.

It wanted her.

"No," Trinity said, her voice dead calm. "You don't get me. Leave. Now. I know *exactly* what you are."

She wondered, later, where the words, the certainty, had come from. Wondered how she had known what to say even while her conscious mind had been trying its best to understand the extraordinary, to define the unknown, to label the uncanny.

She spoke without thinking about it, commanded without wondering what gave her the will or the authority to command.

But she was obeyed.

As she gazed upward, the orb above her head floated several feet from her, toward the altar and the rainbow of light there.

"I know," Trinity repeated, "*exactly* what you are. Leave."

The faint sparkles within the orb brightened for a moment, and then, without warning, it went black—and the rainbow of light at the front of the church went black, starting at one side and rushing to the other, like a gush of oil through some invisible conduit.

And then it was gone. The dark orb, the arch of

darkness, the light that had been there before, all gone, everything gone with a suddenness that made Trinity's ears pop.

She stood there for several long moments, vaguely aware that Braden was no longer growling, aware that her sense of *wrongness* had faded—but not disappeared entirely.

She forced herself to walk forward. To examine the podium, the organ, the entire front area of the church. Even opened the curtain to see the baptistery, empty of water.

For good measure, she went back there and looked around, even opened the back door and looked out on trees climbing the mountain slope above the church. She studied the area for a bit, then closed and locked the door and went back to the front of the church.

Braden never left her side.

They walked steadily down the center aisle to the still-open front doors, and only then did Trinity turn and look back. A normal church, lit only by the light that found its way through the stained-glass windows, so that the interior of the space seemed almost to dance with soft colors.

Peaceful. Pleasant.

A holy place.

Once, perhaps. No longer.

Trinity left the church with her dog, closing the doors behind them after reaching around to flip the catch so that they would automatically lock.

She tried them when they were closed, and they resisted her attempt to open them again.

She stood on the porch for a long time, looking around. Looking at the small graveyard that lay between the church and the parsonage. Everything looked normal, undisturbed.

But that wasn't why Trinity decided to wait and check out the parsonage another day.

She was not a woman easily shaken, but she felt she needed to think long and hard about what she had just experienced. Because although there had been many things in her life she had found difficult to explain, this was . . . something else.

She had no memory of ever seeing true evil.

But what gave her greater pause than that, what bothered her a great deal, was the fact that she had recognized it.

She had recognized true evil because she had, somewhere in her life, encountered it before. She was certain of that, utterly certain.

Even though she had no memory of when, or where, it had happened.

"What's so damned frustrating," Hollis said that evening as she, DeMarco, Miranda, and Dean Ramsay, the fourth member of their current team, sat eating a very late supper at an all-night pancake house just off the interstate, "is that we can't track this guy."

"So far," DeMarco reminded her.

"Well, yeah, but that means we have to wait for him or evidence of him to turn up again. Which means bodies or abductions. Am I wrong?"

"No, unfortunately," Miranda responded. "I doubt we'll find anything in the autopsies that offers any new or helpful information. His comfort zone seems to be a wilderness even the rangers have trouble navigating at times."

"We can be pretty sure he's heading south," Dean Ramsay pointed out. "With or without an accomplice. There is that."

Hollis shook her head. "Even if he is, and even if he stays in the mountains, that's still thousands of acres, all the way down into Georgia. He's avoiding cities. He's even avoided towns so far —that we know of, at least. So—what? We just trail along behind him, jumping from one off-the-highway motel to the next, collecting crumbs of evidence and hoping he makes a mistake?"

"If that's what we have to do," Miranda said. "It's how most serials are caught."

The restaurant was practically deserted, but Hollis nevertheless lowered her voice when she said, "You haven't seen anything?"

"Afraid not. You?"

"I," Hollis said, "haven't seen a spirit in months. Not since that energy vortex at Alexander House.[1] I know Bishop said it might change me to channel

---

[1]*Hostage*

43

all that energy, but he didn't say there was a chance I wouldn't be a medium anymore."

Miranda looked thoughtful. "It wouldn't be the first time one of us had temporarily burned out because of too much energy. Still, I don't think that's it—because you *did* see the spirit of Mr. Alexander after it was all over."

Hollis was honestly relieved—which rather surprised her. "You're right, I did. I'd forgotten that."

DeMarco said, "Maybe the spirits are just giving you a break."

"Spoken by someone who is *not* a medium," Hollis said dryly. "Trust me, spirits are not that generous. They have things to do, unfinished business, unhelpful hints to drop here and there while the medium fumbles along in the dark."

Gravely, Dean said, "It doesn't sound like you miss them all that much."

"Well, they can be annoying."

Miranda said, "I have a hunch they'll be back. In the meantime, use your other senses and your mind. Those are tools as well."

"Tools to help find a murderer."

"Yeah. Preferably before he drops more bodies for us to find."

THREE

January 27

Trinity smothered a yawn as she started her Jeep early on that Tuesday morning. She hadn't slept well, which wasn't surprising; she hadn't slept well since a killer had begun roaming in the mountains far too close to home for her peace of mind.

Especially now. The bastard's body count was up to at least four dead—and he had abducted two more girls on Sunday, just two days ago.

"I don't know how he's finding girls that age out alone at all with the news blaring warnings nearly every hour on the hour," she said to her dog as she backed the Jeep out of her driveway. "I mean, they're all being told this is not a situation where the buddy system works unless your buddies are a crowd—"

Braden suddenly nudged her arm. Hard.

Startled, Trinity slowed the Jeep. "What the hell?"

The dog looked at her but didn't move again until the Jeep had to stop at an intersection. Then he again nudged her arm.

Trinity had known from the outset that her dog was unusual in quite a few ways, but this was something new.

"You want me to turn left?" She guessed.

He nudged her arm.

"Well, let's see," she murmured. And turned the Jeep left. Two streets later, Braden grasped the arm of her jacket in his teeth and tugged gently.

"Right it is," Trinity said, shaking her head. "People would think I'm nuts, you realize that, don't you?"

Braden didn't answer except to nudge her arm again, and Trinity turned obediently. She made several other turns, and frowned when at last she was turning into the small parking lot of an apartment building.

"Wait a second. This is Scott's building. What—"

Her dog began pawing at the passenger-side door handle.

"Okay, okay. Let's get out on this side." She turned the Jeep off and got out, barely fast enough to avoid the near charge of her very strong dog.

He led her straight to the door of Scott Abernathy's second-floor apartment.

Wondering what she was going to say, Trinity rang the bell. After a minute or two, she rang it again.

Braden looked up at her and whined softly.

Trinity banged on the door, beginning to feel more than a little worried. Scott was an avid runner, always ran early before work, and by her watch he should have been downing his orange juice now and getting ready to head out the door.

But there was no answer.

There wasn't a front window for her to try to peer in, and Trinity hesitated only an instant before stepping to the side and carefully prying a loose brick from the facade. There was a key behind it.

"Don't ask," she said to her dog.

He lifted a paw to scratch at the door.

Trinity unlocked the door and went into the apartment, calling out, "Scott? It's Trinity."

No answer. And her voice nearly echoed, the way one's did when nobody was home.

She was familiar with his place, and not only because she'd spent quite a few nights there a couple of years back. Scott hosted occasional parties; he enjoyed cooking and was good at it, so his friends were always happy to attend.

Even if he did make them clean up after.

The apartment was neat as a pin, a fact Trinity noted only in passing. Scott was neat as a pin; he was infamous for not being able to sleep if there were dirty dishes in the sink, and he expected people to actually *use* coasters.

Living room, neat. Kitchen, neat. Guest bathroom, very neat. Guest bedroom, very neat.

Master bedroom door closed. And locked.

Trinity banged on the door. "Scott? You all right?"

She put her ear to the door and listened but didn't hear the shower running. If it had been

47

running, she would have heard it. And by now, she was uneasy enough to really need confirmation that Scott wasn't here, and if he wasn't here, she damned well needed to know where he was.

She looked at the door handle, then stood on tiptoes and felt along the top ledge of the door frame, producing the odd little hooked emergency key designed mostly for situations in which young children locked themselves in bathrooms or bedrooms and didn't yet know how to unlock the doors.

Trinity was able to unlock the door easily. But for some reason she could never explain afterward, she didn't just barge in. She turned the door handle and pushed the door open.

She thought later how odd it was that after all his impatience, Braden sat just behind her in the hallway and never tried to go into the bedroom.

Trinity took one step in. She didn't need to go any farther to see what there was to see. The bedroom was neat, bed made, everything in its place. Except for Scott. Dressed for his morning run, he was lying in an oddly twisted position on the rug at the foot of his bed. His head was turned, and his open eyes seemed to be staring straight at Trinity.

Except that they weren't, because Scott was dead.

Dr. Richard Beeson was hovering around retirement age but refused to give up medicine completely; being the coroner for Crystal County suited him. It was, mostly, an easy job, respectfully bagging up folks after accidents and helping morticians carefully wrap elderly "retirement home" residents in pristine white sheets for their trip to the mortuary.

He'd never handled a murder before. And he wasn't too proud to share that information with Sheriff Trinity Nichols—whom he had delivered with his own hands thirty-odd years ago.

"I don't see what he died of, Trinity. Body temp and rigor indicate he's been dead no more than an hour. It was sudden, but he just had a complete physical with a stress test; his heart was in great shape, and so were his arteries. Told me he smoked a joint now and then, but that was it as far as recreational drugs went. I don't think he lied to me about that."

Trinity nodded. "He liked wine, but it was about taste, not getting drunk. Didn't like losing control." *Unless it was for effect, for show. He could fake losing control with the best of them.*

Unaware of her silent musings, Doc Beeson nodded in turn. "No health issues showed up in his physical, so I'm stumped. His head's at an odd angle though not extreme, but seems to me if he'd fallen somehow, at least that rug would have a wrinkle or two in it."

Trinity wasn't tempted to laugh. "I thought the same thing, Doc. You'll do the autopsy?"

He grimaced, which didn't really change the expression of his thin, craggy face. "Man, I hate doing posts on people I delivered. Haven't had to many times, 'specially considering how many babies I delivered over the years."

"But you'll do his autopsy."

He nodded. "Yeah, I'll do it. Dammit. Meantime, I'll get out of the way so Lexie and Doug can do their jobs." He looked at her directly. "I know you got them trained special as crime scene technicians; you think Scott was murdered?"

Trinity chose her words carefully, even knowing with absolute certainty that Beeson was the soul of discretion. "I think that if you find something other than an accident or a natural death in the autopsy, I want all the i's dotted and t's crossed."

"Guess I'd feel the same in your place. I'll wait out in the living room."

"Thanks, Doc."

Lexie Adams and Douglas Payne, who had been standing silently just inside the door holding their kits, nodded to the elderly doctor as he shambled past them.

It was Lexie who asked, "You want the works, Sheriff?"

Trinity nodded slowly. "Yeah. Photograph everything, print everything, take fiber samples. Scrape under his nails. Use every tool the FBI taught you to use. I want to know what happened here."

"You bet, Sheriff."

She stepped out of the bedroom, reasonably sure her young crime scene unit "team" would feel much more comfortable and assured if she wasn't breathing down their necks while they worked. Not that she felt the need to do that; she had gone to considerable trouble and expense to make certain they were very, very well trained and able.

Doc Beeson was sitting on Scott's sofa, leaning forward, elbows on his knees while he petted Braden. The doctor loved dogs, and Braden loved attention, so the bonding experience was no doubt keeping both of them calm.

Leaving the front door open, Trinity stepped out onto the walkway that dead-ended at Scott's apartment. She leaned on the railing and looked around, the idle glance showing her that there was no one about, so no sign of undue notice. The mortician's wagon hadn't arrived yet; she had called to alert them but asked that they not come until later, and to be discreet.

Discreet. Oh, yeah. Right.

She reached into the pocket of her jacket, drawing out something that lay in the palm of her hand, glinting silver in the morning sunlight. Something she had seen herself before anyone else had arrived at Scott's apartment.

Something she had, against all her training and police protocol, removed from Scott's body. She'd seen the faint gleam between his slightly parted lips, vaguely puzzled at first because she knew Scott had no silver or gold caps on his teeth. And then she had realized it was something else.

A silver medallion. A cross.

She stared down at it for a long moment, then used her other hand to reach for her cell phone.

She had no idea where he was, since he was seldom in his office; for all she knew, she could have been dragging him out of bed somewhere.

She didn't care.

She scrolled through her contacts and hit send. And wasn't surprised when he answered on the first ring.

"Bishop."

"Hey, it's Trinity. We need to talk."

January 29

Deacon James had grown up in a small town, so he didn't exactly feel out of place when he followed the winding mountain road out of fairly dense forest and rather suddenly into the three-block-long downtown area of Sociable, Georgia.

North Georgia.

Remote north Georgia.

And the town seemed to cling to the mountainside, a unique but surely impractical place on which to site a town.

Aside from that, it looked somewhat the way

many small mountain towns looked, with the "major" local businesses on the relative flat of Main Street while smaller businesses as well as a scattering of apartment buildings, Victorian homes, and a few startlingly contemporary ones on climbing side streets appeared to perch precariously behind and above.

Probably have a hell of a view.

Because it was a one-side downtown; that was the real difference. Across the street was a fairly wide swath of well-kept grass striped with the occasional neat and carefully graveled path leading down a gentle but boulder-strewn slope to a wide and apparently shallow mountain stream, which, given its location, almost seemed even more than the town itself to defy gravity and sense.

The town had clearly taken advantage of what could only be used as a recreation area, providing across from Main Street scattered attractive shelters with picnic tables beneath, and benches, and the aforementioned well-kept paths, as well as at least two comfortably wide footbridges across the stream. There was even what was obviously a small park with swings and other rides for the kids plus a big jungle gym, an attractive wrought-iron fence with a gate for safety around the play area.

But there wasn't much else on that side of Main Street, because there wasn't a whole lot of room.

Beyond, on the other side of the stream, were a few smallish trees on an even more narrow strip of grass, a couple of benches facing the spectacular view from an as-close-as-you'd-want-to-get perspective, planting beds covered with mulch hinting at flowers to come in the spring—and then, bordered by a different and stronger wrought-iron fence to prevent a tragic slip, a pretty sheer drop to the bottom of the valley at least three hundred yards below. The valley stretched out for miles and seemed to be mostly pasture dotted with cows and horses, a few fields obviously farmed, and widely scattered older homes holding the people who farmed them.

With the mountains ringing the valley, it really did present an extremely attractive view. And no doubt a pleasant place to live for many reasons, among them the absence of any industry producing pollution of the air or groundwater, and a population small enough that most knew each other but not so small that there was nothing better to do than to nose into each other's business. Most of the time, at least.

Still. It was an odd place to put a town, Deacon thought, but he had seen odder, especially along the Blue Ridge, with its old mountains and old towns that had sprung up generations ago around now long-defunct mining camps or trading posts, or to serve the many farmers in the valley—where tillable land was too valuable a resource to waste on businesses and official buildings that could easily perch on the mountainside above.

Well, not *easily*. But from a practical standpoint, if farming and ranching served the local economy well enough, then sensibly.

Deacon knew that many towns like Sociable pretty much depended on a local-driven economy supplemented by seasonal tourism sparked by this or that "festival" or other annual draw besides the scenery. Most such small towns, in these difficult economic times, struggled to remain viable, and most watched the younger generations move away after high school because there was so little to offer them in the way of a career or even a good, steady job that wouldn't keep them in a small office or behind a counter for the rest of their lives.

But it appeared that Sociable was doing all right for itself, or at least all right enough that all the buildings Deacon could see on Main Street appeared to be attractive and occupied, at least surviving if not thriving. He couldn't see a single vacant building, at least along the main drag. And there had to be some money about; he had passed both a high school and a middle school on the drive in, both newish and sprawling buildings less than five miles from downtown, both with well-designed and well-maintained athletic fields.

Probably the latest thing in tech as well. Couldn't send your kids out in the world these days without education in all things digital, after all—even though plenty of kids knew a lot more about cutting-edge technology than did their parents because they'd grown up with so much of it in their lives.

Deacon had passed a couple of car dealerships, too. A few recognizable chain restaurants off the highway. A couple of small motels tucked away close to the highway, one at least outwardly respectable and one clearly the sort that charged by the hour.

He had also passed churches. Several churches.

And there was one downtown, perched high above Main Street, the highest visible point of downtown, the whiteness of its slender steeple almost shining in the afternoon light. Maybe watching over the town and valley below.

Maybe.

There was a bed-and-breakfast literally at each end of downtown, with a well-kept and attractive building housing a three-story hotel smack in the middle, which included a restaurant on the ground floor. There were numerous stores, at least three other restaurants or cafés, a couple of banks. A sheriff's office apparently shared a fairly large building with the town post office and courthouse, and he could see at the far end of Main Street what looked like a fire station. There were two doctor's offices visible, a pawnshop that looked less seedy than many, a bookstore, and two different coffee shops, one chain and one local.

He wondered idly which got the most business; it was difficult to tell at first glance.

Deacon, not making a community statement, parked in front of the first of the coffee shops he came to, mildly surprised to find no parking meters. He got out and closed the car door without bothering to lock it; his luggage was in the trunk, and Sociable really didn't look like the sort of town where cars were jacked right off Main Street.

At least not in broad daylight.

He stretched absently, a bit stiff after the long drive, and looked around with casual interest for a few moments. There was a fair amount of activity in the area on this Thursday despite the January chill in the air, and as far as he could tell, no one paid him any special attention.

They were polite, though.

"Morning," one middle-aged man said pleasantly as he walked past.

"Morning," Deacon responded.

Not really a booming tourist town, Sociable, but the scenery and small-town charm did bring enough visitors that the arrival of one more clearly caused no particular notice.

Even now.

Which, Deacon thought, was a bit surprising. The people he saw went about their business, expressions preoccupied but not especially tense or uneasy. When two met in passing, they appeared to exchange casual greetings, but no one lingered to talk.

He would have expected that.

Then again, what he was seeing might very well be the citizens of Sociable being uneasy and on edge. Maybe they generally did stop and talk to each other, get coffee, shoot the breeze, discuss local events.

Like murder.

Deacon frowned a bit but decided to get out of the chilly air while he considered the matter. He went into the coffee shop, which he found to be typical of most he'd been in: small tables with minimalist chairs, a long banquette along one wall with evenly spaced tables in front of it, and in one rear corner a tall counter with glass cases showcasing various sandwiches and pastries. There was a drop to a lower counter on either end, where a customer ordered and then picked up said order.

There were signs advertising free Wi-Fi, and at least two customers sipped coffee or tea as they worked at laptops, while two others appeared to be reading, one with a hardcover and one with an e-reader. There were even three independent "stations" just past the banquette with laptops set up for customer use.

A pleasant young woman took Deacon's order, and since it was a no-frills black coffee and a large wedge of apple pie, he was able to carry both to a table in the other back corner in only a couple of minutes.

He settled into his chair and sipped the coffee, which wasn't bad. He sampled the pie, which was excellent.

And he watched, without being obvious about it.

More customers trickled in and out over the next half hour. Some came for coffee and left with their ubiquitous paper cups and preoccupied expressions; a few lingered to chat with the staff behind the counter, which included several young women and only one young man.

A couple sat enjoying coffee, pastries, and a quiet conversation, clearly in no hurry to leave.

A woman with a laptop arrived to get coffee and settle down to work, or check her e-mail or social media sites, or surf the Net, or whatever she was doing. A teenager showed up, bought what he and the staff laughingly referred to as "milk with a little coffee," and then went to one of the provided laptops and settled down to what looked like an online game.

Just as outside, no one appeared tense or on edge. In fact, the occasional chats at the counter erupted more than once into quiet laughter, and the staff behind the counter appeared unfailingly cheerful.

Okay, just one odd murder. So maybe that's not so unusual. Nothing worth talking about, for most people. So what if this town hadn't had a murder in a decade or so until two days ago, when they had a really odd one. Maybe nobody's that bothered. Maybe Melanie's wrong in believing it's bigger than murder, worse than murder.

Maybe . . . maybe it's just Melanie.

FOUR

On some level of himself, he was aware of being hunted. Not frightened, because the voices had told him he didn't have to worry about the hunters; there was a place in the plan for them as well.

So he didn't worry.

There were other things to occupy him. At first, it had been much easier to be God's avenging sword. He had felt so powerful, suffused with the light of justice. It had been so easy to snatch the first two from under the very noses of their friends and carry them off. Easy to keep them quiet with the injections. And easy to punish them. Though he was still uneasily confused by the fact that they somehow got all bruised and battered long before he used his avenging sword to mete out justice.

That was troubling.

Even though long distances had to be covered, and quickly even over rough terrain, he thought he slept a lot, because there were long gaps in his memory. That was troubling, too, because he was growing more tired rather than more rested, and sometimes when he woke up his whole body ached, as though he had run a marathon.

And his sleep, though deep, was often restless, his dreams filled with red. Everything red, so much red.

And screaming.

He thought the screaming made a kind of sense, because the second pair of harlots had been a bit more difficult to subdue and had screamed a lot. They had screamed and fought, one giving him a black eye. And that one had screamed even more later. Every time he woke up, it was to hear her screaming.

Still, if he concentrated on a song he liked and kept that music in his head, he could mostly block out the screaming. So he did that, most of the time.

It didn't really help with the smell, though.

He tried to ask the voices when they could leave the place because it smelled so bad, but they were impatient with him for the first time, and that was troubling.

That was very troubling.

The time he liked best was when he was making the crosses. He had always been good with his hands, and the voices hadn't had to teach him for long before he had it all down. He loved melting the silver, bits of jewelry and coins and other things the voices told him to use. And he loved pouring the liquid metal into the mold.

He loved filing away the rough edges, and drilling the tiny, perfect hole for the ring, and sometimes stamping names and messages into the metal.

He felt so much more righteous when he was making the crosses, so . . . in control.

That was it. When he made the crosses, he was in control. He felt like himself.

The rest of the time . . .

Well, it was troubling.

Very troubling.

But he was a soldier of God. He was doing great and noble work, important work.

He just wished he could sleep without dreaming in red.

And he wished he could escape the screams.

And the smells.

Melanie James had worked at the Hollow Creek Bank for more than three years, and she liked her job. The bank truly was a "hometown" sort of place and had been for at least three generations, its canny local investors and managers both smart and skilled enough to keep it prospering even during the periodic economic downturns of the state and even the country.

And since Sociable was a small town where neighbor still helped neighbor and most had very strong work ethics, being the loan officer for the bank seldom involved unpleasant duties such as turning down a request for a loan, whether personal or business.

"It's just for the rest of the winter," John David Matthews was saying in his laconic, matter-of-fact voice. "Got some fine stock to sell in the spring and over the summer months."

"You've always been a good credit risk, John David," Melanie told him with a smile as she gave the paperwork a final check. "Hey, how is that pinto mare coming along?"

"My daughter's training her, says she's smart and good natured. No vices. You still interested in her?"

"Definitely. I've been saying for the last year that I wanted to have a good riding horse, mostly for weekend trail rides." It was a favorite activity among several of her friends, enjoyable because the area was crisscrossed with miles of mountain trails.

Also because there really weren't a whole lot of options when it came to things to do in Sociable.

"The pinto would be a good choice."

"For a Sunday rider?"

He smiled. "I'd say. Sophie trains with kindness and takes her time; her horses always seem to take on her own sweet nature. With a pasture to run in when you aren't riding so she gets plenty of exercise, the pinto's bound to be a calm mount."

"Good. Maybe I'll come see her this weekend, if it's okay."

" 'Course it's okay. I'll tell Sophie you're still interested. You can call the house and let her know if you do decide to come."

"Great, I'll do that. And you be thinking of a price, okay? I'd be boarding her with you, of course." Her downtown apartment was nice but hardly boasted a stable or pasture. And John David provided fine care at a reasonable price for any animals boarded with him.

His rugged face appeared mildly pleased, which for him was as good as a broad grin; training and boarding fees, along with the occasional guided trail ride, made up most of his income from fall to spring, so a prospective new boarder was welcome news. As was the strong possibility of a horse sold.

Still, being a practical man, he said, "You know you can always borrow a horse if you want to ride. Don't have to have the expenses of buying and boarding."

Melanie gathered up the signed paperwork into a neat stack and smiled at him. "Little girls dream of owning their own horses one day. I did. Now I can actually do it. And I've got my eye on that pinto, John David."

"Consider her reserved."

"Thanks. Now—here are your copies of everything, and here's your check. Always a pleasure doing business with you." The words were conventional, but her tone made them friendly and personal.

"Thank you, ma'am." He smiled as he rose, and they shook hands before he headed out into the bank to deposit his check.

Melanie rechecked to make sure all the paperwork she needed was in his file, then closed it and for a few moments gazed down at the folder on her blotter without really seeing it.

Good job. Good town. Good people. She had friends. She had dates when she wanted them. She had a nice home she enjoyed and money enough to live comfortably, even well.

It was a good life.

Or, at least . . . it had been.

Until the dreams had started. Until she'd begun to catch glimpses of . . . something . . . from the corner of her eye, just quick enough to be gone when she looked.

Until she had begun to feel that too-familiar, almost gleeful sense of being watched from the shadows.

Until they started hearing about what was happening in the mountains so near.

Until people started dying.

The cold knot in the pit of her stomach was never very far from her awareness now. Because something was very, very wrong in Sociable, something . . . unnatural was here. Something a deeply primal part of herself recognized.

And she was afraid that meant at least one person in her life wasn't at all who or what she believed them to be. In fact, she was almost certain that was the case.

Not a stranger, Trinity had said, eyeing Melanie calmly. No evidence of that, and plenty going the other way.

It was entirely possible, Trinity had said, that someone in Sociable was a murderer.

It's not natural, what happened to Scott. It's not . . . normal. Normal is when somebody gets mad and somebody else gets dead. Shot. Stabbed. Hit on the head. Somebody gets greedy and somebody else gets dead. Somebody gets jealous and possessive and somebody else gets dead. Simple motives for simple, stupid crimes, mostly obvious right from the start. That's what Deacon says. And he's right. That's the way it works. But this . . .

This was definitely not simple, and if the killer was stupid, he or she was hiding it well.

Even with no experience investigating murder in Sociable, Trinity was no fool and probably better trained to handle the unlikely than most small-town sheriffs, given her background in big-city law enforcement. And she wouldn't hesitate to arrest even a friend if the evidence warranted it.

She was giving Melanie the benefit of the doubt. For now, at least.

Melanie had so far gotten only a few odd looks from some of her fellow citizens, but she knew it was early days yet. There were just a few rumors now, mostly because too many gossips had been in the restaurant when Scott had been so angry and Melanie so icy, their relationship clearly on the rocks.

So gossip said, preferring the drama over the more prosaic truth that a fiery relationship had simply burned itself out.

And long before that public display of . . . emotions.

Just gossip now. But with every day that passed without the murder being explained and the killer being unmasked, let alone caught, she would get more and more of those looks. As time went on and the very air grew thicker and thicker with tension, with anxiety, people would look for a focus for their suspicion and fear.

She was a relative newcomer to the town. And even if they didn't know for sure, people would imagine . . . motives. From the reasonable to the irrational, there were bound to be motives.

Hell, she could think of a few herself.

Which explained her panicked call to Deacon.

Melanie wasn't exactly having second thoughts about that, except that she hated feeling this need for . . . somebody on her side. Somebody who knew her too well to believe . . . even reasonable motives.

Someone who knew she was not a murderer.

Deacon absently tracked a casually dressed woman from the door to the counter. She had dark brown hair, pulled back at the nape of her neck. Hard to tell from the loose, bulky jacket, but he judged her to be slender, average height. He couldn't hear what she said to the staff, but they seemed to know her and be eager to serve her.

It wasn't until she turned with coffee in hand and came directly across to where he was sitting that he saw the gun on her hip.

And the badge.

He began to rise out of automatic courtesy, but she waved him back and took the chair across from him. Since the table was small, they were close enough that he could detect the unusual gold flecks in her rather startling green eyes.

"Sheriff," he said. "Did I park illegally or something?"

She smiled briefly, the expression turning her face from rather ordinary to something close to beautiful. "No, Mr. James, you didn't park illegally."

"How did you—"

"You and your sister favor. The same blue eyes. High cheekbones. Even the way you raise your eyebrows."

He thought about it, sipping the last of his coffee, then said, "And you ran my plates." He was driving his own car.

"And that," she agreed amiably. She sipped her own black coffee. "I'm Trinity Nichols, by the way. But I expect Melanie told you that much. Probably told you a lot more."

He pegged her age at not much past thirty, which was young for a sheriff—except maybe in a small town where her father *and* grandfather had also served as sheriff.

Melanie had told him a lot, including the fact that Trinity Nichols had hardly inherited the job but had earned it on merit; she had spent nearly ten years as a cop in Atlanta, on the streets and as a detective, so she was most certainly not a politician or a desk jockey.

Deacon nodded. "I'm not here to cause trouble. Not here to interfere with your investigation."

"Just here to support your sister."

"Yeah."

"So there's nothing at all official about your visit."

"No. Just visiting Melanie. I had vacation time coming and no pressing cases."

"So a busman's holiday of sorts." Her tone was still affable.

"Brothers worry."

"Do they?" She smiled, something a bit wry in the expression. "I wouldn't know."

Deacon thought that might prove an interesting tangent to explore, but also knew enough about small towns and the people who lived in them to be certain such probing wouldn't be welcome.

Not yet, at any rate.

He hesitated, not entirely sure just how much this keen-eyed woman knew or had guessed, then said, "Melanie can be . . . overly dramatic, especially if an idea takes hold. And she has a very active and vivid imagination. But she isn't capable of murder. I hope you know that."

"I would have said." Her green eyes never left his face. "Still resisting the notion, actually. But—evidence."

"Circumstantial," he said.

"True enough. But about all I've got. And apparent motives all over the place. A romance on the rocks. Arguments in public. Her fingerprints found in the home of the murder victim."

"Well . . . they were involved."

"Yeah. But Scott was a neat freak. And his habit was to make very sure all traces of his latest ex were wiped out of his apartment."

"Still, a little cleaning wouldn't—"

"He hired an industrial cleaning crew. Practically had them on retainer."

After a startled moment, Deacon said, "Wow. That's a little extreme. On retainer? How many exes did he have?"

"A few. But if you're thinking more suspects,

most remained at least friendly with him afterward. And Melanie was the most recent. The one showing anger in public. So . . ."

"So your number one suspect?"

"Not exactly. It's just that his place was . . . awfully clean. And they had that argument in public. So I have to take notice, so to speak."

"I assume you also have to take notice of the unlikelihood that my sister—or any woman without special training—could have broken the neck of a healthy, fit, adult male with plenty of his own muscle. And most especially when his neck is broken with no bruising or ligature marks, no sign of a rope—and the body found in a room with windows and door locked from the inside."

Sheriff Nichols nodded slowly and with no surprise. "It is a puzzle," she conceded. "I've been trying to wrap my mind around it, without much success."

"Then you don't believe my sister killed him."

"The thing is," Trinity Nichols said, "I'm having a hard time believing anyone killed him."

"And yet he was murdered."

"And yet he was murdered."

They were coming.

He could feel it, like a change in the air before a storm, a kind of oppressive heaviness even though the sky was clear. And not just heavy, but more, like power of some kind let loose to roam, prickly, tingling, uncomfortable. Both light and dark energy moving slowly all around him, restless and uneasy.

Like him. The restlessness, at least. And a growing sense of power within himself. He wasn't exactly uneasy, just . . . alert. That was it. He was alert and aware.

Not a bad thing, surely.

An edge.

It fascinated him that he could feel them coming nearer. He hadn't expected that. He'd expected to feel *her,* of course, because she couldn't close herself off, and even though he was being careful that she didn't sense him, he'd always expected to sense her.

Except that she felt . . . different, somehow. More than she had been? Less? Or just different? He didn't know.

Not knowing bothered him.

It was something out of his control.

Then there was *him*. He was different now, too. Shut inside himself like before, protected like before, but . . . connected in a way he *hadn't* been before. Connected to her. So something new there, too. Something he couldn't . . . quite . . . get hold of.

It was irritating.

And if the truth be told, he wasn't sure if this

uncertain sensitivity to both of them, all these changes in what he had expected, would make things easier—or more difficult.

Not that it mattered, really.

He had A Plan. And he intended to stick to his Plan no matter what sort of tricks they brought with them.

A muffled sound drew his gaze from the town and stunning scenery around it to the bound man at his feet. He studied the sluggishly bleeding cut in the center of a swelling bruise on the man's temple, then shook his own head, not so much in impatience as in regret.

"It's a shame you came to," he told the man. "I thought I hit you hard enough to keep you out. It would have been much better for you that way. I'm sorry, I really am. But this one has to look very . . . physical. Because the other one wasn't. I need to throw them off the scent, so to speak. I'm sure you can understand."

The sounds muffled behind the very efficient tape and gag became even more frantic.

"It's nothing personal," he assured the man as he bent and unrolled a soft leather case filled with assorted very shiny tools. "I mean, you didn't do anything to me. You just fit my requirements, that's all. You have a part to play. A Very Important Part. And isn't that better than anything you could have found for yourself in your really boring life?"

Pleading sounds, garbled panic and terror.

"Oh, stop it." He studied his tools for a moment, then stepped over to recheck the rope around the man's ankles. "I know it's terribly undignified, going out like this, and I'm sorry about that, I really am. If it's any consolation to you, I'll do my best to make sure nobody in your family finds you. Of course, the police'll probably take lots of pictures, but I don't think they show the really bad ones to the family, do you?"

A long, low moan, then even more urgent sounds.

"And morticians can do wonders these days, so you'll look good in the box so everyone can pay their respects."

This time, the sound was more a muffled scream.

He looked briefly interested, then shrugged, checked the hoist and rope for a final time, and began to slowly, carefully raise the man until he was hanging upside down with his head not much more than a foot off the ground.

For a few brief moments, he twisted around desperately like a newly hooked fish, but then subsided, still making those moaning sounds.

"I really am sorry," he told the man again as he tied off the rope. "If I had another choice . . . But I don't. It's just something I have to do. You understand that, right?"

A frantic shake of the head.

Again mildly curious, he went around and bent

slightly so he could grasp one side of the duct tape covering his victim's mouth. "You know nobody can hear you up here, right? Just us?"

A jerky nod.

He stripped the tape far enough to one side to expose the mouth, and allowed his victim to push the wad of gauze out with his tongue.

"Well? What are you so desperate to say? And please don't beg me not to do this. That's so boring."

In the upside-down face, terrified eyes stared at him and the mouth worked several times probably just to generate enough spit to be able to speak before a gasping string of intelligible words emerged.

"It's . . . you . . . You're *dead.*"

He didn't bother with the gauze, just smoothed the tape back over his victim's mouth.

"Yes," he said. "That's what makes it all so very interesting. Don't you think?"

FIVE

"It certainly isn't your average murder," Trinity Nichols said.

Deacon wondered how she felt about that, but couldn't tell. Her pleasant expression gave nothing away, and when he let his guard down a bit, that extra sense failed him as well. Not so

75

unusual; he had a fairly narrow range, according to Bishop, able to sense less than half the people he encountered even on a very good day.

Today was an average day, and he could sense only two here in this coffee shop. The teenager who seemed so intent on his online game was worried about flunking out of school, and one of the young baristas was nursing a pretty fierce crush on her boss. With more of an effort than he had expected, Deacon reestablished his shield, and the emotions faded away.

He nodded. "So . . . any suspects other than my sister?"

"I could tell you I wasn't free to discuss the investigation with an outsider."

"You could. Are you going to?"

"Well . . . it *is* up to me."

Having done his research, Deacon nodded. "State constitution grants all Georgia counties home rule to deal with local problems. Do you answer to county commissioners or a town council?"

"Commissioners," she answered readily. "We have a good board, as usual. People who want to serve, not use the position as a stepping stone to something better. Not really the best place to begin an ambitious political career, Sociable."

"I would have said," he murmured.

A faint gleam in her eyes acknowledged his use of the phrase she had used herself earlier, but she didn't comment on that.

Instead, she said, "Since the county sheriff's office is here, there's never been a need for town police, though a few of the smaller townships in the county have small forces. Basically, I'm the law in Crystal County."

"That was my understanding."

Conversationally, she said, "There was no way I was going to call in the state police, even when I realized—which I did well before noon on Tuesday—that whatever's going on here is something we've never had to deal with before. And that we certainly lack any necessary specialized . . . training . . . to deal with it. Bad as the situation was and is, it would be made immeasurably worse by the sort of media attention that always follows big official investigations with multiagency task forces."

Gazing into her intelligent eyes, he said slowly, "So you called in someone else. You called in the FBI."

Trinity Nichols inclined her head slightly. "I was a bit surprised when you turned up today. Having a family connection here, I mean. I assume that would disqualify you from working the case."

He barely hesitated. "Actually, I'm not sure whether it would or not, though there's probably something on the books to address a situation like this one. But the unit I belong to is a bit . . . outside . . . some aspects of traditional FBI procedure, so I'm not at all sure any sort of standard rule would hold true. In any case, I'm definitely not here officially. My boss didn't say anything to me about sending an agent or team down here."

"Bishop?"

That did surprise him, although he wondered if it should have. The SCU was, after all, becoming quite well known within law enforcement all over the country. Even in very small southern towns.

Maybe especially in very small southern towns.

Still, it made him more than a little wary. No matter what she said about media attention, the bald truth was that small-town local law enforcement generally called in federal troops only as a last resort, and the SCU as a *desperate* last resort. Unless, of course, that law enforcement was not too proud to yell for help—and not too closed minded to reject all things paranormal out of hand.

Which appeared to apply to Sheriff Trinity Nichols.

"Yeah. You called Bishop specifically? The Special Crimes Unit, not just the Bureau?"

Her shoulders lifted in a slight shrug, though her eyes never left his. "I know a few other sheriffs and cops in districts along the southern Appalachians. With all the tourists and hikers wandering up and down the Blue Ridge, some of them getting lost or into some other kind of trouble, it pays for law enforcement to keep in touch even across jurisdictional boundaries."

"Especially at times like now?" he suggested. "On the drive down here, all I heard on the radio was about all those young women abducted and killed in the mountains. Four dead so far, with two more missing."

Her face tightened slightly, but her voice remained calm. "Yeah, we're keeping in touch on that account. The girls have been taken along the southern part of the Blue Ridge, with abduction and dump sites miles apart. Hard to track, maybe even impossible, but they think he's moving south."

Deacon half nodded. "I know there's an FBI team working that case, including a couple of very good profilers. But it's the kind of case that can drag on for months, even years."

"God, don't say that," she muttered. "Six women abducted since just after Christmas, four of them already dead—and the last four taken awfully close together in the timeline. That's not just efficient; that's scary efficient."

"And scary prolific," Deacon said. "I don't see how he can keep to this pace much longer, but if he does . . . a lot more women are going to die."

"He's operating in a wilderness, and so far that's worked for him. But all the media coverage coupled with rangers, cops, feds, and even private investigators and bounty hunters crawling all over the mountains, plus helicopters buzzing overhead during the day, is bound to shrink his victim pool."

"They'll stop making it easy for him," Deacon agreed. "No more hikers or motorists stopping at lookouts or even rest stops. I heard the last two were taken from a pretty deserted rest stop."

"Yeah, and now every rest stop along the Blue Ridge and the general area is being manned by state cops or rangers, twenty-four-seven."

"A sensible precaution."

"It could drive him down into the towns to hunt, you know that. And there are way too many small, isolated mountain towns where hunting would be relatively easy for him."

"Like Sociable?" Deacon said.

"Like Sociable."

Cathy Simmons normally took a brisk walk before work nearly every day, weather permitting, and used the gym three times a week, usually after work. But since Scott's death, she had noticed she wasn't the only one electing not to be out walking or jogging alone.

The gym was crowded for a Thursday morning; it was a good thing she'd taken an early lunch, or she probably wouldn't have gotten a treadmill to herself.

Since there was a line waiting to use the equipment, she didn't linger but did a brisk thirty-minute walk, then gave up the machine and went to the locker room for a quick shower. She figured if she hurried, she'd have time to stop in next door for a salad or a half sub, even if she had to eat it in the break room at the bank—

"Hey, Cathy."

She started, swearing inwardly. "Hey, Jackson."

"Did I scare you? I'm sorry." Jackson Ruppe was a big man who towered over most everyone around him, but he was also the stereotypical gentle giant—unless he intercepted a bully or someone otherwise picking on the smaller and weaker.

Cathy could remember at least once in junior high when a couple of the "mean" girls had been verbally picking on her near her locker; Cathy had been to the point of tears when the girls had suddenly shut up and melted into the crowd. And Cathy hadn't been very surprised to turn and find Jackson looming.

He had smiled, winked, and gone on his way before she could even say thank you. And whether he had done something else or merely made his protection obvious, she had never again had to worry about being picked on—at school or outside it.

Smiling, she said, "I'm just jumpy. I think a lot of people are right now. Bad enough Scott's gone, but not knowing who killed him has everyone on edge."

"Yeah, that's all anybody's talking about down in the valley." Jackson worked on his family's horse ranch, raising and training beautiful Arabians that had for generations been so famous that they were shipped all over the world.

Cathy could remember as a child seeing an honest-to-God sheik in town to look at the horses. Flowing headgear and all.

"What're you doing up here in the middle of the day?" she asked.

"Mostly came up to ask Trinity if she had any leads. And to pick up my one good suit from the dry cleaner for the funeral tomorrow."

Making a mental note to check on her own wardrobe, Cathy asked, "What did Trinity say?"

"Wasn't in her office. I gather she's over at Village Coffee talking to a stranger. Except word is, he's Melanie's brother. And a fed."

Cathy blinked. "Seriously?"

"Way I heard it."

"You think he's here just to visit Melanie or because of Scott's murder?"

"He's not talking to Melanie," Jackson pointed out dryly. "He's talking to the sheriff."

Cathy chewed on her lower lip. "Maybe Trinity just needs somebody to talk to, a cop, who didn't grow up here. I mean, can *you* be objective about who might have killed Scott?"

Calmly, Jackson said, "I figure it was a cuckolded husband. Just not sure which one."

"But Scott and Melanie just broke up, and they were an item for months."

"Doesn't mean he was faithful."

Cathy hated finding out bad things about friends. "Dammit, did he cheat all the time?"

"It was his nature." Jackson wasn't in the least judgmental, just matter-of-fact. "I think most of his women caught on pretty soon, and some probably knew going in. Trinity did."

"She did? How do you know that?"

Jackson smiled. "Just do. She's one of the brightest people in this town and very . . . intuitive to boot. She knows people, and without being told. Horses love her. So do cats and dogs. Watch Braden with her sometime. Animals can always tell about good people."

"I know you've always thought that."

"It's true. Take Scott, for instance. Now, we both know I didn't care for the guy, but that doesn't mean I haven't noticed things about him. Telling things. Anytime a group of you went riding, he always had something else to do. Truth is, horses didn't like him. Neither did dogs. Even if he hadn't been a neat freak, there's no way he would have had a pet."

Cathy wasn't surprised that Jackson related people to animals; he'd been that way his whole life, probably not surprisingly given his upbringing on a ranch filled with high-strung horses, numerous other animals, and a family of bedrock-calm people.

She leaned sideways to look around him and

down the sidewalk for a moment. "Yeah, Braden's sitting outside the shop. He doesn't get far away from her, does he?"

"No, and probably a good thing, right now especially."

"I guess." She realized something suddenly and frowned at him. "Wait a minute. If you believe Scott was killed by somebody's husband, then why should Trinity be especially careful?"

"Hear about those women abducted and killed north of here?"

Cathy shivered, distracted from Scott's murder by probably the only thing that shook her almost as much. "There isn't much else on the news. Horrible. But that's miles away from here, Jackson, *and* miles away from any town. Out in the wilderness."

"Yeah. But looks like he's heading south pretty steady, so it might be her headache eventually. And trouble for us. Of all the mountain towns here at the end of the Appalachians, we're at the highest elevation. Closest to that wilderness."

That hadn't occurred to her. "Great. That's just great."

Jackson realized he had shaken her and was immediately sorry. "Look, it'll probably never get that far. *He'll* probably never get this far south. They've got an army combing the mountains for him."

"I wish that made me feel better."

He took her arm. "You need to eat before you go back to the bank. Why don't we get a sub, and then I'll walk you back to work, how's that?"

Even though the sub shop was less than a dozen doors down the sidewalk from the bank, it made Cathy feel better. She managed a laugh as she fell into step beside him. "Still watching out for me even after all these years."

"Maybe I'm just watching out for me," Jackson murmured, but so softly she didn't hear it.

"So that's why you reached out to the FBI?" Deacon ventured. "Less because of this murder in Sociable than because there's a serial in the mountains not so very far from here, maybe heading this way?"

"I had several reasons," Trinity said. "As I've noted, there are some unusual elements about the murder of Scott Abernathy. Enough to make me wonder if his killing was personal . . . or the start of something a whole lot worse."

Deacon hesitated, then said, "According to Melanie, he was the kind of man who might have enemies."

"He was that. A womanizer, everyone knew. But charming, and tended to keep things civil, at least with the women. Though I'm sure there are a few men out there who wouldn't have minded beating the hell out of him."

"But not breaking his neck?"

"No, not in a locked room early one morning. And not without disturbing his very neat apartment. This wasn't a killing in rage."

"Not your average murder," Deacon murmured.

"Exactly."

"So you reached out."

She nodded. "I reached out to some cops I know, asked who I could trust to help me figure out this unusual murder, and without running roughshod over me or this town—or turning it all into a media circus."

"And Bishop's name came up?"

"Quite a few times. Especially when I made it clear I didn't believe I was dealing with an average murder. At that point, most everybody said to call Bishop. And he seemed to almost be expecting my call." She smiled slightly. "I'd say he's earned his sterling reputation in the law enforcement community."

Deacon wasn't surprised. That tended to be a fairly universal reaction—though usually *after* the SCU assisted with a case.

"Did he say who he was sending?"

"Not by name. Said a team, no number mentioned, and they'd introduce themselves when they arrived. Sometime today, he said. You don't know?"

He frowned. "No idea. I just put in for some accumulated leave time, that's all. Officially, through channels, right after Melanie called me about this murder. And after asking Bishop if the timing was okay for me to be away a couple weeks. I wasn't on the team working the serial up in the mountains, and nothing else urgent seemed to be in the offing. He said fine, didn't ask where I was going. I didn't tell him I was going to visit family, or even in which direction I planned to head during that leave time, Sheriff."

"Trinity, please."

"I will if you will."

"Okay, Deacon. So you didn't tell Bishop you were coming to Sociable?"

"No. As I said, no pressing cases and I had leave coming. I had leave time piled up, as a matter of fact. And we're encouraged to take that time, especially doing the type of work we do. We need time away, time to . . . decompress. I hadn't been taking any breaks to speak of, and we've had a few rough cases in the last few months. So I told Bishop I could use a break. When one of his agents says that, he listens."

"He doesn't know you're here?"

After a brief silent debate, Deacon said, "Oh, he probably knows exactly where I am."

"That's the *special* in Special Crimes Unit?"

Deacon wondered just how much she really knew. "You said you talked to other cops. I'm assuming at least some of them know exactly what the unit is all about. Probably from experience."

"Some pretty remarkable experiences, I gather. Details were a bit sketchy, but . . ."

"But at least a couple of cops you trust vouched for the SCU."

"More than a couple. A bit sheepish about it all, but convinced. I gather they all had good reason to be."

He took a chance. "And you? How do you feel about the paranormal?"

"Not really an opinion one way or the other. I haven't experienced anything like that myself." Her tone didn't change, nor did her pleasant but unrevealing expression.

Deacon took another chance. "Haven't you?"

The jingle of the bell at the coffee shop door sounded before she could reply, and Trinity Nichols turned her head as a middle-aged man came in and then held the door for a black dog to enter as well. The man sent her a grin.

"He obviously wanted in, Sheriff."

"It's okay, Jack."

He waved a hand, then made his way to the counter to place his order.

The dog came straight through the shop and sat down at Trinity's side, uttering an odd little sound between a sigh and a sneeze.

Deacon studied him. Gleaming black, medium-sized but muscled, stocky, with very alert and almost eerily intelligent brown eyes. Nobody had cropped his ears, so they stood up almost all the way but with soft tips folded down, lending his wide face a sweeter expression than might otherwise have existed. Because the dog was unmistakably one of that unique mix of breeds commonly recognized as a pit bull.

A pit bull staring back at Deacon.

"Yours?" he asked the sheriff.

"He seems to think so."

Deacon kept his brows up questioningly.

"We don't have strays around here to speak of," she said. "Or abandoned pets. Good people who care, mostly. Good and longstanding laws and ordinances prevent backyard breeders, and the few licensed breeders in the county are good ones. Everybody else spays and neuters their pets, mandatory, even the cats; part of my job is to make sure the citizens comply, and the fines if they don't are pretty stiff and handed out without exception.

"My grandfather was an animal lover, and he believed it was part of his job to make sure people took care of their pets and livestock. Got pretty hot on the subject if he found out otherwise; neglect, abuse, even carelessness wasn't tolerated. Since he was sheriff, and since those were tougher days with fewer . . . constraints . . . on law enforcement, people listened and did what he demanded. Even the mayor and board of commissioners did. Until it simply became . . . the way of things. My father shared his views on the subject, and so do I. We've never even needed an animal control officer or shelter."

"And yet this guy was a stray? Maybe he got separated from his people while they were traveling."

She looked at the dog a moment, then returned her gaze to Deacon. "Well, I thought that might be, so I did the usual things. Ad in the papers all through the region; fliers put up; online posts where people from all over go to look at lost, found, or adoptable pets; phone calls to the three vet clinics in the county and fliers up in those offices. Even followed one lead supposedly to a suspected dog-fighting ring about fifteen miles outside town."

"And found?"

"They weren't fighting dogs, they were cooking meth. Damn near blew the house up before we could get the whole thing shut down and the idiots doing the cooking safely locked away."

Deacon considered. "A lot more money in meth than in dogfighting, especially in a place this isolated."

"Yes, thank goodness."

He lifted his brows at her.

"People making idiots of themselves and risking their own lives for money or whatever to do it is a choice. A stupid choice, but a choice. Abusing animals for *entertainment* or money is unconscionable and torture in my book."

In Deacon's book as well. "Okay." He looked at

the dog again, then back at her. "Well, he certainly doesn't look like he's been in a fighting ring. And I imagine you'd know fast enough if one existed."

"I would."

He didn't question that. "So you had this . . . misplaced dog."

She nodded. "Even notified the ranger service in case a hiker or camper along the Blue Ridge missed him, asked about him. Not a peep. Weeks passed, and nobody claimed him. Which seems to be just fine with him. No tags, but his name is Braden. It's on a little brass plate on his collar."

The dog immediately lifted a paw, directed at Deacon.

He accepted the paw for a brief shake, saying merely, "Hey, Braden." Then he returned his gaze to the sheriff. "So there was somebody who cared. Or did you train him to do that?"

"Must have been somebody who cared, because he's obviously had obedience training." She glanced at the dog. "At least."

Just because Deacon couldn't read her didn't mean he wasn't aware of . . . undercurrents. "So he offers to shake when he hears his name?"

"No, he offers to shake when it's appropriate. Like just now."

"You didn't signal or anything?"

"Nope."

"His idea?"

"Seems to be. He's like that. A mind of his own."

SIX

Hollis Templeton looked at the wide, boulder-strewn creek that seemed just inches from the edge of the winding blacktop road her partner was navigating and said, "Why do we always end up in or near tiny little mountain towns?"

"Is that a rhetorical question?" Reese DeMarco asked, keeping his eyes on the road.

"No." Hollis was a little disgruntled, and it showed.

"Because this is where the SCU-type crimes always seem to be, I suppose. A majority of them, anyway. Always a good hunting ground for monsters, these peaceful little towns. Because nobody expects it, or suspects their neighbors. Because they tend to be isolated and not really on the media radar. Because nobody notices anything is wrong until bodies start to turn up."

"And local law enforcement gets over-whelmed."

Her partner sent her a quick glance. "Yeah, especially when there's a chance of something out of the ordinary going on. They don't exactly teach courses in paranormal investigation at cop school. And locked-room murder mysteries are seldom found outside mystery novels."

Hollis sighed. "I just don't know why Bishop pulled us off the mountain serial and sent us here to investigate a single murder."

"You heard what Miranda said the same as I did. The team needed fresh eyes, so Bishop decided to send down Isabel and Rafe; they're just coming off a break. And since we've been tracking—or trying to track—the mountain serial for more than a month, he thought we needed a break, at least from that case."

"Miranda and Dean are staying," Hollis muttered.

"Miranda's the primary, and we all know one of Dean's strengths is recognizing patterns. Besides, both of them had a break before the mountain serial started."

"Well, our last case wasn't that demanding," Hollis objected. "We had a spree killer who practically had his motive tattooed on his forehead. Took us all of four days to track him down, and only across one state line." She sounded disgruntled. "There wasn't even anything weird about that case. I mean, just a regular FBI team could have caught him."

"Uh-huh," DeMarco murmured.

"I didn't mean it like that."

"Okay."

"Stop humoring me, dammit."

DeMarco sent her a glance. "What's really got you bothered?"

Damn telepaths.

Hollis sighed. "Bishop. God knows he never gives away anything he thinks might . . ."

"Mess up the plans of the universe?"

"Well, yeah. He and Miranda are always so careful when they've caught a glimpse of the future. You can always tell when it's one of *those* cases."

"You can always tell. Me, not so much."

She looked at him in surprise, then nodded. "You were undercover all those months in that church cult, really focused on that. I went through a whole bunch of cases in those two years or so." She frowned.

"So you think the mountain serial is one of those cases Bishop is being careful with? Even though Miranda said she hadn't seen anything of the future?"

"I think I wouldn't play poker with either one of them, because they can lie and have lied to our faces if they truly believe it's for our own good —or the greater good."

"It's necessary sometimes."

"You're former military; of course you think that way."

"It isn't because I'm former military. It's because I stood at the side of a megalomaniacal cult leader with a serious messiah complex and watched very bad things happen when I knew I couldn't intervene to stop them. No matter how much I wanted to. Because some things have to happen just the way they happen."

Hollis wasn't quite sure what she would have said to that, so it was a good thing that her partner went on calmly.

"Bishop didn't say much about this case."

"No. And this time I got the feeling he knows a lot less about whatever's going on here than he usually does when he sends us in."

"That would be a change."

"Yeah."

"Not a change you like," he noted.

"Oddly enough, no. I get as pissed as anybody else when we find out he held back on us, even if his reasons are understandable once a case is done with. But I don't much like feeling that he's as in the dark as we are and might not be able to . . . anchor us if we need it."

After a moment, DeMarco said, "I'm pretty sure we can handle whatever comes on our own, Hollis."

"I'll remind you that you said that," she said with a sigh.

"Well, whatever he knows or doesn't know, Bishop tends to match agents with the situation pretty well, so I'm sure he knew what he was doing when he decided to send us."

"You're sounding a lot more charitable than you have in the fairly recent past. I thought for a while there you were at least going to challenge him to a sparring workout just so you could legitimately get a few shots in."

"Legitimately?"

In an absent tone, she said, "You aren't the type of man to physically challenge another just because you're pissed. And you were pissed. But still respecting of the chain of command. That pretty much has to be the military background."

DeMarco glanced at her preoccupied expression and smiled faintly, but all he said was, "I'm sure Bishop has his reasons. And we'll find out what those are. When we get there. To Sociable."

Gloomy, she said, "You just *know* with a name like that the town will be anything but."

"Probably."

"Especially to us."

"Well, I imagine any strangers are going to be eyed uneasily, given the situation."

She sighed again. "I know. Because nobody in Sociable could have killed, especially like that. Nobody in Sociable is *capable* of that. They all know their neighbors, and there's just no way any of them are killers."

"Except," DeMarco continued in the same vein, "for that one guy. The guy everybody knows. The one who lives in a crappy house or trailer and drives a car that's broken down more often than it's running and who has four more junk cars up on blocks in his overgrown yard. The guy who

96

always gets himself into trouble. Gets thrown in the local jail so often he has his own cell with his favorite pillow on the cot. Maybe has a problem with drinking or beats his wife or has serious anger issues with the world and takes it out on anybody who even looks at him the wrong way. The guy his neighbors will mention because he's made them uneasy. The guy who could turn out to be a killer without surprising anybody."

"Right. The one guy we can usually rule out right away."

"Maybe we should have warned them."

"We couldn't, you know that. They have to figure it all out for themselves."

"But they have no *idea* what they're walking in to. It all looks so simple—and it isn't. It all looks like just another case. And it *isn't*. If this plays out the way we think it will . . ."

"It has to, you know that. We both know that. It has to *end* finally, with no questions left unanswered. With no vague shadow of a threat left out there to haunt us. It has to end. And it has to end on our terms. Not his."

"He'll know they're coming."

"Yes. But I don't believe he'll know what they've become."

"They don't know what they've become."

"After this, they will."

"If they survive."

"They will. They're probably the only two we could send who would."

"They'll be blindsided. God, what a word."

"They'll survive. And they'll win. More than that, they'll emerge even stronger."

"Maybe. But even if they do, this time they may never forgive us."

"Me. They may never forgive me."

"Can you live with that?"

"I'll have to, won't I?"

Deacon wondered if it was a coincidence that they started talking about the dog when he had mentioned the paranormal.

No. Surely not. The dog had come in and they were talking about him. That was all.

Casually, the sheriff said, "He didn't have a rabies tag, so my vet checked him out and vaccinated him. He's in good health, not much more than a year old, well nourished, and he's been neutered. No physical or behavioral signs of neglect, mistreatment, or injury. No microchip, no tattoo, nothing to indicate who he belonged to before I found him on my front porch about two months ago."

"So now he's yours."

"Appears to be."

Deacon still couldn't tell how she felt about that. "You said you were an animal lover," he ventured.

"I am." She paused, then said, "Always had pets growing up. And as an adult. I have a cat, who Braden is very polite to. And two months to the day before Braden showed up, I had lost my most recent dog to age and cancer."

"I'm sorry."

"Yeah, so was I. We'd been together a dozen years." Her shoulders lifted in a slight shrug. "I found him in one of the rural pounds between here and Atlanta. A pit bull or pit mix; the sort I favor. We clicked."

"And Braden?"

"Well, I had just decided it was time to get another dog, because I've seldom been without one and I like my home and my life in general better with a dog in it. I had literally just decided to get online, contact rescues and shelters within driving distance. Then I opened my front door, still thinking about that, and there he was. Sitting on my front porch as though waiting for me."

"Already named and trained."

Her smile was faint. "Yeah. And . . . we clicked. In that first moment, when he lifted a paw to shake. He sleeps on the foot of my bed and comes to work with me every day. Always near, at home or around town, but never underfoot or otherwise in the way. He sits in the Jeep if I'm out on a call—with the window all the way down, at his insistence. And while I'm outside the vehicle, he watches. Our town drunk got belligerent with me one night, and Braden was just suddenly there, between us. Didn't growl or make a sound. But . . . Never seen Amos back down so fast, and he's been known to charge bears unarmed."

"Real bears?"

"When he's drunk, yeah."

Deacon looked at the dog for a moment, noting that Braden at least appeared to be following the conversation, looking at whoever was talking. "Think he has law enforcement training?" he asked, finding those intelligent brown eyes fixed on him.

Until Trinity answered.

"I think he has a mind of his own. Whatever his background, whatever . . . shaped him . . . left him unlike any dog I've ever known. He knows all the basic commands and appears to be not only observant but . . . intelligently so."

Deacon was curious. "For instance?"

"I couldn't find my keys the other day. Didn't say anything, just started looking. About a minute later, Braden came to me with the keys in his mouth."

"So . . . maybe a service dog?"

"Maybe. But mostly he just . . . does exactly what he should be doing at any given moment, to respond, to help if there's a problem, or just to make things easier. Assesses the situation and behaves accordingly.

"He has chosen to be with me, that's clear

enough. He has chosen to be the sheriff's dog. And, so far, I've never had to tell him to do anything. He just seems to know what's expected of him, from walking at heel without a leash and looking both ways before he crosses the street to making sure he's beside me if there's a threat or trouble of any kind."

She looked at Braden. "I have to say, though, always before, if I've been in a restaurant or one of the coffee shops, he waits outside. Sits politely out of sidewalk traffic and waits. No one would object to his presence, but it's supposed to be like most places where food is served, only service animals allowed. Something else he seems to know without having to be told."

"So—what? He came in to meet me? To listen to us talk about him?"

"Maybe." She frowned, then lowered her voice when she said, "From the little I was told, I gather each agent in the unit has a unique ability. Mind if I ask you what yours is?"

"Melanie didn't tell you?"

Trinity said, "We didn't talk about the unit. Plus, from things that have come up in the past, I get the feeling that Melanie isn't all that comfortable with even the idea of psychic ability, never mind talking about it."

He hesitated, then said, "Some abilities are a lot more difficult to learn to live with. Some people struggle with them. Some people try to just ignore them. Melanie belongs in the latter camp."

"She's psychic?"

"We've found it tends to run in families. But having a latent ability, being for all intents and purposes suppressed, is a long way from being able to effectively tap into and use that ability."

Instead of asking about that, Trinity said, "Well, since you're part of the SCU, I gather you use your ability. Which is?"

Deacon didn't hesitate. "Empath. I pick up on emotions sometimes. Not all the time, not with everybody. But sometimes."

She appeared to accept that, nodding. "Do you have to concentrate to do that?"

"I have to drop my guard, usually." He shrugged. "Those of us born with abilities usually build our own individual type of mental or emotional shielding by the time we hit our teens. A kind of self-defense mechanism so we aren't . . . bombarded."

"You were born an empath?"

"As far back as I can remember, I've been able to feel what some other people feel. Especially if the emotions are powerful. Anger, pain, grief, fear. Those I pick up on pretty easily if I pick them up at all."

"I imagine that could be overwhelming."

"Under the right circumstances, yeah, definitely. Hospitals and prisons are the worst, generally speaking, but any situation where emotions run high can be . . . uncomfortable for people like me."

"Prisons?"

He smiled. "I wasn't an inmate, I promise you. Just a visitor. Part of why the unit is so successful is that Bishop . . . challenges and tests us on a regular basis. Sends us to places or into situations where we're able to practice using our abilities. Or not using them, which can often be more important."

Trinity sipped her coffee, her considering gaze on him, apparently not bothered by any of that, and then she asked, "What about with animals? Can you feel what they feel?"

"I don't think I ever have." He barely paused before saying, "You're curious. About Braden. Is he really that strange?"

"He's that . . . unusual."

"Because he has a mind of his own?"

Trinity drew a breath and let it out slowly. "Because before there was any report at all, he led me to Scott Abernathy's apartment, and to the murdered body. As if he knew."

Toby Gilmore laid out the cards for the third time, and frowned down at them.

Weird.

She hardly considered herself an expert at tarot, but she *had* been reading the cards since high school. For fun, of course; it was a good party trick, so she always carried a deck of cards wherever she went, and whenever there was a festival of any kind, her thing was dressing up like a gypsy and telling fortunes.

For entertainment purposes only, of course.

Usually when she laid out the cards in whatever pattern she chose, what she got was a random arrangement, one she interpreted more through knowledge and intuitive guesswork about her friends and acquaintances than any paranormal gift. Usually. And she was good at cold-reading strangers—or seemed to be, judging by their reactions. But sometimes it really did feel like the cards were talking to her, telling her things.

Not something she wanted to admit to any of her friends.

Especially now.

Because this . . . was more than a little unnerving. It had started only a few days before Scott had been found so horribly murdered. She generally "practiced" tarot here in her office, because real estate wasn't exactly a booming business in Sociable, at least not in winter. Even with a storefront window opening onto Main Street, what foot traffic there was to her office tended to be the UPS guy or friends dropping by.

So there were long hours that would have been boring if she didn't do *something* to occupy herself.

Toby stared at the layout and rubbed her forehead, trying to ease the increasing ache there.

The same combination kept coming up—almost exactly. No matter how many times she shuffled, the same dozen or so cards turned up in the same exact place in the layout.

She was experienced enough at tarot not to be disturbed that the death card was always there; that only meant a change, a transition, something as simple as changing jobs or moving house or breaking up with a boyfriend—not literal death.

But it was always at the center of the layout, and that was troubling. And the other cards . . .

Toby had realized not long after Scott's murder, when at least the worst of the shock had passed, that something else had changed. She had. Or how she saw the cards had. She wasn't sure which. All she knew for sure was that when she looked at a layout now, not occasionally but *every single time* she dealt the cards, she . . . *felt* what they meant.

And what she felt were certainties.

There were changes coming—for a lot of people. There was something very bad looming out there, something worse than a killer, and it was . . . old. Ancient.

Scary as hell.

She told herself that it was only a natural reaction to the murder of someone she had known. Scott had been a bit of a ladies' man—well, worse than that, if the truth be told—but even though Toby's fling with him had lasted only a few weeks and was years back, just after college, they had remained friends because Scott was like that and Toby never held grudges.

Despite what gossip said, despite the edgy "discussion" in the restaurant she had witnessed herself, she knew he most certainly would have remained friends with Melanie James, a much more recent fling.

Just as he was still friends with Trinity and with the other women who had shared his bed for whatever length of time. There might have been—probably were—a few men who had been pissed off at Scott, but he had a charming way about him when he wanted, and as far as she knew, there had never been any trouble that had escalated to even a punch.

Even when Scott had probably deserved one.

But that wasn't what bothered Toby right now. What bothered her were the cards.

It had been Cathy Simmons who had, years before, christened them The Group: a dozen or so men and women in their early thirties, actually from the same high school graduating class, who had lived in Sociable their whole lives and had either remained after high school or returned after college.

In Trinity's case, after college *and* nearly a decade down in Atlanta as a cop. But that hadn't changed anything. She'd been born here, raised here, lived and worked here now. So she was one of The Group.

Discounting kids still at home and in school, and the occasional person now and then returning for brief family visits, they were pretty much the youngest group of people in town; after The Group, kids tended to go away to college and stay away.

Or just go away.

As if the town itself had decided there were enough people here.

What a weird thought. It's just . . . no real career choices. Not many good jobs unless you inherit the family ranch or farm. That's all it is. Completely natural.

Toby rubbed her forehead harder.

Most members of The Group were still single, and there had been a fair amount of dating among them, with at least a few bad breakups over the years. But The Group's social lives were still pretty much intertwined—though it wasn't as if the various members didn't also socialize with other friends and family.

We aren't a cult, for God's sake!

Just a group of friends who had gone to school together and got invited to the same parties and worked out at the same gym and known each other their whole lives.

Melanie James was in The Group despite not having been born here. Maybe because she was friendly and personable and simply in the right age bracket. Because she was very attractive and seemed bent on putting down roots here.

Because she . . . fit.

Cathy had brought Melanie into the group, though it certainly hadn't been a formal thing. They had known each other in college years ago, now worked at the same bank, and Cathy had simply invited Melanie along when a few of them had gone on one of their Sunday trail rides. Melanie could ride and had enjoyed it—and they had enjoyed her company.

That's how it had started, and after nearly three years, Melanie was tacitly considered one of them.

Which was interesting, very interesting, because Toby was convinced that it would be Melanie who would be instrumental in finding the murderer doing such horrible things in Sociable.

Melanie was a linchpin of some sort.

A catalyst.

Toby couldn't see it all in the cards, not clearly at least; some things were fuzzy. And outcomes depended on actions, individual choices, which could always change right up until the moment those actions and choices took place.

Some things were always fluid.

Almost nothing was set in stone.

Almost nothing.

But there were things Toby knew, things she was certain were fated to happen.

Toby knew that because of Melanie, a dark man

would come to town. Was, in fact, already here. And at least two other people were coming as well, a tall woman with odd eyes and a big blond man who was rather startlingly handsome. Three people either on their way or already in Sociable. Three people who had things in common, much as The Group had things in common.

But not the same things.

The three strangers had faced evil before, more than once, and survived it. They would face it again, here.

And one of them would be destroyed by it.

That's what the cards kept telling Toby.

SEVEN

"In a small town, the obvious is seldom where we end up," DeMarco agreed. "So *not* that one guy everybody suspects. With our luck, it'll be the mayor or sheriff."

"We've had it be one mayor and one chief of police in past SCU investigations, if I'm remembering correctly. Plus a deputy or detective or two." Hollis sighed, then shook her head. "Probably not the sheriff, though, at least this time."

"It would be nice if we could at least trust the badges," DeMarco observed.

"Ain't that the truth." Hollis opened her tablet and in a moment was studying official documents. "So the sheriff is the one who formally asked for FBI assistance. Trinity Nichols. Unusual name. A woman. Attractive. Young for a sheriff, too. Law enforcement background down in Atlanta, with lots of commendations and glowing reports earned when she was a very young detective. Plus some serious formal training in crime investigation, including courses at the Bureau. Physically, though, just basic cop marksmanship and self-defense training. She excelled at both, says here, but nothing fancy like martial arts. So even if she's physically imposing—which her picture and stats indicate she really isn't—it's a bit hard to see how she could have snapped the neck of a man nearly a foot taller than her. Or . . . snapped a human neck, period. Last I checked, they don't teach cops how to do that."

"Granted. How's the mayor look?"

Unsmiling, Hollis checked the files. "Late fifties, married, kids *and* grandkids, never so much as a parking ticket. No military background. And not exactly physically imposing. Or even physically fit. Says here his doctor has ordered him to watch what he eats and to exercise. So His Honor signed up for a gym membership. And visited exactly once, last month."

"New Year's resolution," DeMarco murmured.

"Probably. Gym memberships always pick up around the New Year. And before swimsuit weather."

"Uh-huh." He paused, then added, "I'm not going to ask how we got our hands on medical records."

"Best not," she agreed.

"Okay, so there's two possible suspects mostly ruled out, and we haven't even hit town yet."

"Yeah, but . . ." Hollis continued to study the file, the reports, the crime scene photos.

"But?"

"But, we have an unlikely victim who lived in a small town—a young, fit adult male found with his neck snapped. In a locked room in his own locked apartment. No signs of forced entry into the apartment *or* the room. Room is neat. Victim shows no signs of being strangled, no ligature marks, no signs of trauma. No signs of a blitz attack to subdue him. And no signs he even tried to put up a fight. There was certainly no disturbance that attracted attention. Even though he lived in a second-floor apartment, the bedroom of which is where the body was found.

"You saw the crime scene photos when we got the case," Hollis finished. "Awfully peaceful and neat, this guy's bedroom."

"I just glanced at them but, as you said, no visible signs of struggle. Was he drugged?"

"Tox screen isn't back yet, says here. Forensics went to the state lab, and they're busy."

"Usually are. I'm betting Bishop will have whatever they've got shipped to Quantico ASAP."

"That would be my guess. So we'll probably have tox screen results and any other forensics within a few days."

"You don't think those results will be helpful," DeMarco noted, guided by her tone as much as his own logic.

"Well, I doubt he got drunk or high and managed to break his neck without leaving even a bruise. And if he *had,* there still would have been signs of some kind of disturbance, surely. A chair knocked over. A wrinkle in the rug at the foot of his bed. *Something.*"

"Granted. Unless a drug was used to knock him out so he could be more easily dispatched." DeMarco added, "All signs of which the killer then took with him after making sure the room was left nice and neat and then using his mad skills to throw a security deadbolt from outside the apartment door without leaving so much as a scratch on the metal."

"It's a puzzle," Hollis agreed.

"Who found the body?"

Hollis read, then let out a little sigh. "The sheriff. An anonymous tip, she said."

"So maybe the killer wanted his handiwork found and appreciated. And sooner rather than later."

"Maybe. According to their coroner, who is also apparently the most senior doctor in town, the victim had only been dead an hour, two at most, when he was examined at the scene."

"Interesting," DeMarco said.

"Weird is what it is. Aside from the whole locked-room thing, I don't like anonymous tips; it means somebody knows something or saw something that they are not willing to be public about. And that is never good."

"Secrets."

"Yeah. And small-town secrets can be doozies."

Melanie had only one appointment that morning, and since foot traffic into the bank was very light and she hadn't been sleeping well, she went to her boss and asked if she could take a sick day.

Bank manager Gary Martelle was immediately sympathetic. "Of course you can go home, Melanie. I told you yesterday you could take the rest of the week, if you needed it. I know you and Scott had your problems, but it had to be a horrible shock for you, his murder."

She couldn't tell if he was fishing for information or genuinely sympathetic, but neither interested her, given her present mood. So she merely smiled and thanked him.

Cathy appeared in the doorway of her office as Melanie was gathering her things, her usual sweet expression disturbed by worry. "Hey, are you going to be okay? I mean, do you really want to be at home alone?"

Melanie didn't really want to go into long explanations or protest what she knew would be

Cathy's offer to accompany her, so she said what she knew would most likely reassure her friend.

"My brother's going to be visiting for a couple of weeks, so I won't be alone. I'll be fine, Cathy."

Visibly relieved, her friend nevertheless said, "We'll go to the funeral together, okay? And . . . visitation is tonight. Are you going to go?"

"I haven't decided yet. I guess the rest of The Group is going?"

"Far as I know. I'm not sure about Trinity; it probably depends on how her investigation is going. And when the feds get here."

Involuntarily, Melanie said, "Man, news travels fast."

"Well, federal agents in Sociable? Just a couple days after the first murder in these parts for a decade?" Cathy smiled wryly. "You should be glad of them coming, you know. It's at least taking some folks' minds off whether Scott killed himself because you broke his heart."

"Seriously?"

"Afraid so."

Melanie's strongest reaction to that news was the realization that Scott would have *hated* anyone believing that a woman had dumped him, driving him to suicide.

Cathy's smile widened. "I know I shouldn't be amused, but . . ."

"Yeah." Even as she said it, Melanie shook her head. "I bet gossip has it both ways. He dumped me, so I killed him—somehow; I dumped him, and he killed himself. I really come out on the lousy end of things no matter which they believe."

"Well, if it helps, most of The Group I've talked to have every intention of spreading the word that you two broke up—and that you were both fine with it. End of story."

Except it wouldn't be, Melanie knew. Not with Scott dead.

Murdered.

"I'm going home and taking a nap," she announced.

"I'll call you in the afternoon to check on whether you want to go to the funeral home tonight."

"Okay."

Melanie lived close enough to work that she only bothered to take her car if she knew she'd be leaving the bank to go out of town for some reason. Shopping out by the highway. The multiplex out by the highway.

Even the funeral home was out near the highway.

For some reason, that really depressed Melanie. But the chill in the air served as a handy excuse for her to avoid pausing to talk to anyone on her way home, walking briskly down one block and then back just one street to her apartment building. Rather than external apartment entrances like Scott's building had, Melanie's boasted a lobby with a manned security desk and an elevator.

She waved to the security guard but didn't pause to talk to him, either, going straight to the elevator and up to her apartment.

It was a nice place, and she had furnished and decorated it with a lot more care—and more taste—than she had put into the tiny apartment in Atlanta where she'd lived during and after college. This was her home, a place she intended to live in and enjoy for a long time. Maybe for a very long time.

She was reasonably sure she had already dated all the men who interested her in Sociable. The men who had attracted her. Of course, maybe one would come along later, or get divorced or widowed . . .

Jesus. It's not like I mind being alone.

She turned on the TV because she didn't really want to nap, then went into her bedroom to change out of her work clothes and into jeans and a sweater.

The day stretched before her. She was ruefully certain that Deacon was already in town and was not at all surprised that she hadn't seen him yet. He'd get the lay of the land first, get a sense of Sociable and its citizens, probably even check in with Trinity and the investigation into Scott's murder, before coming to tell her all the reasons why the panic that had caused her to call him was nothing but her fevered imagination.

Not that he'd put it that way. No, he'd be more

subtle than that. More caring. But the gist would be the same.

Are you taking your meds, Mel? Are you getting enough rest, enough sleep? Eating right? Because you know what the doctors said about stress and how the mind can play tricks . . .

Swearing under her breath, she turned toward the elegant little desk in her living room, where she usually used her laptop for work—or for fun. She took one step toward it.

And then froze.

Gooseflesh spread over her entire body, and she almost felt her heart stop.

No. It isn't. It can't be.

Scott. Standing not a foot from her desk, looking at her, his expression anxious. He reached out a hand toward her. To her.

She could see through him.

"Scott," she whispered. Every instinct urged her to run or scream or even close her eyes again. But she couldn't.

He seemed to be trying to speak to her, but there was no sound, and as she stared he faded away until there was nothing.

No image of a murdered one-time lover.

Melanie still couldn't look away from where he had stood, where she had surely imagined him to be standing. She didn't know how long she stood there, staring at the spot, almost willing him to return.

But he didn't return.

Something else came.

A hint of motion near the wall drew her gaze a foot or so to the right of where Scott had stood, and as she watched, something black seemed to ooze through the pretty wallpaper she had chosen with such care, slowly taking shape as though filling an invisible mold. Melanie grew colder and colder, unable still to scream or move or even look away.

It became the shape of a person, but distorted, larger than Scott had been, looming. And it was utter, complete blackness. It was blacker than it was possible to be, so black she could see nothing through it, see nothing else as it loomed over her.

Hungry. Needing. Evil.

"Secrets do tend to be magnified in small towns," DeMarco observed to his partner. "To at least appear to be bigger or more tangled than secrets in other places."

"I doubt it's an optical illusion," Hollis said dryly.

"Maybe another kind of illusion. No anonymity in a small town. Everybody knows—even the secrets. Maybe especially the secrets. They just usually agree to keep them. At least from outsiders."

"Which we will be."

"Which we will definitely be. Outsiders with badges. And questions they won't want to answer."

"Standard police work," Hollis said, acutely aware of the lack of enthusiasm in her voice. "Looking at reports, interviewing witnesses, asking all those questions nobody will want to answer."

"Building a profile," DeMarco reminded her.

"Given the file we've seen so far, the glaring lack of any evidence at the scene, I don't see how I'll use that particular tool from the toolbox. Not unless there's another murder. And it does seem unlikely that two serial killers would be operating so close to each other at the same time."

"True. But possible."

"You're thinking of why Bishop sent us here."

"Well, he rarely sends a team to investigate a single murder, even if it's an odd one."

"True."

"And even if this really is a simple police investigation without any psychic frills, you have been working on building a shield," DeMarco said.

"And you know damned well I'm still broadcasting like a beacon more often than not. Which means nada on the shield." She sounded frustrated.

When he glanced at her, the same frustration was written clearly on her expressive face.

Choosing his words carefully, DeMarco said, "I'm sure you remember that Miranda also offered a theory about that."

"Yeah. That all my abilities, including initially becoming an active rather than a latent psychic, have been triggered by . . . events. By need." Her voice was calm and even wry and offhand, the way it always was whenever she mentioned the subject of her developing abilities.

DeMarco wondered if she realized how much she distanced herself emotionally when she spoke of them, especially when the subject was the devastating attack that had triggered her latent abilities as a medium.

Though God knew it had to be a survival mechanism for her to say as little as possible—and that, light and almost flip. The report of that attack had held only the cold, brutal facts, but those had been enough to shock and sicken even a man who had been to war.

Knowing what had been done to her gave DeMarco horrific nightmares—and if some of those were her nightmares, unremembered in the sane light of morning, it was something he would never tell her about. Because she would only take another step away from him, guarded and wary.

Not ready to truly face it herself, far less ready to share it with the man who loved her.

It didn't help DeMarco to know that the serial

rapist and murderer who had brutalized Hollis, leaving her terribly injured body and soul, even her sight, *her eyes* taken from her, had paid for his crimes with his life. It didn't help him to know that Maggie Garrett, a gifted empathic healer, had helped ease the worst of the pain and trauma so that Hollis had emerged from the horror of that attack able to not only continue to live her life but also thrive and grow, reinventing herself rather than retreating into darkness, as that monster's other surviving victims had done.

It didn't even help that a gifted surgeon—and, DeMarco suspected, her own innate healing abilities—had given her back her eyesight.

None of it helped.

Because Hollis had been hurt terribly in ways no human being should ever be hurt, and no matter how deeply buried the agony of that was, no matter how easily she seemed able to refer to "the attack" almost as if it had happened to someone else, the truth was that she would live forever with a dark knowledge of true evil and unspeakable loss, and that might never, ever heal.

And there wasn't a goddamned thing DeMarco could do to help her deal with that.

Unaware of his thoughts or the pain they brought him, Hollis was going on in that almost flip, uncaring tone she invariably used when discussing the evolution of her psychic abilities.

"The first new sense opened up because of

extreme trauma and because I'd lost one of the original five, and nobody knew it'd be a temporary loss, even my own mind. Later I apparently needed to see auras, so I did. I needed to be able to heal myself because I'd be dead otherwise, needed to be able to heal others because Diana would most probably be dead otherwise—and I'm not going to let a friend die if there's anything I can do to stop it."

"I don't think there was a 'probably' about that one," DeMarco murmured. "Without you, she would have died."[2]

Hollis half nodded, acknowledging that. "And I needed to be able to channel pure energy, dark energy, *and* scrub it clean, because it was causing all *kinds* of trouble and threatening more; someone had to take care of it, and evil has a nasty habit of deceiving most people, even most mediums. But not me, I'm not deceived, mostly due to that first traumatic event in my life, where I met evil up close and intensely personal, so the evil behind that energy at Alexander House couldn't trick me, couldn't hide itself from me."

She frowned suddenly. "I wonder if channeling energy like that was a one-time deal for me? An extreme situation demanding an extreme ability? Or whether it's in the toolbox now."

"Bishop didn't say?"

"No. Though in fairness, I didn't ask."

[2]*Blood Ties*

"Then I imagine," DeMarco said, "you'll find out soon enough."

"Yeah." Still fretting about her inability to construct for herself any kind of reliable psychic protection, she said, "But a shield . . . that really does tend to be a necessity for us. You telepaths block out the chatter of minds all around you. Precogs, most of them, try to keep up some kind of barrier against seeing the future when they aren't looking for it so that they aren't always blindsided by visions they aren't braced for. Clairvoyants block out bits and pieces of information that can come at them like bullets. And we mediums . . ."

"Usually have to open a door. Consciously. Which you've sometimes been able to do. But especially these last months you've been pretty much wide open. So you don't need a shield so much as a lock and key."

"Yeah, but if I've ever had a lock or key, I've never been able to consciously use them. I mean, at least before I'd concentrate and I'd *think* I'd opened a door, but the longer I do this the less certain I am that even that much control seems to be present in me. It's more like . . . I show up, and some spirits are able to come through, usually because they need to, because they have unfinished business."

"That plus you," DeMarco pointed out. "Bishop seems convinced that your very presence attracts spiritual energy."

"It hasn't attracted any lately," she retorted, then went on before he could respond. "But no matter why I see and talk to spirits, they aren't a dangerous drain on me."

"It does drain you," he pointed out. "To varying degrees."

"Yeah, but not enough, apparently, for me to feel the need to shut them out at will. I haven't *needed* a shield so far. Not like that, not to protect myself. Not out of the desperate need to . . . close out all the spiritual signals I'm such a dandy receiver for. I've always needed to be open, not closed. Even in the beginning, when I was resisting, I didn't have a shield—I just refused to listen. Until I didn't have a choice. Eventually, according to Miranda, I'll discover a reason why I really, really need a shield. And when I *do* that, when I badly need a shield, I'll have a shield. Presto, just like magic."

"You know better than that."

Hollis sighed. "Yes. I do. Which is why I can't decide whether that possibility sounds too simple or just scary as hell. Because we both know how strong past events were to trigger new abilities in me. How extreme. Mostly traumatic. Mostly painful. Events that nearly got me killed. Should have gotten me killed. Several times. So what's it going to take to create that shield, Reese? How bad do things have to get before my mind decides to protect itself?"

EIGHT

Sheriff Trinity Nichols said dryly, "I'm sure you understand why this is the first time I've . . . shared this information in Sociable."

Deacon glanced at the dog, who returned his gaze intently, then looked back at her. "So none of your deputies know."

"I told them an anonymous tip led me to the body. That's also what I put in the file, the official report. So nobody knows. Except you. And Bishop."

"So you told Bishop." Deacon frowned slightly. "I wonder if he's sending Callie, then."

Trinity raised her eyebrows.

"Callie Davis. She's the only one in the unit, to my knowledge, who has experience communicating with animals telepathically." He kept his tone completely matter-of-fact. "Her only true SCU partner has been Cesar, a Rottweiler she raised and trained. I'm told it's pretty remarkable to watch them work."

"So she talks to him. Telepathically." Trinity didn't sound doubtful, just as though she wanted everything to be perfectly clear.

"Definitely. In complete sentences or close enough, according to what's known within the unit. I've never worked with her, so I don't know for sure. But last I heard, she was working with at least three other dogs to find out if her bond with Cesar is unique."

"What's the verdict so far?"

"The bond seems to be unique, but she's nevertheless been able to communicate, on a far more basic level, with at least two of the other dogs. Only been working at it a few months, and her bond with Cesar was developed over years, so there's every chance she'll be able to improve on the basic communication."

"I see. So maybe she could . . . communicate . . . with Braden."

"Maybe." Deacon frowned again. "Although when I was told she was working with the other dogs, I was also told she was—more or less—on extended leave. Or the more typical SCU version of it, anyway. Not working on active cases but working on the psychic toolbox."

"That's what you guys call it?"

"Well, it fits. Bishop started the unit because he believed psychic abilities could be used as investigative tools. Not that we'd ride in on our white horses and solve everything with a single *reading,* dazzling the locals with our seemingly magical abilities, but just that we'd be cops, trained investigators, with a few extra investigative tools we could use to help hunt down and catch the bad guys."

"Any edge is usually welcome and often makes

all the difference between success and failure," she agreed.

"And sharpening or improving control over those tools is usually a priority, though it tends to be done in the field and through sheer time and experience."

"Makes sense."

"Yeah, but we generally fly under the radar, so to speak. It's the usual type of police work observers see, not the psychic abilities. We tend to be not real open about those extra tools, even quite often with the law enforcement people we're working with. I mean, it's getting more common now for us to encounter members of the law enforcement community who do know about us, and who accept what we do even if they don't believe in it, but that's because we have a high success rate, a strong reputation for discretion, and we don't ride roughshod over the locals. If anything, we go out of our way to stay . . . back in the shadows and out of the media spotlight. If there is one. Will there be here?"

"Not if I have anything to say about it." Trinity's tone was just a bit grim. "The local newspaper hasn't gone digital and has kept reports low-key at my request. No local TV or radio. We're isolated geographically, miles off a main highway, and those serial killings of women in the mountains north of us are keeping the national and most of the regional media occupied for the moment. This time of year isn't part of the major tourist season for us, not without a ski slope within easy driving distance. If anything, uncertain weather can make driving treacherous in a hurry and without much warning, and so tends to keep visitors at a minimum in winter. But you know as well as I do that one kid with a cell phone can upload an image or video to YouTube, Twitter, or Facebook—and the whole world knows what's happening in Sociable."

"So you've done what you could to keep access to the crime scene restricted, especially visually?"

"And threatened my deputies with firing or worse if any of *them* leaks information. In any way, shape, or form." She paused, then added, "We were lucky that this killer left his victim inside a locked apartment rather than in some high-traffic public area. If we have a one-time murder, that may take care of any publicity worries. But . . . if he is a serial and kills again, if he evolves the way I was taught that serial killers evolve . . ."

"He may want media attention sooner rather than later. Hey, look at me. Look at what I can do. Can't catch me."

"Which is what I'm afraid of."

Deacon brooded for a moment, glancing once or twice at Braden to find the dog looking steadily back at him. "So . . . the body was found in a locked room, which is about as private as it could be."

"Scott Abernathy. In his own bedroom in his own apartment. If I hadn't been . . . alerted . . . as quickly as I was, the first person there might have been the building manager or a concerned coworker. Or relatives; Scott has—had—a few locally. Widowed mother, brother. A cousin, I think."

"You knew him?"

"I know most everybody in Sociable. Grew up here. Left for college and to be a cop in Atlanta for a few years, but I came back here. And I still know most everybody."

Deacon nodded slowly. "So family might have discovered the body, but instead of any of them finding him, it was you and Braden."

"Yeah. Far as I can tell, no family was expecting to visit him or expecting him to contact them, so it likely would have been the apartment manager, urged on by a coworker concerned when he didn't show up for work. Had a spotless work record and had never failed to call in on the rare occasions when he was sick. He would have been missed that day, certainly by the next day; he was killed early on a Tuesday, apparently about to go out on his regular morning run."

"Habits," Deacon murmured.

"Habits the killer would have known about, if he lived here and paid attention. Or just if he'd watched for any length of time," Trinity agreed.

"Any signs he did?"

"Not that we could find. No vehicle loitering, no place within view of his apartment where there was evidence someone had spent some time lurking and watching. No neighbors who noticed anything odd in the days and weeks leading up to the murder, or even that day. And his usual running route was almost all public, one used by most of our regular runners. There was about a half-mile twist through the woods where he might have been alone at that hour, but otherwise he was in full sight of plenty of people. When he usually ran, I mean. Not that morning."

"Anybody else know you and Braden found his body? Your coroner? Some of your deputies?"

"Doc Beeson didn't ask who, just when. Of the deputies, only two were allowed into the apartment. Lexie Adams and Douglas Payne make up my crime scene unit, such as it is. I sent them up to Quantico to be trained and equipped nearly two years ago, shortly after I took office, and roughly every four months since I've sent them down to Atlanta to work on a case for a week or so and keep their skills sharp, since those skills are rarely needed here. Or were rarely needed. Nobody else got close, it's locked up, taped off, and under guard, and the crime scene photos are Need to Know."

She paused, then added, "Far as I'm concerned,

nobody outside the investigation needs to know, and precious few inside the investigation do."

"Is the mayor happy about that?"

"I didn't ask him."

"Or the county commissioners?"

"Or them. My job, not theirs."

He decided not to comment on that. "How're the families taking it?"

"Still in shock. Scott Abernathy's widowed mother is still under a doctor's care, heavily sedated. His brother, older, has been drinking. A lot."

"It's been noticed, I take it."

"Yeah. The only alcohol served in any restaurant or café here in the downtown area of Sociable is wine or beer, but there's a liquor store out near the highway—and he's been making regular visits out there, then back here and brown-bagging wherever he goes. Also spent a night in my jail for drunk and disorderly. Nobody blamed him for being upset about his brother, but he was talking wild about getting his guns and going looking for whoever murdered Scott."

"So you let him spend a night in jail?"

"Yes. And then talked him into surrendering his guns once he'd sobered up. I don't think he would have done anything crazy sober, but drunk is another thing entirely. Drunk makes all kinds of crazy possible." She paused, then added, "Other gun owners who know him, especially his friends, have been warned against allowing him to borrow one of theirs, no matter how sympathetic they might feel. We have a lot of hunters in the area."

"He's the only one with . . . notions?"

"So far he's the only one who's voiced them, at least within my hearing. But I can feel people getting edgy. This needs to be over and the killer behind bars before others start eyeing their guns. And having notions."

Deacon noted her very emotionless voice, and wondered what would happen when Trinity Nichols finally let go of the pressure undoubtedly building inside her. She was clearly a strong woman, and when strong people held their feelings in check too long . . .

He couldn't decide if he wanted a ringside seat for that or not.

The sheriff's Jeep was easy enough to spot parked in front of a coffee shop, especially since there weren't a lot of vehicles parked on Main Street, and by mutual consent that's where DeMarco parked their SUV.

"Because we don't know how official she wants us to be," Hollis had remarked. "Bishop said it's up to her whether we're just consulting, here to offer a profile or Bureau assets, or to be truly active in the investigation. She might prefer to meet up casually rather than at the sheriff's office. And besides, I could use some coffee."

They got out and stretched cramped muscles; even though they had been less than a hundred miles away as the crow flew, they weren't crows, and the winding mountain roads had taken a toll. Stretching felt good.

A nice, hot bath would feel better, Hollis thought, hoping the downtown hotel where they'd booked rooms would provide an opportunity for that. Later, of course.

They had barely reached the wide sidewalk when the coffee shop's door opened and the sheriff emerged. Along with a dog—and a familiar man.

"Hey, Deacon," DeMarco greeted him, calm.

"Reese. Hollis. So it's you two Bishop sent."

Before the other two could wonder, Deacon added, "My sister Melanie lives here and called me when Scott Abernathy was murdered. He was . . . a friend. And Melanie was spooked, like most of the town. I didn't think of it as a case, just supporting family. So it's only annual leave time for me. But Sheriff Nichols has been kind enough to bring me in . . . unofficially."

"I still don't know how official *we're* supposed to be," Hollis complained mildly. "Up to you, Sheriff."

"Trinity, please. I think we'll play the question of your status by ear, if you don't mind. I gather you're the team Bishop told me to expect today?"

They introduced themselves, and it wasn't until

then that Hollis said. "Beautiful dog. Why is he staring at me?"

He was, Deacon noted with some surprise.

"He's Braden, my dog." Trinity frowned down at him. "And the staring is a bit . . . unusual. He usually just focuses on whoever is speaking." She glanced around to make sure they were pretty much alone on the chilly sidewalk, then said, "You aren't a telepath, are you?"

"Medium," Hollis replied without a blink. "With a few bells and whistles."

"Meaning?"

"I'm assuming you know about the SCU? Hence the question about telepathy?" Hollis's voice wasn't low so much as it was utterly casual.

Trinity nodded.

"Well, very few of us do . . . just one thing. One primary thing, which tends to be our strongest ability, but sometimes other things as well."

"For instance?"

It wasn't a challenge so much as genuine curiosity, so Hollis responded more openly than she might otherwise have done. "One of my other things is the ability to see auras. The electromagnetic field common to all living things, but as unique as a fingerprint."

"Unique?"

"Yeah. To the person, but also changing with mood and . . . circumstance. You have a troubled aura, Sheriff—I mean, Trinity. A lot of energy close to you, very positive reds and yellows and some bright blue, which I'm thinking is your natural state, but right now all the colors are brighter than they should be, more intense, and the whole aura is mostly enclosed, tamped down closer to your body than it should be, with heavy, dark blues, almost navy, forming a thin sort of barrier along the outer edges, probably a hell of a lot stronger than it looks. Which in my experience tends to mean either unusual stress or a high degree of natural energy. Which also tells me you have a pretty dandy shield, not so uncommon in small towns, and also that you're holding in way too much for your future mental or emotional health." She paused, adding, "I can also heal a bit if you start having headaches. Which you will, holding in that much energy."

Trinity stared at her for a moment, then drew a breath and let it out slowly. "Well, I asked."

DeMarco murmured, "She's nothing if not honest."

Hollis gave him a look, then shivered and zipped up her fairly light jacket. "What I am right now is cold. I want coffee, and it's clear we have things to talk about before we see the crime scene. Can we do it inside?"

"I'd suggest the conference room at the station, at least to get things going," Trinity said, nodding down the block at the building only about four doors away. "More privacy there, which is what

I'd prefer. But I'd advise you to get your coffee here. Cop-shop coffee is lousy no matter who makes it. I went through three expensive electric coffeemakers and one very expensive cappuccino machine before I figured that out."

So it was about fifteen minutes later that the sheriff and her three Special Crimes Unit federal agents—two of them official and one not so much —settled into very comfortable chairs around an oval conference table in the smallish private conference room, all with files and/or tablets before them and coffee from the local coffee shop.

Except for Braden, who had neither files nor coffee, but nevertheless occupied one of the chairs. A nimble feat he managed despite the chair's tendency to want to swivel.

Intercepting a look from Deacon, Trinity said, "A mind of his own."

DeMarco was looking at the dog with interest. "Does he usually join you for meetings?"

"Not like this. Usually on his bed over there or the matching one in my office if that's where I happen to be." She nodded toward a thick and obviously comfortable dog bed in a corner by some filing cabinets.

"He's still staring at me," Hollis noted, curious rather than uncomfortable. She liked dogs, animals in general, really, and they tended to instantly like and trust her—a trait she had in common with Bishop, oddly enough.

Trinity said more than asked, "I don't suppose you're picking up anything from him?"

"No. Should I be?"

"I have no idea," Trinity said frankly.

"Well, he's alive. There's that. So I wouldn't be seeing his spirit. Like all living creatures, he does have an aura." She studied the pit bull thoughtfully, obviously concentrating as she had when she'd described Trinity's aura. "Calm. Bluish-green. Huh. Silvery streaks. I don't see that very often even in people."

"It means something?"

"Well, bearing in mind that all this is a learn-as-you-go sort of thing, in my experience so far, it seems to indicate positive power—and a kind of primal sensing ability."

"He is a dog," DeMarco pointed out.

Hollis looked at her partner, seemed about to say something, but then just nodded.

DeMarco smiled faintly, then looked at the sheriff and said, "One of my extra bells and whistles is something Bishop calls a primal sense, the ability to feel it if a gun or another weapon is pointed at me. Maybe from years in the military at a fairly young age, from being under threat for long stretches of time. Wherever it was born, Hollis has seen it as a series of silvery streaks in my aura."

Rather apologetically to the sheriff, Hollis said, "In a unit full of psychics, privacy is sort of at a premium. So we try to respect each other's boundaries, at least as much as we can. It was up to Reese whether to tell you about his primal sense, at least in part because it's one of his extra and unique abilities, just like it was up to me to tell you I'm a bit more than just a medium."

Trinity nodded. "I get that."

Mildly, DeMarco said, "So is the interest in Braden because he sits up in a chair like people?"

Deacon briskly explained the dog's role in the investigation so far, including his somewhat mysterious arrival in Sociable.

Neither DeMarco nor Hollis looked much surprised by the information; Trinity had the feeling that very little would ever surprise these people, both because they'd seen too much and because they knew only too well that the world was filled with the inexplicable, much of which they were called on to investigate.

Hell, they lived with the inexplicable every day, apparently.

And at the very least, that made her more grateful that she had elected to call in specialized help. But also more wary.

DeMarco said to his partner, "So no anonymous tips. You should feel better about that." He glanced at the sheriff, adding, "Too often anonymous tips mean people who quite likely have more information they aren't willing to share."

"It was bugging me," Hollis confessed. "Why

not come forward if one of your own neighbors or friends is horribly murdered?"

"Unless you're somehow involved?" Trinity offered.

"Sometimes. Though more often it's only protecting personal secrets that have nothing to do with the crime. But it's something to weed out, and that just gets in the way."

"True enough," Trinity agreed. "I've run into that sort of thing more than once."

Getting back to the subject that had sparked the brief discussion about anonymous tips, Hollis looked at DeMarco, her brows rising. "Are you picking up anything from Braden? He's the telepath, it's his primary thing," she explained in an aside to the sheriff.

DeMarco looked at Braden and shrugged. "I've never connected to an animal. At least . . . not individually."

"Then how?" Trinity asked, curious.

When her partner remained silent, Hollis hesitated, obviously thinking about those boundaries and whether this was a good enough reason to cross them, then said, "There was a case a while back during which a number of animals died all at once. Unnaturally."

"I sensed that," DeMarco said, somewhat remotely.

Trinity frowned. "You sensed—"

"In my mind I heard them scream."

NINE

Melanie had rapidly talked herself out of believing that she had really seen Scott's spirit, so she told herself that wasn't the reason she didn't want to stay in her apartment.

Alone.

Instead, she went to her usual spot at the Downtown Café for lunch, head high and rather prickly in her determination to face down anyone who so much as gave her a suspicious look or even hinted that she might have either driven a man to kill himself or somehow managed to break his neck herself.

But gossip had other things on its mind that day, and not even Melanie's uncertain status as Lead Suspect of Something could prevent Lynne Dunbar, the young, most gossipy waitress in town, from spilling all the news even as she poured Melanie's coffee.

"I heard two, but then somebody said one got here sooner, by himself. Three FBI agents! In Sociable. Everybody's saying the sheriff called them in, not because she couldn't've solved the murder herself but because it's just so strange and awful, and maybe even part of something bigger going on that the FBI would know more about. Like those murders up in the mountains, those poor girls? Maybe it's the same killer, that's what people are saying. And that'd make sense, wouldn't it, calling them in because of that?"

Melanie made no attempt to respond or interrupt in any way; she knew too well it would be virtually impossible until Lynne had said everything she wanted to say.

At least for the moment.

"I heard the guy agent who came with his partner is really big and powerful, and drop-dead gorgeous, seriously, seriously hot, like blond-Greek-god hot, and no wedding ring, but a gun. Big gun."

For just an instant, Melanie forgot all the horror and had to fight her instincts to burst out laughing.

Unaware, Lynne was going on in her single-minded determination to share and speculate. "His partner is a woman, doesn't look like any kind of cop, even less than the sheriff—taller but really slender, sort of pretty, but with odd eyes, like she's wearing tinted lenses that stare back at you, and with a funny shine, like they aren't really a normal, human color, you know?"

She paused, presumably to take a breath.

Melanie merely nodded, wondering if the colorful descriptions in any way resembled reality.

"Not one of them wearing suits or even sunglasses." Lynne sounded distinctly disappointed by that. "Very casual, all of them. The one that came alone, and *not* in a black SUV, they say he sat in the coffee shop for a while before the sheriff joined him, just drinking coffee and watching people before anybody knew who he was. Then the sheriff just walked up to his table and sat down, and they were there for a long time. Talking like they knew each other, maybe a cop thing, I dunno." She frowned. "Nobody's sure what they were talking about, though, 'cause nobody was close enough. Probably the murders, though."

"Probably," Melanie said dryly, even as her mind raced. *Dammit, is he here officially? That's not what I wanted. But maybe inevitable . . . Did Trinity call in the SCU? Why? Why that unit? Because there was more odd about Scott's murder than even gossip knows about? Did I see Scott's spirit? Could I have?*

She forced her attention back to Lynne.

"Yeah, probably the murders. Anyway, they're all at the station now. Jeff came in a bit ago on his break, and he said they're in the conference room with the door shut. And said the sheriff didn't introduce them to anybody at all, just took them straight back to the conference room. What do you suppose that means, Melanie?"

"That they have a case to investigate, which means they have work to do," Melanie said, taking advantage of the break. "Which can also be said for you and me. Could I have my usual, please, Lynne? I don't like to be away from the bank more than an hour." She lied without a blink.

"Oh, right, sure. Sure." For just an instant, it was written large on the waitress's young face her sudden memory that she'd been standing here talking to a Potential Murder Suspect, possibly even the Prime Suspect, but then she pasted on a totally fake pleasant smile, gave the immaculate table a quick wipe, then bustled off to place the order.

And undoubtedly to spread more gossip.

Melanie didn't have to look around to know that other members of the late lunchtime crowd were watching her now, if they hadn't been before. Not openly, of course. Only with sidelong glances, curious, speculative. Adding up the few pieces of information they had and coming up with a much more damning total.

That a man was dead, horribly dead.

Mysteriously dead.

That Melanie had known him—and in the biblical sense.

That she had been overheard having an icy "discussion" with him shortly before he had been murdered.

And suddenly, Melanie didn't feel so brave anymore.

Even though Hollis had been present—and very actively involved—in that final confrontation at Samuel's "church" just over a year before,[3] she

[3]*Blood Sins*

hadn't talked much to her partner about his much more lengthy and deeper involvement in the investigation and in the church. He hadn't seemed to want to talk about it, for one thing. And for another, Hollis herself had shied away from what was bound to be a discussion that would undoubtedly open painful memories he really didn't need to relive.

Like the mental screams of hundreds of dying animals.

She had been telling the truth when she'd explained to the sheriff about boundaries. SCU team members were careful as a rule not to cross them, because everyone *did* deserve at least some privacy, and that was hard to come by in their unit.

So Hollis kept her tone calm and steady when she spoke into the rather shocked silence to say, "Obviously, that was an extreme case. To my knowledge, there's only one telepath in the unit who's been able to establish a telepathic connection with a dog—"

"I told her about Callie," Deacon said.

"Did you? Good. Wish she was here. Has anybody thought about inviting her?"

"She's at Haven," Deacon told her. "Working with a few of the dogs there. Official status is inactive."

With a sigh, Hollis said, "Only Bishop would have the nerve to put an agent on the inactive list and still expect that agent to work."

"In fairness, I gather he's calling it administrative leave, so she's still getting paid." He frowned. "Though how anyone could call working with three dogs administrative beats me."

Trinity asked, "What's Haven?"

It was DeMarco who answered. "A kind of civilian sister organization to the SCU, headquartered in New Mexico."

"I'm surprised the government allows that," Trinity said.

Deacon grinned faintly. "I sort of doubt anybody asked permission."

"Bishop's like that," Hollis added. "In the course of an investigation he met a billionaire who, sort of like Alexander, had at a fairly young age already conquered the known world—in his case the business world—and wasn't finding many challenges left. By the end of the investigation, the billionaire had a very psychic wife, a fascination with all things paranormal, and had been challenged to build the civilian sister organization that came to be known as Haven."

Trinity blinked. "I would imagine it comes in handy."

"Oh, yeah. Licensed private investigators, which all Haven operatives are, can go places and do things we federal cops can't. They work independently of the FBI, though we've had occasion to team up with one or more of their operatives from time to time.

"The thing is, Haven operatives tend to 'mirror' SCU agents when it comes to psychic abilities. So they have telepaths and empaths and mediums, too. Along with some . . . unusual variations, some of which are very difficult to contain, much less control. And quite of few of the psychics lack the temperament for even an unusual law enforcement position."

Trinity nodded immediately in understanding. "So in looking for people to build his Special Crimes Unit, Bishop had found himself quite a few psychics who just didn't fit into the FBI mold."

"You've got it. Being Bishop, he didn't want to waste all that talent. I'm sure it was in the back of his mind to try some means of utilizing it. And then John Garrett came along, the perfect ally. So—Haven. We often pool resources, from information to advances in how to better control our abilities. But Haven operatives, most of them based in different places all over the country, tend to have assignments that look more like a series of temp jobs. It suits them. It suits the organization, gives them a lot of flexibility."

"So, anyway," Deacon said, "Callie isn't really available. Unless communicating telepathically with Braden becomes imperative, we're on our own there."

"Lovely."

"Well," Hollis said, "you never really know about us. We learn new things all the time."

"You aren't a telepath," DeMarco told her, a faint warning note in his even tone.

"I know that. I wasn't actually talking about myself."

"No?"

"No." Avoiding his steady gaze, she realized that the dog was still looking at her intently, something in those brown eyes almost eerily intelligent, and even though she liked dogs, she was nevertheless vaguely surprised that it didn't make her uncomfortable.

In truth, it bothered her far less than DeMarco's watchfulness.

"Generally speaking," she told Trinity, "it's difficult enough to have a mental connection with another person, even when you speak the same language and understand the same concepts. Another species . . . Well, you can imagine. As smart as they are, and as long as they've been domesticated—living with us, learning to work with us, understanding at least some of our language, and watching us the whole time so they catch even nuances of expression—dogs still don't think the way we do. Communication has to be . . . fine-tuned on both sides. So far, Callie's the only person Bishop has found with that ability, and like we said, she's still exploring the limits of it."

"So what you're telling me is that it doesn't really matter to the investigation that Braden apparently knew about the victim before anyone other than the killer knew about him."

Hollis returned the dog's steady gaze for a moment, then looked at the sheriff. "Oh, no. No, that's not what I'm telling you at all. What I'm telling you is that telepathic communication with him probably won't be the way he helps us."

Somewhat warily, Deacon asked, "What other way? You mean leading us to more murder victims?"

The words had barely left his lips when Braden's head almost whipped around, his gaze directed toward one of the windows. And then he was out of his chair and at the door, looking back at the sheriff with so much meaning that every single one of them recalled an old TV series about an uncannily intelligent collie able to guide people in and out of dangerous situations.

"Timmy's down the well," DeMarco murmured.

Toby Gilmore had never really *believed* in fortune- telling, not really. It was just a fun thing, the tarot cards. Like the Ouija board she sometimes produced for parties.

Just something fun. And something a bit out of the ordinary for a place like Sociable.

Maybe her way of rebelling, however minor the rebellion. Or maybe just her way of having a "thing" all her own.

But this . . . there was nothing fun about this. This was different.

This was something new.

She looked at the clock on her desk, then lifted her gaze to note that not even foot traffic passed her window on this chilly February afternoon. She knew it wasn't the chill of the weather keeping people inside so much as the chill of murder.

Surely I don't see in the cards what I think I see.

She gathered up the cards, shuffled them briskly, her eyes closed as she concentrated on something very specific this time. The Group. Not victims or killers or strangers. Just The Group. She thought of them one by one, named them in her mind, thought about personalities and expressions. Strengths and weaknesses.

She dealt her favorite layout.

By the time she placed the last card carefully, she could see her fingers quivering.

Same thing. The same dozen or so cards. The death card central to the pattern. Three strangers coming, because of Melanie. Three people who . . . were different. Because they had faced evil and because of something else as well.

Because they hunted monsters. Not the monsters of legend and fairy tale, not those. Real monsters. Human monsters. They didn't run from them as most everyone else did. No, these three sought out monsters, deliberately, facing them. Hunting them. Fighting them.

And defeating them, at least so far.

But not without cost. Each of the three bore scars, inner ones if not outwardly visible ones. Bad. Bad scars. Each, in their own unique way, had suffered from the touch of evil. And yet they elected to continue, to center their lives around a battle against monsters.

A battle they would never truly win.

Because evil had always existed, and always would. No matter how many times they hunted it, fought it, defeated it. No matter how much of themselves they risked in the battle. No matter how many friends and comrades were lost along the way . . .

Toby sat there at her desk for a long time, staring toward the front window without even noticing the occasional car passing or the spectacular scenery that was the valley below Sociable and the mountains in the distance.

She didn't believe.

Not *really* believe.

So it didn't matter, did it? Whatever the cards showed her—whatever she *thought* they showed her—didn't matter. Because it wasn't real. They were just cards, and what she felt was only fear because a friend—a former lover—had been murdered.

Something horrible had happened in her normal world, and she wanted to understand, to see, to maybe know how to make things all right again.

That was all it was.

Still, it took every ounce of strength and courage Toby could summon to force herself to look down at the tarot layout she had dealt moments before.

It was different. Not the layout she had dealt.

Worse. So much worse.

Toby felt as if something invisible were squeezing her, because it was hard to breathe. She had to concentrate. She had to make herself breathe.

She had to force herself to look up again.

Outside the window, a couple passed, talking to each other. A car drove slowly down Main Street.

Everything looked . . . normal.

Except that nothing would ever, could ever, be normal again. Not for Toby. And maybe not for Sociable.

Toby looked down at the tarot layout and rubbed her forehead again. *Damn. Damn. I'm imagining this. All this. I have to be.*

Because the layout, though different in other ways, still showed her the three strangers coming here to battle evil. But this time, all around this battle with evil, their lives and fates entangled with a monster who had just begun to kill horribly in Sociable, was The Group.

• • •

Trinity said, "It's like I was telling Deacon, Braden can be very insistent and always seems able to make his wishes known. In fact, it's almost impossible not to know what he wants, even without an ability to read his mind."

"What does he do if you don't follow him?" Deacon asked.

Braden immediately left the door, went to the sheriff, and grasped the sleeve of her jacket in gleaming white teeth. He tugged, gently.

"I should keep my mouth shut," Deacon said.

Hollis picked up her unfinished coffee with a sigh and said, "Well, I'm really hoping it isn't another victim, but my vote is we go see whatever it is he wants us to see. Especially since he clearly knew what he was doing when he guided Trinity before."

Jesus, not another body. Trinity felt grim and hoped it didn't show. "I'm assuming you guys brought along some equipment and supplies?" she asked them as she also rose to her feet—and her dog released her sleeve and returned to the door.

"The SUV is packed," DeMarco confirmed. "And one of these days I'm going to ask Bishop how he always manages to have the things waiting for us at a moment's notice."

"He's Yoda," Hollis said.

Trinity looked at her, decided that despite the grave face it had been a stab at wry humor, and decided to ask later why a unit chief in the FBI would be compared to a wise and powerful but inscrutable movie alien.

"Okay," she said briskly. "Then you two follow my Jeep; I'd rather not alert my crime scene unit unless and until I have to. This little parade could cause enough attention as it is. Deacon, you can ride with Braden and me, so we at least keep it down to two vehicles."

"I am curious to know just how he guides you," Deacon said.

"I have a hunch you'll be impressed. I was." Without another word, the sheriff led her guests back through the relatively small bullpen, where four deputies and several administrative staff members worked industriously.

"We're finally in the process of digitizing old case files as well as historical records," Trinity told the others as they emerged onto the sidewalk. "Once that's done, my civilian administrative staff will consist of a tech or two to keep entering current data, my usual assistant, and two receptionists to cover the first two shifts; third shift is covered by a deputy. I have twenty full-time deputies and usually have half a dozen cruisers patrolling the county at any given time. There's another half-dozen part-timers I can call on at need, most of them semiretired but experienced, a few very trustworthy younger hunters who can be counted on to obey instructions and not decide to mete out justice on their own terms. Usually I have more than enough manpower to do the job."

"Still," DeMarco said, "a decent-sized department for such a small town and county."

"I have a decent budget. The city founders and subsequent leaders have been bright and dedicated, and keeping the peace and maintaining a good quality of life for our citizens has always been a priority." She looked down as Braden gave an insistent tug on her sleeve and sighed. "It was such a nice, normal little town."

Following her down the sidewalk toward their vehicles, Hollis said earnestly, "You'd be surprised how often we hear that. Such nice little towns. Such kind, *normal* people. Everything all nice and tidy. Until monsters come hunting. On top of being a tragedy it's just a shame. I really hope Sociable isn't much changed when it's all over and done with."

She didn't add that in her experience that was, unfortunately, seldom the case. Evil acts always changed people and places, and never for the better.

"I'm just hoping against hope that this monster isn't somebody I know." Trinity opened the front door of her Jeep to admit Braden, adding to Deacon, "Mind riding in the back? He generally gives way like a gentleman to a passenger, but he needs to sit in the front seat to guide me."

"I wondered if he'd lead the way on foot. Now I'm just more curious than ever," Deacon told her, climbing willingly in the back.

"If he led the way on foot, the whole town would be talking about it," Trinity responded somewhat grimly. "Whether it's deliberate or my good fortune, I'm just glad he's more subtle than that."

"So far, anyway."

"You had to say it, didn't you?"

"Well, somebody did." Deacon had been in enough grim situations to know that they were both using wry humor almost on automatic, their minds ranging ahead and already speculating about what they might find.

What neither one of them wanted to find.

Trinity backed her Jeep out of its parking place, then started it forward slowly.

Immediately, Braden leaned over and grasped the arm of her jacket, seemingly careful to get only material between his teeth. He tugged gently.

"Right turn?" Deacon guessed.

"Let's see." She took the next right, which was onto one of the side streets that seemed to climb straight up behind the town toward the top of the mountain.

Trinity kept the Jeep moving below the posted speed of twenty-five, but not so slow as to attract undue attention, and they passed one cross street that ran parallel to Main Street. Just before the next cross street, Braden leaned over again, this time nudging her arm with his nose.

"Left turn," Deacon murmured.

"Sort of hard *not* to know what he wants," Trinity agreed, turning left onto the next side street. "Like I said. He's been like that about a lot of things, though this guiding thing is new."

These streets were lined with assorted buildings, some homes, the occasional small business such as an insurance office, a doctor's office, and a couple of crafty gift shops.

At the next stop sign, Braden tugged again for a right turn. Trinity obeyed, and again they climbed the slope upward. It appeared to be growing steeper.

Thinking about those slick roads she had earlier alluded to, Deacon said, "Jesus, if it's snowy or icy, how does anyone keep from sliding straight down to Main, across it, and down into that stream on the other side of the road? Four-wheel drives even with tire chains would have trouble on streets this steep."

"It's a bit easier to zigzag using the cross streets," she said. "Takes longer, but is at least a bit safer."

"Not very much safer, I'd guess."

"Most locals have the sense to stay put," Trinity answered over her shoulder. "Or walk, if they have to get out, at least down to Main. Visitors are warned not to drive unless it's an emergency. And we use sand and salt on the roads, especially these."

"Still, I bet you've fished a few cars out of that stream."

"Every time we get a winter storm," she confirmed. "Average is four or five times a year. No fatalities so far, but some serious injuries and totaled cars."

"I bet." He watched the dog in the front passenger seat, noting his fixed attention straight ahead. "Are we going straight up? What's at the end of this street? Does it go all the way to the top of the mountain?"

"You can't get to the top of the mountain from any of these climbing streets," she told him. "All of them either turn right or left, or just dead-end. Sociable backs up to about a thousand acres of forest between us and the top of the mountain. Walking, hiking, and riding trails crisscross the forest, with a few of them leading eventually to the summit. Great views."

"I would imagine. No homes up there?"

"Part of a national forest, so no building."

"Does this street dead-end?"

"In a manner of speaking. It ends at an old church, one of our historical buildings no longer in regular use." She paused, then added somewhat dryly, "Trinity Church."

TEN

As she climbed out of their SUV, Hollis said, "Is it superstitious of me to say that if we find a crime scene or dump site at a church, it *has* to be a bad sign of worse to come?"

"You're the profiler, not me," DeMarco reminded her as they walked the few steps to join the sheriff and Deacon James.

And Braden.

Obviously hearing that, Trinity said to Hollis, "Everything I've learned about profiling, admittedly not much, is that it's a process, a bit like putting together a jigsaw puzzle. Evidence, facts, information, experience, speculation, and educated guesswork. With a lot of pieces that don't look like they fit. Until they do."

"That describes it pretty well." Hollis held on to her warm coffee cup with one hand and put the other in her jacket pocket; it felt a good twenty degrees colder up here. And she wasn't really tempted to turn back and look at the view down to the valley and beyond.

"It'll be interesting to see how this one comes together," Trinity said, but absently. "Well, Braden isn't leading, but I'm not much inclined to stand around and wait him out."

The street had dead-ended into a relatively

small, graveled area about twenty-five yards from the southern side of the church, presumably used as a small parking lot. And from where they stood, old overgrown shrubbery blocked their view of the front of the building—though they could easily see the tall, very white steeple stretching into the sky, brightly lit by the afternoon sun.

Stained-glass windows were also visible along the side facing them, the only sign of ornamentation on the white clapboard building that had to be well over a hundred years old. It had a plain brick foundation, and the simple steps of a small rear entrance were only just visible from this angle.

There was no shrubbery close to the building, just the pale, almost colorless grass of winter, worn here and there by a path or just a seemingly random bare spot where no grass grew. It was clear the wilderness rising behind the building hadn't been allowed to encroach, and yet there was an odd air of abandonment about the place.

"The church isn't very large," DeMarco said. "Looks like only two entrances?"

"Yeah, just two."

"We split up, front and back?"

"Sounds good to me," Trinity said. "On the other side of the church is a small graveyard, and then the old parsonage. The parsonage is private property but a historical building like the church, so maintained but not occupied. I have standing permission to enter both buildings."

"Good," Deacon said. "Especially since we don't have probable cause to enter. I don't see anything suspicious."

Hollis set her coffee on the hood of Trinity's Jeep, then adjusted her jacket so that her sidearm was visible. She flexed her fingers absently. "Did something bad happen in the church?" she asked Trinity.

"Yeah, years ago. You sensing something?"

"Not sure. We'll take the back."

Deacon was just about to admit that his weapon was locked in the trunk of his car down on Main Street when DeMarco bent and removed a Glock from an ankle holster. He straightened and handed it to Deacon.

"Thanks."

"Don't mention it." DeMarco unzipped his jacket, revealing a very large silver pistol in a shoulder harness.

Deacon had heard that this former military man carried a cannon and was uncannily accurate with the powerful weapon. He'd thought the first part an exaggeration. He saw Trinity's brows rise slightly, but she didn't comment on the gun.

Instead, she said, "There's a key to the back door on top of the door frame. I have a key to the front doors."

"Let's go," Hollis said.

All four moved toward the church, Hollis and

DeMarco following one of the faint paths that appeared to lead straight to the small back porch, while Trinity and Deacon followed another that led to the church's front doors.

They were all alert and watchful, but only Deacon carried his borrowed gun in his hand.

They had moved no more than a few yards when Trinity glanced to her right—and then came to an abrupt stop.

Deacon, a step behind her, stopped automatically and followed her fixed gaze. "Oh, shit," he breathed.

Hollis and DeMarco were just suddenly there, with them, also staring at what the shrubbery had hidden from them when they had first arrived.

"Too late," Hollis said.

Without discussing it, they all moved very slowly toward the end of the main walkway that led from the street in front of the church to its front doors.

In a very steady voice, Trinity said, "I hope to hell he was already dead before—before that was done to him."

Just a few yards from them, straddling the main walkway that led to the front door of Trinity Church, someone had constructed an A-frame structure, like a child's swing set, only larger. It was made of heavy, old timbers, the sort common in an area with many barns and old buildings about, fastened together with a certain amount of care with heavy bolts that also looked old.

In the exact center of the top crosspiece, a heavy rope was tied without any particular skill, the other end wrapped several times around a man's bare ankles.

He was naked. His eyes were wide open. Duct tape covered his mouth. His arms dangled, the limp fingers just touching the ground.

The very bloody ground.

He had been gutted with a single long slice from crotch to rib cage. His intestines spilled out. Organs glistened wetly. Blood was still dripping sluggishly.

"He was still alive," Trinity said. "Wasn't he?"

"Yes," DeMarco said. "The killer was careful. None of the organs look cut, damaged. Just the skin and muscle. Just enough."

"How long could he live like that?"

DeMarco turned his head and looked at her. Evenly, he said, "Someone can be disemboweled and live a long time. Hours. Even days. But this killer was impatient. Or maybe he knew we were coming. It isn't obvious with so much blood and—tissue—from the gash everywhere, but he opened the carotid arteries at some point. This man bled to death within a minute or two. He was gone before we started up the mountain."

Deacon said, "You couldn't have saved him, Trinity. We couldn't have saved him."

She drew a breath through her mouth, as though

instinctively trying to avoid the smell of death that was, here, mostly the smell of blood and terror and pain. "He—the killer—took something again. From the body. He was still alive when that was done to him, too, wasn't he?"

It was Deacon who said, "That was probably done first. A . . . special kind of torture to a man."

The victim's penis and testicles had been removed. Not neatly.

They couldn't assume that the killer wasn't still somewhere about, perhaps even watching to see the reaction to what he had left for them.

Her voice steady, Trinity said, "The parsonage is a lot larger, just two entrances, front and back. You three take it, and I'll take Braden and go through the church."

Hollis noticed only then that the black dog had joined his mistress, standing exactly at the "heel" position. "Key to the parsonage?" she asked.

"Under the back flowerpot in that grouping beside the front door is its key. The back door just has a kind of trick handle. Lift up and lean in."

Deacon murmured, "Some security."

"We've never really needed it up here."

All four of them had their guns drawn now, and with a nod to Trinity, the three federal agents made their way cautiously toward the parsonage. They gave the body a wide berth to avoid disturbing any evidence there might be, though just a few steps showed all of them that the ground was all but frozen up here, and dry, and they weren't likely to find any footprints.

It was almost eerily silent, even for a winter day. They all looked at the small graveyard as they passed, its no more than two dozen headstones very obviously old. Some were crooked, some were almost absurdly decorative, and some were . . . very small.

"Anything?" Deacon asked Hollis.

"No. But I've only rarely seen spirits in graveyards or cemeteries. Not exactly where they want to hang out, I gather."

"Always wondered about that. First chance I've had to ask." Deacon paused, then added, "I'll take the back door."

"Watch yourself," DeMarco advised.

"You, too." He split off from them, moving swiftly but cautiously along the edge of the graveyard on the parsonage side.

Hollis said to her partner, "I gather your primal sense hasn't offered a warning?"

"Not exactly. No weapon pointed at us. But . . ."

"I know. Feels weird, doesn't it? The energy in the air is way above normal."

They were moving cautiously toward the front door, both of them watchful.

"Geographic?" DeMarco suggested.

"Maybe. I noticed an awful lot of lightning rods

on the drive up here. But it's something else, too. I just can't put my finger on it."

They reached the porch, and Hollis found the key to the door while DeMarco kept his wary gaze roaming all around them. Within a minute, they were standing inside a dim foyer.

Hollis looked at her partner. "Well?"

He was frowning. "There's nobody here. Just us and Deacon."

"Sure?"

"Positive."

Hollis reached over and flipped a light switch beside the front door. Immediately, the overhead light fixture in the foyer came alive, as did a lamp on an entry table against the stair wall—and sconces going up the stairs.

"I'll check upstairs," Hollis said.

"We'll check upstairs." DeMarco raised his voice. "Deacon?"

"Yeah?" His voice was distant but clear.

"Don't think there's anybody in the house but us. We'll check upstairs, you take this floor."

"Got it."

Hollis briefly considered being indignant about DeMarco refusing to leave her side but discovered she couldn't work up much enthusiasm for being in here alone.

There was something distinctly . . . odd . . . about this place.

So she didn't object as they went up the narrow

staircase together, and together checked out the landing, four bedrooms, and two bathrooms. All the rooms were furnished plainly and simply, with quilts on the beds and rag rugs on the dull wood floor. Nothing matched or looked too elegant for its place; this had been a home, the furnishings assembled from family and thrift stores and a few precious things bought new.

A long, long time ago.

They discovered a door that opened to a second set of stairs, these even more narrow, and found a huge attic space with three windows and, oddly, nothing else.

"I don't think I've ever seen an empty attic in a furnished house," Hollis murmured. "There always seems to be piles of broken and discarded furniture, and boxes and old picture frames."

"I guess they used all they had and fixed what got broken," DeMarco responded. "Let's get out of here."

They holstered their weapons, both of them, Hollis noted, doing so almost reluctantly.

There was no one here, they were sure of that. No killer lurked in this house.

And yet . . .

They met up with Deacon at the foot of the stairs.

"All clear," he said. "But my skin's sort of crawling. Hollis, is that you?"

It took her a moment to understand, but finally

she shrugged. "I dunno, maybe. It feels weird in here. It felt weird outside. I don't like this place."

DeMarco took her hand. "Let's get out of here."

They did, and Hollis didn't try to pull her hand free of her partner's even once they were outside.

Trinity and her dog had clearly finished their sweep of the church and were standing several yards away from the hideous contraption where a dead man hung.

"Church is clear," she said steadily.

"Parsonage, too," Hollis reported.

Trinity's face was pale, but her gaze was as steady as her voice. "I need to go back to the Jeep to use the radio and call in Doc and my techs. Cells don't work up here. Neither do walkies."

DeMarco turned his head to study the position of the body relative to the streets below, then said, "If you want to keep the details of this scene quiet as long as possible, better tell them to bring a tarp—or a tent. In the meantime, I can park the SUV over there, in front. It won't contaminate the scene, but it should help block the view from anybody close enough and curious enough to see anything once other vehicles get here and people below notice the commotion."

Trinity nodded and took a couple of steps toward the vehicles before Hollis's voice stopped her.

"Trinity? Do you know who he was?"

"Yeah. His name is Barry Torrance. We were in high school together."

• • •

Melanie really didn't want to go back to her
apartment after she finished lunch. She had
lingered as long as she dared but finally made
herself leave. And she considered several alterna-
tives to going home before finally sighing and
heading for the bank.

If she was lucky, her boss had already left for
the day; he generally did unless he had late-
afternoon appointments. And nobody else would
probably notice or care if Melanie slipped back
into her office. Especially since it was near the
front doors and sort of back in a niche, so she
could pretty much come and go as she pleased.

But she had barely settled behind her desk when
a brief knock made her jump and brought her
attention to the doorway. She frowned slightly at
Toby Gilmore.

"Hey. Something up?"

Toby was chewing her bottom lip, a sure sign
she was upset. Not that she was ever able to hide
her feelings. Dark and exotic-looking she might
be, but there was nothing in the least mysterious
about Toby.

"I'm not really sure. That is . . . Melanie, have
you got a minute?"

"Sure. Don't have any afternoon appointments
scheduled, and so far it hasn't been a day for
drop-ins. Have a seat." She was slightly surprised, and more than a little uneasy, when her

friend closed the office door before sitting down.

"What's up?" she more or less repeated, warily this time.

"I've been reading the cards."

Melanie sighed. "Toby, why can't you just play solitaire when you're bored, like everyone else? Or mahjong. I know you have both on your computer at work and your tablet for home."

"That's not why—I wasn't reading the cards because I was bored, Melanie. I was reading because of the murders."

"Murder," Melanie said, automatically. "Just one."

"No. I think there's been another."

"The cards tell you that?" Melanie asked dryly.

Toby flushed a little but kept her gaze steady. "They did. And then just a bit ago, when I was coming here, I saw Lexie and Doug leave the sheriff's office. With their kits. They looked grim, Melanie. I didn't see where they went; I don't think they wanted anybody to see where they went. But I think it's up at the old church."

"It?"

"The body. The second victim." She swallowed hard. "Somebody else we know."

Melanie hoped her own face didn't look as closed as it felt, but judging by Toby's unhappy expression, it probably did. "You can't possibly know where Lexie and Doug were going, or why. As for tarot, they're just cards, you say so yourself. Just for fun."

"Yeah, but . . . This time, what I saw . . . It was dark, Melanie. It was really dark."

"You're upset. We're all upset about Scott. Of course whatever you *think* the cards told you was something bad."

Toby bit her lip again, then said, "I thought it was just a dark man, but when I looked closer . . . Melanie, is your brother coming to Sociable? Maybe already here?"

"Is that what the cards showed you?"

Toby nodded. "The dark man, connected to you. Brother to you. And he's some kind of cop, isn't he? FBI? It's all over town that Trinity called in feds to help." Almost to herself, she added, "Maybe she knew, too. Or suspected. That there'd be more. That Scott was just the beginning."

Carefully, Melanie said, "Deacon is only supposed to be here as family. Not official. I called him because . . . Well, because. I had no idea Trinity would call in the FBI."

"But since she did . . . he's official now?"

"Maybe. Probably. I haven't talked to him yet." Dryly, she added, "I heard from Lynne at lunch that there were three FBI agents in town."

"Monster hunters," Toby said quietly.

Melanie frowned at her. "All cops are really monster hunters, aren't they?"

"Not like them."

"Meaning?"

Toby chewed her lip a moment, clearly worried.

"Your brother, the other two . . . they don't just hunt killers. Murderers. They hunt the true monsters humanity produces—or allows to exist—from time to time. The dark ones. The evil ones."

It didn't sound melodramatic. At all.

Since Melanie knew what Deacon's job consisted of, and more than most people would ever guess about an FBI agent, she couldn't really argue. So all she said was, "Killing Scott in a locked room. And now you say he's killed someone else. Up at the church? Another weirdly broken neck?"

Toby looked suddenly queasy. "No. No, worse than that. I saw blood, a lot of blood. And . . . other things. Awful things."

Melanie wished she had stayed in the restaurant. Or even in her apartment. "Look, if he's done what you say, on top of killing Scott like that, I'd say those things easily put this killer into the creepy *and* truly evil category. So? Is it so surprising federal agents would be hunting him?"

"Not that. I mean—"

"What *do* you mean, Toby?"

"I mean it's one of us."

Melanie sighed. "I know Trinity pretty much ruled out a stranger. And I know how hard it is to accept that somebody we might know, even think we know well, could be capable of murder at all, far less like that, but—"

"That isn't what I'm saying."

"What, then?"

"I'm saying it's one of *us,* Melanie. The murderer. It's one of The Group."

He frowned as he considered them. He had tried and failed to reach any of them, even Trinity, something that bothered him more than he wanted to admit to himself. He had the uneasy sense that the very energy that fed his abilities also enhanced theirs.

Whatever protected them, at least.

He had not factored that into his plans. This was supposed to be *his* edge, not anything that would help them. Protect them.

His gaze fell on the black dog sitting quietly at Trinity's side, and he felt his frown deepen. Something else he hadn't expected to be a factor—that dog. Because while he was surely protection against an admittedly unlikely nighttime break-in of her home, or if Trinity encountered the normal sort of relatively tame trouble in her job day-to-day, he wouldn't be able to protect his mistress from the fate designed for her.

The fate he had designed for her.

Except . . . the dog had led her to the first body, and that hadn't been part of the plan.

And now they were here, had come up here when they had no reason to. Unless they had known, or suspected. He'd planned to do something a bit later to call attention up here, judging the time right to let more of the fine citizens of Sociable have a better look at his handiwork. Maybe start a small fire . . .

Even fireworks. To draw the kids later in the afternoon, after school.

But that would be a problem now. Because here they were, a cop and three feds. A cop, a sheriff, who had shown her hand plainly: She would do everything in her power to shield her town from at least the worst details of horrible murder.

A sheriff who did not yet know she was part of this.

A fed who was connected to Sociable by blood.

And two other feds who had no idea what it was they had come here to face.

His frown faded, replaced by a smile. And he began to quietly hum under his breath as he settled down to watch them.

ELEVEN

They stood several yards away and watched as Lexie and Doug did their work with grim white faces. None of them wanted to look over at the steps of the church, where Doc Beeson sat hunched, his craggy face ancient now and his eyes curiously blank.

It felt like an intrusion, looking at him.

"Did you arrive with a preliminary profile?" Trinity asked almost mechanically.

"Not one ready to share," Hollis answered. "Bishop felt we needed to learn more about the victim and have a better feel for the area. Not just facts in a report or photographs, but . . . a sense of here. The place. The people. A sense of Sociable. Sometimes these extra senses of ours provide information most standard profilers never get. And sometimes we really need that."

"So Bishop does believe a local is committing these murders," Trinity was saying.

It was DeMarco who said, "Well, a stranger would stick out, that's fairly obvious. I'm betting most of the townsfolk already know the three of us have arrived, and have been discussing us, and we've only been here a few hours."

"Probably so," Trinity acknowledged with a sigh that misted the air before her.

Deacon shrugged. "I didn't come in a black SUV, so not so obviously a fed. I doubt Melanie told anyone her brother was coming for a visit, not if she didn't tell you." Half under his breath, he said, "Knowing her, she probably started having second thoughts the moment I said I was on my way."

Hollis looked at him curiously but didn't ask.

Trinity merely nodded. "But I bet it's already known you're FBI. I did run your plates. Which means my office knows. And it's well past lunchtime, so most of the first shift have left the office on break or for lunch. Or both. So, yeah, word should be spreading."

But her gaze was on Hollis, and she immediately added, "What is it?"

"Hmmm?" Hollis looked at her, then blinked. "Dunno."

"Not a spirit?"

"No. I haven't seen—or felt—what I would normally with a spirit nearby, and definitely haven't seen a spirit." She didn't add that that particular sense had been AWOL for months now. She shifted slightly, as though physically uncomfortable, and she was frowning. "This . . . Something feels . . . off."

"A murder victim isn't enough?" Trinity asked warily.

"Oh, it's enough. But this is . . . something else. I've felt it since we got up here. Really felt it in the parsonage. Something is just . . . off."

"Off, how?" her partner asked her. "Your sense of a place tends to come from normal observation—or a spirit energy."

"This is different. You still don't feel a threat?"

DeMarco glanced around them, inwardly checking with the primal sense that virtually always warned him of danger, then shook his head. "No, same as before. No weapon pointed this way. You think we're being watched?"

"I know we are." Hollis was momentarily

surprised by her own certainty and frowned at the sheriff before allowing her restless gaze to roam around the area, suddenly conscious that there was nothing on the slopes above them but forest, dense and dark even in winter, and that it seemed to loom over them. "Like Reese said, I don't usually feel things like that unless there's a spirit somewhere about. But this feeling is getting stronger, and I still don't see anything the rest of you don't see." *Except a really creepy forest looming over us.* "Or anyone."

Calm as always, DeMarco said, "Maybe energy of some other kind. You could be more sensitive to energy in general now. Can you tell if it's positive or negative?"

"Negative." She had answered without hesitation and frowned again as she looked at him, repeating more slowly, "Negative."

Trinity said, "That doesn't sound good."

"No, it usually isn't. But not necessarily . . . damaging."

"You mean to the general populace, or psychics?"

Hollis was faintly surprised for a moment, then said wryly, "I seldom think of how energy affects non-psychics. But of course it does, it affects all living things. And electronics, of course; they can go haywire in a place like this, or just not work the way they're supposed to work."

"What about people?"

"Just taking a guess based on how uncomfortable I feel, and with no idea how long it's been in the area, I'd say the non-psychics in this area, especially the ones more sensitive to energy fields, could be dealing with short tempers, maybe depression or just a general anxiety."

"And you psychics?"

"Varies, depending on the individual. Some of us feel it, some don't." She eyed the two men and raised her brows.

DeMarco shook his head. "I don't feel anything odd."

Deacon hesitated, then said, "I might be picking up on Hollis, but my skin still feels like it's crawling a bit."

Hollis sighed, then said dryly, "And people wonder why I'm still single." Without waiting for a response or reaction to that, she went on immediately. "Like I said, it's making me feel just mildly uncomfortable, at least right now. But even if psychics aren't consciously aware, energy can affect us and usually does. There's just no way to predict how."

"Wonderful," Trinity said.

Hollis eyed the others, one by one, obviously concentrating. "Your auras have changed a bit. Sort of a metallic shimmer on the outer edges. Metallic usually means energy; I'm guessing we're all instinctively blocking that."

"So far, at least," DeMarco murmured.

Trinity asked Hollis, "Can you see your own aura?"

"Usually not, even in a mirror. And I don't block too well; being psychic is relatively new to me, and I haven't been able to build much of a shield. Plus, I broadcast, which is why Deacon is probably feeling uneasy."

Trinity lifted her brows in a silent question.

"Broadcasting is another one of my bells and whistles. Other psychics tend to pick up my thoughts or emotions on some level. Even through their own shields sometimes, especially if I'm really upset about something." She sighed. "I don't like it, and I'm working on a shield, but in the meantime I have moments where I feel . . . very exposed."

"Wouldn't that mean negative energy would affect you more than anyone with a shield?"

"You'd think. But not so much. Not really many absolutes with this stuff, just what each of us has experienced to date." Hollis shrugged, adding briefly, "It has to do with how I became a psychic, and it's a long story. Short version is that I'm sensitive to negative energy but I deal with it better than most other psychics. So far, it hasn't been damaging."

There was a moment of silence, during which Hollis became conscious that she was being stared at.

"What?"

DeMarco stepped closer and held out his handkerchief. In a very level voice, he said, "Hollis, your nose is bleeding."

Hollis checked the handkerchief, then refolded it and stuck it into her pocket, making a mental note to have it cleaned before returning it to Reese. Not that he cared. But she did.

"I think it's stopped."

They were all watching her as if she were a fragile vase on a shaky shelf, and it irritated her. "Really. I think it's stopped. I'm fine."

Deacon said slowly, "I think maybe the question should be, why did it start?"

"I don't know. Hell, we're halfway up a mountain; maybe it's the altitude."

"Never bothered you before," DeMarco said.

Traitor.

Hollis wondered if she was broadcasting, and rather hoped she was. She couldn't tell from his face, which was as impassive as it generally was. "I have a slight headache," she confessed finally, feeling sulky as a child for that moment. She jammed her hands into the pockets of her jacket, resisting the urge to rub the back of her neck—or bang her aching head against something. Because it was more than a *slight* headache, it was a wall banger, and it had started abruptly just about the same time the nosebleed had started.

And she had no idea why she didn't want to explain any of that.

Instead, she said, "I probably shouldn't have pushed so hard to see your auras."

"You had to push hard?" Again, DeMarco.

"Yeah." It wasn't until she said it that Hollis realized. "But that's usually the easiest thing I do. I mean, I concentrate, but it doesn't take anything out of me, not like dealing with spirits does. Not like healing does." *And you were letting me see your aura, so I didn't have to push harder just for you.*

Him and his double shield.

She was still wondering if she was broadcasting. Or if he was just reading her. Because even when he said he *wasn't,* she had to wonder about that, especially when something about his eyes told her he knew all the things she wasn't saying out loud.

Damn telepaths.

DeMarco and Deacon exchanged looks, and the former said, "You said the wrongness you felt was negative."

"I also said I deal with negative energy well, never mind the nosebleed. I deal with it very well, in fact. You of all people should know that."

A very slight frown drew his brows together, for DeMarco the equivalent of a scowl. "That was spiritual energy. Even the negative stuff. Right?"

"Yeah. At least . . . I'm pretty sure it was."

180

"But you said whatever you feel up here isn't that kind of energy."

"Well, one of us said that." It was her turn to frown. "Maybe it's the geology of this place; didn't you bring that up? Trinity, are there a lot of metals in this mountain? I mean, do you get an unusual number of lightning strikes, serious problems with electronics, compasses that go nuts?"

Trinity didn't hesitate, clearly relieved to talk about anything other than the second murdered friend this week. "Down close to Main Street, no problems to speak of. The higher you climb, the more likely you are to run into the sort of things you listed." She paused, then added, "Virtually all the buildings along the top dozen or so cross streets have lightning rods, securely grounded, and more than the average number of surge protectors for their electronics; our electronics store is one of the most successful businesses in town, as a matter of fact."

"Yeah, I saw some of the lightning rods. They made me wonder even before we got up here," Hollis said almost absently. "We have plenty of experience with how energy can interfere with and even destroy electronics."

"Glad there's at least a reason for it," Trinity said rather dryly. "I've often wondered, even though there's always been a lot of energy up here. Sometimes you can stand down on Main

Street totally in the dry, and watch a storm up here. A bad storm."

Hollis nodded slowly. "Which could explain why I didn't feel anything odd down on Main. Maybe it *is* just the geography of the place."

Trinity asked, "Would that make you feel as though you were being watched?"

"I have no idea—though I imagine negative energy could make me feel any number of negative things. As I said, this is a learn-as-you-go sort of thing, figuring out the abilities, what they can do, what causes or triggers them. If they are triggered."

"Are they triggered by energy?" Trinity asked directly.

"We think so. Rarely. It's more likely to be triggered by physical or emotional trauma, a head injury, that sort of thing. It isn't often that we encounter energy fields powerful enough to affect us."

"But you have," DeMarco pointed out. "At least twice before that I know of. And both times the energy was negative."

Hollis was faintly surprised that he mentioned that, but she had learned over time that her partner never let something slip by accident; for whatever reason, he felt it was an important bit of information the others needed to know.

To Trinity, Hollis said, "I've been psychically stable for months now, but I have a history of developing additional abilities during highly stressful situations or when there's excess energy about. At first, I was just a medium; that was triggered by physical and emotional trauma. Then came the other stuff, popping up almost always during intense cases. Broadcasting—sometimes as if I'm powerfully telepathic and able to send thoughts, though never receive—and seeing auras and healing myself and others. Most recently, we discovered I could channel energy, even dark energy, and more or less make it positive energy instead."

"How?"

"Beats me. All I know is that it comes in dark and leaves bright."

After a moment, Trinity said, "Forgive my saying, but that sounds weird as hell."

"Pretty much the way it feels. Although it had a temporary strengthening effect on me physically, which was a nice change." She didn't mention the other physical change, which was not as intense as it had been but was still present: Her eyes had literally turned a different shade of blue. *Also weird, a very long story to explain it, and so why even mention it?* "Mostly, using our abilities leaves us tired at best and drained at worst, especially if it's a dangerous situation."

"Sorry to keep harping on the subject," Trinity said, "but if you channel dark, negative energy that's bright and positive when you release it— what happens to the dark? I mean, do you literally change positive to negative? Because I didn't think that was the way energy worked."

"Neither did I," Hollis answered frankly. "But if you're asking me if anything dark remains in me afterward—no, it doesn't. We have people in the unit who can sense that kind of thing. Several. Bishop is very careful about that given the work we do, making sure we're monitored in every way possible to be sure we aren't being harmed by using our abilities. And I've been assured that nothing negative was left behind in me."

After a moment, Trinity nodded. "Okay. What about this negative energy you're sensing here? Can you channel that? Change that?"

"Probably not. The one time I did that, I was . . . connected. Standing in a kind of doorway where the energy was tightly focused so it was relatively easy to draw in. Up here, this is diffused, for want of a better word. No purpose, no direction, nothing guiding it. It simply . . . is."

"Yeah, I was afraid you'd say something like that."

"Why?" Deacon asked.

She drew a breath and let it out, then settled her shoulders with the air of someone facing something she'd rather not have had to face. "Because with a few rare exceptions, most everything really bad that's happened in Sociable has happened in the higher elevations. It's something that goes back as far as the town does."

He lost interest in watching them after a while. The coroner looked depressed, the crime scene techs scurried around taking care of their minutiae—one of them retiring off to the side behind a bush to lose his lunch before grimly resuming his duties. And the others . . .

The others.

He still couldn't reach them as he'd expected to be able to, and that was troubling. It was also troubling that his strength seemed to come and go.

He was going to need all his strength to finish this. To be the sword hand of God and deliver justice.

More justice.

There was a part of him that knew, that *understood* how to harness the power all around him. Incredible power, more power than he could ever need, ever use. That part of him had the most insistent voice and was the one he tried his best to ignore. Because no matter what the voice said, he didn't think *he* was strong enough to do that. To . . . hold that.

To master that.

He was afraid to try.

And right now, he was tired. He was tired and he needed to sleep.

Everything would make sense again if he could just sleep . . .

"Really bad things?" Hollis asked a bit reluctantly. She was avoiding as much as possible even a glance toward the body and the crime scene techs still working.

Definitely a bad thing.

But Trinity was saying, "The church itself has a few stories attached to it, but it's the old parsonage that's legendary."

Deacon was curious, and it showed. "Any particular legend you want to share?"

"Well, there are lots of old stories going back nearly two hundred years. Hard to document those, since not many records exist. But some survive. It's an official historical building; in the summer, it and the church draw a few tourists if they pick up maps in town showing sites of local interest, or they already know the history of the area. Or if one of those ghost-hunting outfits is in town."

"You seriously get a lot of those?"

"Usually a few every summer. Occasionally a group comes up here in winter. Deliberately."

DeMarco guessed, "The legend you have in mind has something to do with a winter event?"

"The most recent one, yes, though it's not really a legend. I know it actually happened, because it happened about ten years ago. There was a young preacher living in the parsonage with his wife and baby daughter; the church was being restored after decades of not being used for anything except for the local kids to scare each other. The town had put out feelers to see if any preacher was interested. We got one taker, it would have been his first church, and he was due to resume services in the spring."

"I have a bad feeling about what's coming," Hollis said.

Trinity drew a breath and let it out, misting the air. "There were no warning signs anyone saw. They seemed like a . . . very happy little family. They'd lived in the parsonage since just before Christmas. They'd been attending another of our churches until this one was ready for them, so the townsfolk had been getting to know them. Friendly people. Nice people. A couple very much in love."

"I know I'm going to hate this," Hollis muttered.

"It was about this time of year, and it had been a bad winter. There was a snowstorm, but not without warning; most people had been able to stock up on supplies so they could shelter in place, especially up here. The young preacher and his wife certainly had; several people had talked to them before the storm hit. The workers for the church had even left one of their generators for the family, in case they lost power."

"Did they?"

"No. That seldom happens up here, unless there's a lightning strike. We just got a lot of snow.

And nobody got back up here for four days." Trinity drew a breath. "According to all the evidence, sometime during the early hours of the storm, the young preacher strangled his wife— and then killed their child on the church altar before returning to the parsonage and slitting his own throat."

"God," Deacon said.

"I don't think God was here," Trinity responded in the same steady tone with which she had related the horrific story. "I don't think God had been here for a long time."

"No one was ever able to find out why he did it?" Hollis asked.

"No. He didn't leave a note or message. And there was no evidence to indicate why it happened. Just that it happened, and how. My father was sheriff then. And that case haunted him the rest of his life." She frowned slightly, her gaze fixed on Hollis now. "Do you think it could have been this weird energy?"

"I don't know," Hollis answered, honest. "Right now, it doesn't feel . . . dark enough to trigger that sort of horror, but I suppose it could have a cumulative effect. He might have been exceptionally sensitive to electromagnetic fields, to energy. Or maybe the seed of that violence was in him for a long time before he came here. Evil can hide itself. It's something it does very well."

After a moment, Trinity nodded. "The case was

something of a sensation in the area. And it's the sort of case, the sort of crime, that people seem drawn to."

"Tourists and ghost hunters?" DeMarco asked.

"Yeah. A couple of middle-aged sisters with family ties to the place take care of tours if any are needed."

Seemingly idle, Hollis said, "They're always in the house together, right? Never just one of them?"

"You've got it. I asked once, and both sisters seemed amused by the idea that the parsonage or the church could be haunted. But they're always together when the place is open, in the parsonage or in the church. And they don't live together. One's a widow, the other never married." She frowned. "Am I offering puzzle pieces or just running my mouth to avoid thinking about poor Barry?"

"About puzzle pieces, we'll find out by the end, when everything fits into place," Hollis told her, serious.

"And makes sense?" Trinity asked rather plaintively.

"Well . . . makes whatever sense it can. His sense."

"The sense of a psychotic killer?"

"Even madmen," Deacon offered, "have their own mad logic."

Hollis smiled ruefully. "Anyway, I still feel

189

like we're being watched, but . . . it's different somehow. Not a sense of danger, exactly. Just that negative feeling." *And gleefulness. But I don't think I want to tell them about that just yet. There's something scary crazy in that glee.* Despite uncertainty, she adjusted the hem of her jacket so that the gun on her hip remained exposed and easily within reach.

"You said it was getting stronger before. Is it still?" DeMarco was frowning. "Because something's definitely bugging you," he added.

"Stop reading me."

"I'm not. Deliberately. You're broadcasting, but faintly. I can't really *not* hear it, Hollis."

Hollis wondered why she ever bothered to protest. "Yeah, yeah. So, okay, something's bugging me. Can't explain, though. It's more than negative energy—which *is* getting stronger, by the way—or at least different from any I've felt before. Not an active danger to us, at least not now, but . . . not right, either. Not natural."

But familiar. Strangely familiar . . .

TWELVE

"Sheriff?"

Trinity hadn't heard Douglas approach and hoped she didn't look as startled as she felt. And that her suddenly sharp anxiety didn't show.

Is it time?

Shouldn't I tell them?

Some things have to happen just the way they happen . . .

"What is it, Doug?"

He held out a small plastic evidence bag. "We finally got the duct tape off his mouth. This was inside."

"Inside his mouth?"

"Yeah."

Trinity kept her gaze on the bag. "Come back for this a little later, Doug, okay? I want to talk to the agents."

"Sure." He returned to his duties.

"My God," Hollis said, her voice numb. "It's him. But it can't be. Unless . . . unless we were right. It is a team. Only now they're both killing."

Trinity drew a deep breath and let it out slowly. She held her hand out, palm up, the evidence bag holding a small silver cross visible to all four of them.

"I knew Scott's murder was anything but ordinary right from the beginning. When I found one of these in his mouth."

DeMarco frowned at her. "We tried to keep it quiet, but I suppose with so many people around those bodies, it could have been leaked at least among law enforcement that we found a cross like that one in the mouths of two of the four girls killed by the mountain serial."

"That's not how I knew," Trinity said. "I recognized it. From another place. And another time."

"What are you talking about?" Hollis demanded.

"I'm talking about a place in Atlanta, just a little more than three years ago. I'm talking about a cult masquerading as a church, and a very charismatic and very dangerous man who had the ability to . . . brainwash people. Especially women. Especially women who had some psychic ability. Because that's what he fed off. That's how he grew powerful, by stealing their power."

Hollis became aware of her partner's arm around her and wondered vaguely if he had known or guessed that her knees were about to buckle.

"Samuel," she said.

Trinity nodded.

"The church . . . it wasn't in Atlanta," Hollis said, still numb. "It was in North Carolina. It was near a town called Grace."[4]

"His major church was there, yes. The church he always came back to. The one where he planned to make his stand." Trinity looked deliberately at DeMarco. "But he had churches all over the country. Some with a dozen followers. Some with a hundred. The one in Atlanta was . . . big."

---

[4]*Blood Sins*

"Yeah," DeMarco said. "A hundred and three followers, if I remember correctly. "I never saw the place, but I saw the lists. The numbers. And I knew what Samuel told me."

"Bet he never mentioned the one that got away."

Hollis was staring at her. "You?"

Trinity shook her head and looked, finally, at Deacon. "Melanie."

"I don't understand," he said. "Melanie had a— a kind of emotional breakdown in Atlanta. She was in a hospital when I went down there."

"Yes," Trinity said. "That was after we got her out."

"Out?"

"Out of Samuel's so-called church. His cult. We had to pretty much kidnap her. Her will was gone; she couldn't make rational decisions for herself. They had armed guards, for Christ's sake, keeping everyone in that compound. And—he was draining the life out of her."

Deacon was staring at Trinity. Evenly, he said, "I think we need to go somewhere and talk. Right now. Because all of this is new to me. And I need to understand."

Hollis half-lifted a hand. "Same here. Really."

"Let's go," Trinity said.

It wasn't quite so simple as just leaving. Trinity had to call down for a couple of her toughest and most trustworthy deputies to come up to the church and help her crime scene techs and poor Doc Beeson with the body of Barry Torrance. And have them bring a truck of the appropriate size so that the contraption Barry had died on could be taken, adequately covered, to the securely fenced and guarded compound of garages and other storage facilities set up for the town of Sociable— out near the highway.

Then, after some discussion, the sheriff and her three federal visitors returned to the sheriff's department, settling down eventually in that very private conference room. With coffee.

It occurred to Hollis only then that they had been in Sociable considerably less than twelve hours.

They hadn't even unpacked.

"If anybody's hungry—" Trinity began, unsurprised when all three of the agents simply shook their heads.

She sighed. "No, me, either. The family is having visitation tonight at the funeral home for Scott. And before that, I have to go down into the valley and tell Sophie Matthews about Barry. They were engaged. God, this has been the longest week of my life, and it isn't even over yet."

"I want to be sympathetic," Deacon said, "but . . ."

"Yeah, I know." Trinity sipped her coffee for a moment, then set the cup down and said, "Okay, quick background first. Cathy Simmons and I grew up here, and after graduating high school, we both attended Georgia Tech in Atlanta. It's a big school, easy to get lost in, so even though we were taking different classes, we made it a point to have lunch every week, catch up, talk about home if we felt like it.

"Of course we both made new friends, especially in our chosen studies, but we kept those lunch appointments all the way through school. At some point, Cathy told me about Melanie. A new friend, a friend she was worried about. Because Melanie was fragile. And because Melanie was a psychic."

"Why did she tell you that?" Deacon asked. "It wasn't something Melanie ever accepted, much less talked about."

"Cathy was a good friend to Melanie, and eventually Melanie opened up. Cathy told me because she knew I was very . . . accepting . . . of psychic abilities."

"How'd she know that?" Hollis asked.

"We grew up together, remember? We knew each other's secrets. So I knew that Cathy sometimes had dreams about things that came true. Over the years she had a lot of those dreams, and I was convinced very young that she had a gift. By the time we were in college and I was planning to be a cop, I was advising her to be . . . discreet. Like any other talent, psychic abilities could be exploited. She knew that; she has a lot of common sense."

"And Melanie didn't," Deacon said.

"It wasn't a matter of common sense, not for Melanie. She was emotionally fragile, vulnerable. She had abilities that frightened her. She was going to be a target. It was only a matter of time."

"So Cathy—what?—became her watchdog?"

"Cathy continued to be her friend. They were both studying banking and finance. They had hobbies and other interests in common. So they spent a lot of time together. When we all finished college, we also stayed in Atlanta. Me to be a cop, and the two of them to work at the same large investment firm."

Trinity shook her head slightly. "Life happens, and you get busy. The lunches gradually tapered off, and finally weeks and then months would go by between phone calls and even e-mails. We lost touch. Our lives went in different directions. Before I knew it, years had passed, and I was thinking about coming back here and being a different kind of cop.

"It was then, about three and a half years ago, that Cathy got back in touch. She had actually come back home a year or so before that, deciding to settle here among family and friends. She told me she had believed Melanie was going to be just fine, that she had a job she enjoyed, a man in her life, that she seemed to have come to terms with her abilities."

Deacon made a rough sound. "Yeah, by pretending they didn't exist."

"Well, apparently she thought of it as control. But, of course, it was only an illusion. And there were people out there who could see through it. And did. Within a few months, Cathy realized that Melanie was . . . different. She said she was fine, but she managed to avoid several planned meetings over the next few months.

"And then, suddenly, she just wasn't there. She had quit her job, moved out of her apartment—and vanished. All Cathy had to go on was the vague memory of a name. Samuel. So she called me, asked if I'd look for Melanie."

"How'd you find her?" DeMarco asked.

"Legwork, mostly. I talked to some of her former neighbors and former coworkers and learned that a number of them had been worried about Melanie. They'd seen other women with her, coming and going, almost secretively, their expressions guarded. Then someone remembered the mention of a church."

"And from that, you found Samuel?" DeMarco shook his head. "You're good. That was one church that never advertised, never had a phone number, was never listed anywhere."

"Yeah, it wasn't easy. But I found it. And it didn't take a cop's nose to recognize the smell of a cult. Problem was, finding the place was only the first step. The real trick was going to be getting her out of there. And before *that,* the trick would be just getting in. I didn't know enough about the setup to believe I could fake being a convert to get through the gates.

"I got back in touch with Cathy, told her what I'd found. What I knew damned well that place was. And she gave me a name. Someone who she said would help me."

Hollis stared at her for a moment, her mouth open, and then she said, "Don't tell me . . ."

"Yeah. Bishop."

"All I'm saying is that you might have dropped by to say hello before . . . diving in." Melanie's voice was a little tight despite all her efforts to keep it relaxed.

Deacon kept his walls up and made sure they were as strong as he could make them; picking up his sister's emotions had always been the easiest thing in the world for him to do—and had caused friction between the two since childhood. And since he now knew a lot more about her life in recent years than she would be at all happy about, he intended to play his cards very close to the vest.

"That was the plan," he repeated patiently. "I just stopped for a cup of coffee after the drive, figuring I'd come to the bank around lunchtime, when you could take a break. I didn't expect to meet Trinity, and I damned sure didn't expect two more SCU agents—and another murder victim."

"Quite a first day in Sociable you're having," she muttered.

Deacon leaned back in her visitor's chair, glad the office door was closed. "Yeah, it's been peachy. Believe it or not, a peaceful lunch with you would have been my preference." Despite all his efforts, that statement was a grim one.

After a moment, Melanie grimaced. "I know Trinity did everything possible to hide the scene, but it's already all over town that Barry was . . . horribly mutilated."

Man, talk about setting a land speed record.

It had been hardly more than three hours since Barry Torrance's body had been found—and quickly hidden from view in case someone got curious—and a bare half hour since his body had been taken to the town's one medical clinic—in a black hearse and by way of back streets.

"You knew him?"

"It's a small town, Deacon, and from what I've been able to gather, most years the graduating class of East Crystal High moves on to college or finds jobs that take them away from here—and they seldom come back. Maybe one or two kids graduating each year hang around, for a few years or for good, serving coffee or waiting tables or working on one of the farms or ranches."

"But most leave."

"Not many opportunities here, especially for

stable long-term employment, much less a career. The valley below is farm and ranch land, all owned by fourth- or fifth-generation family operations. The farms and ranches help support the town, but as you've seen for yourself, there isn't a whole lot of room—literally—for the town to expand. And even less property any new business would find attractive, especially with national forest topping this mountain and several others in the area."

And with a very, very weird energy zone over part of this town to boot.

Melanie shrugged. "Sociable is a very small town perched precariously on the side of a mountain, fairly remote and isolated in more ways than one. It is what it is. Before this maniac started killing people, it was a nice, peaceful place to live. Beautiful scenery, friendly people, enough diversity of opinion to keep conversation interesting, and enough entertainment options to keep most of us from getting too bored."

Deacon frowned. "You've been here—what? About three years?"

"Almost exactly. And I'm a very rare bird, being a newcomer; not many strangers move here to live, though a few retirees have settled here since I came. I wasn't happy at the bank in Atlanta—not happy in Atlanta, really—and when a friend from college visited and told me there was an opening at a bank in her hometown, I came here to check it out. It felt . . . right. From the moment I got here. So I took the job, and I stayed."

Deacon wished he could tell her he knew the truth, but after the conversation with the others, he had most certainly been convinced that it would not be in Melanie's best interests to say or do anything to disturb the careful "tapestry" of protective memories and experiences that Bishop's empathic healer had woven into his sister's very fragile psyche.

"Probably the same person who helped me," Hollis had said. "If so, you can be sure she did everything possible to heal Melanie's wounds and help her cope the best way possible for her."

Deacon had to trust in that. His sister had a happy life here—assuming they could stop a vicious killer from adding her to his hit list—and he was willing to do whatever was required of him to insure that her life was still happy when he left.

"I'm glad, Mel," he told her. "It seems like a good place to have a good life."

"If you cops can stop this killer."

"Working on that, I promise." He smiled faintly.

Not quite ready to let her own guard down just yet, Melanie said, "When I called you about Scott's murder, did you believe me when I told you it was strange? That there was something unnatural about it?" Her eyes narrowed suddenly. "Or were you convinced it was just me being dramatic?"

He chose his words with care, more the SCU agent now than the older brother who had been, growing up, baffled by her occasional almost hysterical outbursts, emotional storms that inevitably occurred when her inborn abilities tried to force their way to the surface despite all her attempts to deny and suppress them.

"I wondered if you might have relaxed a bit in recent years. If maybe you were . . . listening with more than your ears."

She avoided his gaze suddenly. "I don't know. I mean, I didn't think much about—that. Until I started having nightmares. Until I sometimes felt like someone was watching me."

"Then you tried to tune in?" He kept his tone matter-of-fact.

Melanie grimaced. "Tune in. Makes me sound like a damned radio or something."

"You know what I mean."

She did. "I just started paying closer attention to what I saw and heard, that's all. What I felt. And there was . . . it was nothing I could put my finger on, but something felt wrong. Then Scott was murdered. And a *lot* felt really, really wrong."

DeMarco finished with the third evidence board, then took a couple of steps back and half sat on the conference table. They were a bit crowded, with the three boards added to the relatively small room; Trinity had sent in a couple of subdued deputies to remove anything not essential and to help set up the boards nearly an hour earlier.

Then she had told her people nobody entered this room without being invited. Period.

Almost as if she could read his mind, Hollis murmured, "I know Trinity wants to limit the number of people, even the number of her deputies, who see these pictures and know all the details of the murders. I can't second-guess her, I suppose. She knows her people, and she knows this town."

"But?"

"But . . . if this killer is evolving, I can't even guess what he might do next. From a bloodless, *bruiseless* broken neck to a disembowelment? Even if this guy is the mountain serial's teammate, Miranda was absolutely sure he didn't kill those girls. She was sure the dominant did—and since two more girls were abducted eighty miles from here at about the same time Barry Torrance was being killed, it seems pretty clear she's right about that."

"So our guy is the submissive. Not exactly acting like one, is he?"

"That depends."

"On?"

"On whether he's acting on his own initiative."

DeMarco gestured to a small evidence bag pinned to the board, the silver cross inside it gleaming dully. "Even though the victims are wildly different, the crosses do seem to link both sets of murders. Either that, or we've got a very knowledgeable, very talented copycat who just wants to kill who he wants to kill—and pin it on somebody else."

"That's probably as likely as anything else. The mountain serial *moves,* shifting his hunting grounds and his dump sites up and down the Blue Ridge. Maybe only one relatively small part of it—but that's a long way from setting up shop in a small town."

"Yeah." He brooded for a few moments, his gaze roaming over the evidence boards. "Killing fit, athletic men—so far, at least—rather than slight young women. The mountain serial is all about physical and sexual dominance, about control—but he grabs victims of opportunity and doesn't give a damn about displaying his handiwork; when he's done with them, his victims are dumped like garbage."

"While here," Hollis finished, "one was left in a rather conspicuously locked room, while the second was hung from a homemade torture device."

"Look at what I can do," DeMarco murmured.

"He does seem to be preening, doesn't he? I wonder if it's for us . . . or for his master."

DeMarco shook his head. "I don't think his master would care. The victims are just too different. If he were . . . I don't know, grabbing women who *weren't* just thrown in his path, then doing something to them that would attract the attention of the dominant, maybe that would make more sense."

"To us. Whatever he's doing, it makes sense to him."

"Don't remind me." Studying the board in front of him, DeMarco said, "At least Trinity's people were able to start background checks on the victims. Both men worked out at the same gym. Popular place with their age group, looks like."

Hollis was seated in a chair on the other side of the table, but closer to the door. She still had her jacket on, and her hands remained in her pockets. A fresh cup of hot coffee sat before her, almost untouched.

She hadn't said very much at all about the revelation of Bishop in the pasts of Trinity and Melanie, except to note that since Bishop had his psychic radar out at all times, it only made sense that he would have known about Cathy—and possibly Melanie as well.

DeMarco was a bit surprised that she had not taken the opportunity to talk about spiderwebs or rats in a maze, something of that sort. As she usually did when the fine hand of Bishop showed up at any point in one of their cases.

He was also a little surprised that he couldn't get a clear reading on her. Not that he was *trying* to read her—but he generally didn't have to try, especially when a twist in a case had caught her off guard.

Unless . . .

"You knew Bishop would show up somewhere in this case, didn't you?"

THIRTEEN

Hollis smiled very faintly. "Well, he really went out of his way to make us believe we were just getting a break from the mountain serial case to investigate this puzzling little homicide. I was suspicious. And even more so when we got here."

"Why?"

"Trinity. She was just a bit too accepting of psychic abilities for a small-town sheriff. Even one who did street time in a big city before coming back home. She asked some really interesting questions about psychics and how our abilities work."

Hollis shook her head. "I do wonder, though, if Bishop knows about Braden. Think Trinity told him about her dog? Because I think that would make him curious. It's almost worth calling him to ask about it."

"Almost?"

"I don't want to give him the satisfaction. Isn't that childish of me?"

"It's an interesting response," DeMarco said cautiously.

She laughed suddenly. "You should see your face. Not nearly as impassive as usual. I've figured something out. If I'm broadcasting, no shield. Just nothing there to stop my being upset from spilling out all over the place. But if I keep my mind very quiet and calm . . . I don't think you can read me. Not, at least, with one or both of your shields up."

"Not ready to test your theory with my shields down?"

Hollis reached for her coffee cup. "No. Besides, I still feel a little weird from that energy up there."

"What, still? Down here?"

"Headache that won't quit. I'm probably just tired. It feels like we've been here forever. And a day."

"Maybe we should call it a day," he suggested.

She moved slightly, almost a physical protest. "Levity aside, this guy . . . he's just moving too fast. Whether he learned his trade at the master's knee, or is taking orders from the master, or is totally off the reservation on his own, he's a monster. He's a monster, and this is a nice little town that shouldn't have to be afraid of a monster."

"It's not all on your shoulders," he told her.

"I know that. But I've been hunting monsters a

while now. I should be good enough to catch this one."

"We just got here," he reminded her. "Barely long enough to have even a handful of facts with which to speculate."

"Well . . . let's use them. We have two murders in a week—here. Virtually no cooling-off period. Two very different murders of two fit adults in their early thirties. Two men. Both white, which is the majority demographic of Sociable, so maybe that means nothing. They probably all went to the same high school, because there's only one for the town. And Trinity said her preliminary investigation of Scott turned up no enemies pissed enough to kill, let alone kill with this sort of violence. I'm betting Barry didn't have any enemies, either."

"The key word being 'preliminary,'" he reminded her once more, this time more for emphasis than anything else. "This investigation has barely gotten off the ground."

"Yeah. But in a town this small, I would have expected someone to have come forward by now, even before we got here. Maybe especially before we got here. Someone who saw something at one of these places, something unusual, even if they didn't think that at the time. Something useful."

"You said evil hides. This evil clearly did just that."

"Yeah. And it's still hiding. Probably in plain sight."

Prompting her before she could fall silent again, DeMarco said, "Sure the killer is male?"

"Reasonably. That contraption displaying Barry's body took muscle to build, even if he was only bolting together the pieces."

"Granted. What about the rest?"

"The mutilation of Barry's genitals gave me pause, it's something a woman might do—but likely out of rage. Hate. In that case, it would have been . . . the main show. And I doubt she would have removed the severed genitals afterward. Women don't take trophies. More likely to drop them on the ground—where he could see them. And let him bleed to death from that wound."

DeMarco said, "And a woman isn't likely to disembowel a victim."

"Not likely, no. Women have cut up their victims into pieces, but seldom if ever motivated by hate or sadism, only to help them dispose of the body more efficiently. Disemboweling a living victim . . . that's pure sadism."

"The first real sign of sadism," DeMarco pointed out.

"Yeah. Well, arguable, I suppose. I don't know why there was no violence in Scott's murder, but if this guy *is* a student or disciple or, hell, even a victim of the mountain serial, he's studied sadism up close and personal. Bound to rub off on him."

"Not a woman's type of crime."

"No, not really. Which is not to say women aren't capable of sadism. It's just that when women are sadistic—not being paid to be, I mean—it tends to be emotionally, psychologically. They get off on control, on power, but it's rarely a physical thing. Women generally don't kill *because* they're sadistic; for women, murder is usually a means to an end. Murders this violent, this . . . messy . . . are virtually always committed by men."

"So we've already narrowed the field of suspects."

Hollis turned her head and stared at him. "Great. Men roughly between the ages of twenty-five to forty-five. I'm figuring at least a couple hundred."

"Well, since both victims fit a narrower age range, we'd probably be safe in narrowing it down for the profile. Maybe between thirty and forty-five."

Hollis considered for a moment. "You're shifting the low end a bit higher because you believe he's not a kid. Because . . . there's been too much control."

DeMarco nodded. "He got into and out of Scott Abernathy's apartment without leaving any forensic evidence behind, including any sign of just how he managed to break the guy's neck."

It was Hollis's turn to nod. "And after watching

Trinity's team work today, I doubt very much they missed any evidence at that crime scene. Still, we need to see where Abernathy died. And like you said, we need to get a timeline of their movements up on the board. That means we have to start talking to people."

Entering the room just in time to hear that, and closing the door firmly behind herself and her dog, Trinity said, "Which means I haven't got a hope in hell of keeping a lid on this."

Serious, Hollis said, "It isn't just two murders, Trinity. This is definitely a serial killer, if only because we can connect him through those crosses to the mountain serial."

"Okay. And so?"

"Leaving his victims the way he did, even though each scene looks different, each method of killing is different, means something to him. He's getting more brutal, no question, which means an escalation. But . . ."

"But?"

"This doesn't feel like a killer . . . learning his craft. And it doesn't feel like a submissive—unless he's had a psychotic break of some kind. This feels like something very carefully thought out, planned, maybe for a long time. He's on some kind of mission. I don't know what it is yet, but I'm betting his victims have something in common, some connection to him, and that's why he killed them. Maybe even why he killed

each the way he did. But we can't begin to understand him until we understand each of them."

"He won't stop?"

"Not until we stop him—or until he's finished."

Slowly, Trinity said, "I thought serials killed
out of some kind of twisted psychological or
sexual need?"

"Most kind of serials do, yeah. The mountain
serial is that type. And most of them go on and on
until they're caught or killed. But I don't think
this guy is a typical serial killer. These aren't
stranger killings. A stranger hanging around long
enough to gather the sort of intelligence I believe
he had to have would have been noticed. He
isn't killing them because they fit some private
fantasy or because it's the only way he can get
off; he hasn't shown any sexual interest in them
at all. He has a different reason. He's on a
mission. I'm even betting he has a list."

"A list," Trinity said slowly.

"Yeah. His hit list. Don't know why he's killing,
but we can make an educated guess about who his
next targets are just based on who he's killed so
far. Men in their thirties, though we can't rule out
possible female victims, not when he's just getting
started. But both were locals. People he knows.
Went to school with, played sports with—maybe
even still works out with at the same gym."

"Why? Why people like that?"

"Because," Hollis said, "they're people like

him. Or were like him. Somewhere along the way, something happened. To him, to his life, his sense of self. To someone he cared about. Right now, I have no idea what that might have been, but I know something changed in his life."

"A trigger," DeMarco said. "A stressor."

Hollis nodded. "Something that turned a man you probably know or knew from a seemingly nice guy into a vicious killer."

Trinity said, "I can have my people start running more detailed backgrounds on all the victims. I know you guys probably prefer to do your own background checks and interviews, but we can at least have more detailed preliminary data for you to work from."

"That would help a lot, Trinity," Hollis said with clear gratitude. "We do prefer to talk to people ourselves as a rule, but the more information we can gather beforehand, the more productive those interviews are likely to be—and the less stressful for all concerned."

"The second shift's just coming on; I'll put a few of my brighter boys and girls on it."

Hollis was surprised. "The second shift?"

"Yeah, it's around four o'clock. And in case you haven't looked outside, it's already getting dark. The sun sets behind this mountain, so night comes early, especially this time of year. My advice would be for you two to get settled into the hotel and have an early night, try to get some rest. And eat something. I know we've all avoided food after what we found at the church, but all this coffee on empty stomachs isn't going to help any of us."

"What about you?" Hollis asked.

"After I brief the second shift, I'll probably head home for the night. There really isn't much we can do tonight anyway. My people will begin gathering more information, and Doc said we'd have the post on Barry Torrance by morning. I don't know if he'll find anything other than what we all saw, but at least we'll know if there's something new to factor in."

Curious, DeMarco asked, "Will he pull an all-nighter?"

"Probably." She sighed. "He delivered both victims, and though he's a tough guy, a former corpsman in the navy, this hasn't been easy on him. He's thorough, and very professional, but I know he wants to do his job and get it over with. Then go home and get drunk. It's the way he was after he did Scott's post."

"Can't say that I blame him for that," Hollis said. She added to Trinity, "We'll need to establish a timeline for each of the victims. Going back at least a week or two before the first murder. Where they were, what they did, what was habit and what wasn't."

"Where and when they crossed paths with their killer?"

"Hell, they might have seen him every day. Until we get a feel for their lives, their routines, we can't know much more than we do now. With the timelines, we may be able to figure out whether Scott actually let his killer in. Or where Barry Torrance was grabbed. Or maybe . . . see that they weren't where they should have been at a particular time. Sometimes what isn't there is just as helpful as what is."

DeMarco wanted to make some comment about just how expertly Hollis was beginning her work as a profiler on this case, but he knew her well enough to keep his mouth shut.

"Makes sense," Trinity said. "In the morning, I'll take you to Scott's apartment. I know profilers are trained to see things average investigators aren't trained to look for, indications of behavior and personality. And I know your unit is trained to make use of those extra senses. One way or another, I'm hoping you'll see something I've missed."

"We'll have to wait and find out," Hollis murmured.

"In the meantime, the hotel is nice, and room service is from the restaurant on the first floor. Nothing fancy, but good food. Deacon left to check in and then go visit his sister. I gather they have some catching up to do, especially since he knows now what really happened to her before she came to Sociable, so I don't expect him back here before morning. There are a couple more restaurants in the downtown area, but everything's pretty sedate—and most of the townsfolk will probably stay in for supper tonight. My advice, we all get some rest and come back fresh tomorrow."

DeMarco nodded, then looked at Hollis with raised brows.

"Might as well pack it in for now," she said. "We've done all the speculation we probably should with the information we have so far. Even as quickly as this bastard is killing, he's been taking at least a couple of days between murders. Who knows, maybe he's tired enough to give us all a break."

Half under her breath, Trinity said, "After what he did to Barry, I'd expect him to need more than two days. A lot more."

"That," Hollis said as she rose from her chair, "all depends on the why of this. Once we know why he's doing what he's doing, a lot of puzzle pieces should start to fall into place."

Miranda listened to the rather terse report, then said, "It sounds like you've got everything under control, Hollis."

"Yeah, right." Hollis was still dressed even though it was after ten, but she'd kicked her shoes off and was leaning back on several pillows piled at the headboard of her bed, a muted news channel on the TV. And she was using the hotel's landline.

She'd discovered her cell phone to be dead as a doornail, which, between the normal "psychic drain" and all the energies up the mountain, hardly surprised her. It was charging on the dresser across the room. For all the good it would do her tomorrow.

Her tablet was also charging; like everything else electronic that the SCU agents used, it tended to have a very short battery life—even inside its specially designed cover.

"It's a rough case for your first time as a primary and profiler," Miranda conceded. "Serial killer investigations are always rough. But certainly not beyond your abilities."

"Well, it might have helped if you or Bishop had told us we were investigating the flip side of the mountain serial."

"What, and spoil your fun?"

Normally, Hollis appreciated Miranda's wry humor, but tonight her head was pounding and she was still uneasily sure she was not qualified for the job she'd been tasked for.

"I just . . . I want to do right by these people. They're good people. Even if Trinity *is* still holding out on us."

There was a brief silence, and then Miranda said, "You think she is?"

"I know she is. Just not quite sure what it's all about. Something she doesn't think matters to the investigation; she's too good a cop to keep something like that to herself."

"Mmm. What do you think of the town?"

"It's gorgeous—but a lot of odd stuff has happened here over the years. Most of it decades ago if not longer, admittedly, but we should have known. And we damn sure should have known about that strong electromagnetic field from somewhere at or above the old church down at least a half dozen streets below it. It's like the top part of this town is . . . almost in a world of its own."

"How did it make you feel?"

"The energy? Uncomfortable. Bothered. Deacon said it felt like his skin was crawling—but he also said that was probably what he was picking up from me." She considered. "Though I suppose that's what a tough manly man would say. Is he one? I don't know him well enough to guess."

"Not like you mean. He's tough enough to not worry about protecting his image. Or even projecting one."

"Okay. Then maybe he *was* picking it up from me. Reese didn't say, but I was probably broadcasting like crazy."

"What else did you feel up there?"

She drew a breath and let it out slowly. "We were being watched."

"By?"

"I thought at first the killer. And maybe it was

him. What I felt was something almost . . . gleeful. Almost like it was a game, and he was watching to see how we'd react to what he left for us. Nothing threatening, just curious and . . . gleeful. Which was creepy enough, I can tell you."

"But it changed?"

Hollis scowled as she stared at the muted TV. There'd been a blizzard in the Northeast. Probably a foot of snow even at Quantico. Not that Bishop was there. She hadn't asked, but he'd been heading out to a new case the same time they had. She couldn't remember where. Maybe California.

She wondered if Tony was complaining about the weather.

"Hollis?"

"Yes, it changed. You're getting as bad as Bishop. Why do you ask me questions when you know the answers?"

Not being her husband, Miranda answered.

"Because I don't know the specifics. Did it feel like someone or something else watched you later?"

"Yeah."

"Did you see something?" She was patient.

"No. No, I didn't see anything at all. Not a spirit. Not even one of those orbs that keep showing up on the ghost-hunting TV shows. I didn't see a damned thing, Miranda. Just like I haven't seen anything spiritual for months. And it's beginning to scare me."

● ● ●

"So," Tony Harte said when Bishop's phone call with his wife had ended, "did you *know* this case would force Hollis to face a few things she's avoided facing until now?"

"We knew it was possible," Bishop said.

"You didn't warn her."

"Some things have to happen just the way they happen, Tony. You know that."

"Yeah." Tony was more resigned than sarcastic. "We all know that."

It was considerably earlier in San Francisco. It was also a very, very foggy night.

Gloomy, Tony turned away from the window that had shown him only a view of the dim glow of a few nearby streetlights and one weirdly garish glow from the neon sign of a bar just slightly down the block.

"I'd rather have rain," he said. "At least then you can *see*. Fog is just creepy. It distorts or hides everything."

"We don't have to be out in it tonight," Bishop said. "Count your blessings."

He was sitting at what was a rare luxury for them when on a case, a very spacious table in their small hotel suite, more of a conference table than one designed for eating.

Two-bedroom suites generally didn't have to seat eight people for dining. And this particular suite was currently occupied by only two people.

"I thought Maggie helped Hollis heal," Tony said, referring to Maggie Garrett, one of the founders of Haven and a quite extraordinary empathic healer.

"She healed the worst of the damage," Bishop said. "But physical scars fade a lot faster than emotional and psychological ones, even with help. Emotionally . . . Hollis was given the gift of being able to heal physically and move on and adjust to her psychic abilities without the additional burden of memories too painful to bear."

Tony frowned. "Maggie took away her memories?"

"You know better than that. Nobody on our side has been able to develop that ability. No, Maggie just . . . pushed the memories into the distance. Made it feel to Hollis as if more time had passed. But it was a temporary fix."

"Did anybody tell Hollis that?" Tony asked dryly.

"We weren't sure ourselves. Hollis has been amazingly resilient, with some of the strongest survival instincts we've ever encountered. As Quentin is so fond of pointing out, she should have died half a dozen times by now."

"Okay. And so?"

"And so . . . we've worried. Her abilities have grown in ways no one could have predicted, and most are extremely powerful, even more so than Hollis knows."

"How could she not know?"

"Do you know if you can lift a car with your bare hands?"

"Well, yeah," he said. "I can't."

"And if someone you loved was trapped under that car? If the situation was extreme, and you had to do something incredible in order to save them?"

Slowly, Tony said, "It's been done. So I suppose under those conditions I probably could. Are you saying Hollis doesn't know her limits because they haven't been tested? Even with all she's been through?"

Bishop's voice was grave in a way it seldom was. "Every situation is unique, and if we're tested, it tends to be in ways specific to whatever's happening."

"Okay. I think I get that. And so?"

"She's the only recipient of an eye transplant who can see. Why do you suppose that is, Tony?"

He had to think about that for a moment, but then it came to him. "Because she was a medium-healer from the very beginning. We just didn't know—she didn't know, at least consciously—that the first person with an injury she healed was herself."

"The first sense she healed. Changed," Bishop said. "Maggie helped her with the initial physical and emotional trauma, but her sight was gone. Her eyes were gone. There was no healing that, not by the strength of any empath we know. And by every medical and scientific measurement we know or think we know, an eye transplant will always fail unless and until science develops the knowledge to hardwire the optic nerve born in one person into the brain of another—and somehow teach those two separate organs to work as if they were born connected."

Tony stared at him, then said, "I never thought . . . but that sounds really creepy."

"A lot of people walk around with organs they weren't born with inside them, Tony. Transplants are routine. We've developed drugs to trick the body into accepting organs it wasn't born with, and allow them to function normally. Hearts, kidneys, lungs, livers. Even corneas. But the eyes themselves? No drug known to our science can forge that connection and make it function."

"But Hollis needed to see," Tony said.

"She was an artist before the attack. Her sight was more important to her sense of self than it would have been for many people. If she hadn't lost her sight, she might never have become a healing medium, but simply a medium. Because that was the first extra sense that made itself known. She heard spirits. One, in particular, at least at first. A spirit that would help her avenge many women, including herself. Still, despite what she might have been capable of doing blind, Hollis needed to see. A doctor performed the transplant, made all the physical connections he was capable of making, sewing together severed ligaments and muscles and nerves—which had never been connected to each other. So it should never have worked."

"Hollis made it work."

"Without even being consciously aware of it. The spirit told her she could see if she wanted to. She wanted to. And maybe an artist's trained knowledge of how every part of the body fit together helped her. She finished what the surgeon began. She healed the severed and damaged connections between eyes and brain. And then she somehow convinced her brain to accept and process images from those new eyes. Eyes from a donor she convinced her body and her brain to accept completely."

"She could see." Tony frowned again. "She's said things now and then, offhandedly, about seeing things differently. That her sight is different now."

"Not only different," Bishop said. "Changing. It was a bit off in the beginning, judging by what she told me, and what little she admitted to the doctors. Not enough to impair her vision, but enough to distract her from time to time. Then various cases brought her into contact with energy fields. Sometimes sheer electrical energy, like storms. Then there was Samuel, with his incredibly powerful and incredibly dark energy. Then there was what happened at Alexander

House, when she channeled an enormous amount of energy."

"I know Samuel literally hit her with a blast of his energy," Tony said slowly. "One of those things that should have killed her and didn't. But it changed her. Or . . . it woke up that other psychic ability, self-healing. Good thing, too."

"Definitely," Bishop agreed. "And even though she didn't literally channel energy then, she did absorb dark energy and use it to heal herself."

Tony blinked. "That's what she did?"

"We believe so," Bishop said. "It's what helped make it possible for her to do what she did at Alexander House. She's unique, Tony. She's the only psychic we know of able to actually use dark, negative energy—absorb it, channel it, change it, expel it, possibly even shape it to her needs—in a productive way and without herself being harmed in the process."

"Not harmed. But . . . ?"

Bishop nodded. "Always a price. For Hollis, the price isn't clear, at least not all of it. But there will be a price."

FOURTEEN

Annabel Hunter was regretting her decision to decline her friend Toby's offer of a sleepover. Not the sort of sleepover a couple of teenage girls would have, of course, braiding each other's hair and playing loud music and talking about boys.

No, a much more mature version. Just two adult female friends nervously keeping each other company because a killer was on the loose.

And probably drinking a lot of wine.

Annabel broke out an unopened bottle of her own stock by nine thirty, and by ten thirty had consumed half of it. Maybe that's why the old movie she had on television was so funny.

Because she had the vague idea it wasn't really supposed to be a comedy.

She thought she was probably getting drunk, then decided that was a good idea. She'd sleep better. Maybe even not dream. And it might be early for bed, but she figured extra sleep was bound to do her more good than harm.

Especially after hearing about what had happened to Barry.

Especially after Trinity's call.

And most especially after what Toby had shared.

Damn tarot cards.

The thought had barely skittered across her

mind when the TV suddenly developed a mind of its own.

The old movie vanished, channels scanning past in a blur. Stopping on a sitcom. Then scanning again, stopping this time on a music channel. Seconds later, on again to pause briefly on a science documentary, before settling for way too long on a movie about demonic possession.

Annabel fumbled for the TV remote, but before she could do more than grasp it, channels were scanning by again, but slowly now, and pausing for long seconds on each of a series of movies she recognized.

One about a haunted house. One about a psychotic murderer. One about supposed witches being horribly—and graphically—tortured during the Inquisition. One about a group of teenagers on an ill-advised weekend party trip to a creepy isolated cabin, where a lunatic machete-wielding killer stalked them. One about a seemingly simple, innocent game that ended in terrifying, bloody death. One about an extremely disturbing little Asian ghost girl with long, stringy black hair and the seeming ability to drive people out of their minds with terror.

Annabel wasn't so drunk that she didn't catch the theme emerging. In fact, she didn't think she was drunk at all. Not now.

Not any longer.

In fact, she was certain she was cold sober

when she began pushing buttons on the remote—and the TV continued to wend its way through a series of nightmarish images.

"Dead batteries. That's all it is," she muttered to herself, trying to ignore the screams from the TV.

Never mind that the light indicating the remote had power was bright green.

Had to be the batteries. Dead batteries. She'd just get up and go find fresh ones, and—

"I'm coming for you next, Annabel."

She froze, her eyes on the remote, listening to the utter silence that had followed that sinister male threat. And it was a long time before she was able to force herself to look at the TV.

The dark black screen of which showed her nothing now except her own reflection in the lamplit room.

January 30

Reese DeMarco stood in the doorway of the bedroom and studied the very, very peaceful space. If he hadn't known better, he would never have guessed someone had died in this room. It was the bedroom of a very neat man, almost compulsively neat, with not a thing, seemingly, out of place.

"You seeing anything I'm not?" he asked his partner.

Hollis was a few steps into the room, turning slowly as her gaze roamed over furniture and prints on the walls and simple blinds on the windows and muted rugs on the polished hardwood floor. "No," she said finally. "Neat, wasn't he? Trinity?"

DeMarco stepped inside the room to allow the sheriff to come in, and found himself looking down to see that her ever-present black dog had moved as well, but not into the room with his mistress. Instead, he was sitting beside DeMarco, exactly on the threshold. Before DeMarco could ask the question tickling the back of his mind, Hollis spoke to the sheriff.

"When you got here, when Braden led you here—the front door was locked?"

"Yeah." Early night or not, Trinity didn't look as if she had slept very well. "I knocked, rang the bell, no answer. He kept a spare key behind a loose brick in the facade."

"Who knew that?"

"Anyone who knew Scott. This was a very safe town, remember? Beyond a little occasional teenage vandalism, we don't get break-ins." She shrugged. "I was wearing leather gloves when I used it, because it was cold that morning. I had the key printed later. A couple of clear prints. His."

"And this door locked from the inside."

"Yeah. I had a locksmith check the front door

and this one. He said there were no signs any-thing other than the key had been used to unlock the front door."

"And this door?"

"No signs it had been tampered with. But you can see it's a typical sort of modern bedroom door, with a turn lock on the inside but not a deadbolt, and not really a keyhole on the outside. A tiny slot for an emergency release key in case a kid gets locked inside, or the door's locked accidentally."

"Let me guess," DeMarco said. "It was on the top of the door frame."

"Yeah. Where we're all told to keep them: handy, but not visible or in the way. This apart-ment complex isn't that big, but there are two families with kids, and safety is a factor. The owner is in residence and serves as the building's manager. He told me he makes very sure to tell each tenant where the emergency release keys are to be kept. And that he checks between tenants, and replaces any keys that are missing. They're more or less universal with this type of door."

Hollis was frowning. "If a door can be unlocked from the outside, it can be locked as well."

Trinity nodded. "Locked-room murder mysteries aren't what they used to be, at least not in newer buildings where safety concerns triumph. The killer could have used the emergency release key to lock the door from out in the hallway. Probably what he did."

"I had a feeling the how of that locked door wouldn't be as interesting as the why of it," Hollis said.

"The why of it?"

"Yeah. Why lock the door? What was the point? Most everybody knows how this type of door works, so finding it locked wouldn't be a big deal. Mildly puzzling, but not a barrier to discovering the body, not anything that would have slowed anyone down—or impeded the investigation if it was a question that went unanswered." She paused, then added slowly, "It was almost . . . childish, locking this door from the outside. And mocking, because the killer took the time to do it when he didn't have to. When there was no point in it."

DeMarco said, "Especially when the big mystery was how he managed to break Abernathy's neck without leaving so much as a bruise."

"Misdirection?" Trinity suggested. "Hoping we'd be so preoccupied with the locked door that the manner of death wouldn't seem as interesting by comparison?"

"Not unless he knows virtually nothing about police investigations," Hollis replied. "I mean, people not trained in crime scene investigation might have dwelled on something you generally hear of only in mystery novels, but cops? No. You noted it in your report, but you didn't give it much importance. Neither did we. Why would we? We concentrate more on time of death and cause of death, on possible enemies, possible motives, possible witnesses. Who saw him last, what was the last thing we *know* he did. Who cares whether the door was locked?"

It was Trinity's turn to frown. "Good point. I just considered it another oddity in a very odd murder."

"Natural enough, especially given the murder that followed this one. And maybe I'm missing something, maybe there *was* a reason. But I can't think of one."

"Neither can I," DeMarco said.

Trinity sighed. "Then I vote we put it in the column of mildly puzzling things and get on with the bigger puzzling things."

"You won't get an argument," DeMarco said.

Hollis opened up the tablet she'd carried in with her, swore under her breath as she noted the already-diminished battery life, then studied the ME's report for a moment, using two fingers to enlarge a particular section. "He wasn't strangled, manually or with a rope or garrote, and his neck wasn't exactly broken, not the way we've been talking about it. Literally, his spine was severed."

DeMarco took a step into the room, noting abstractedly that Braden remained exactly where he was. "Wait a minute. His spine was severed? Not fractured or crushed or torn? Something that couldn't have been done by twisting? Because that's the only method I thought might possibly have broken his neck without leaving even a bruise, at least if it was done very quickly by someone who knew what he was doing."

"Severed." Hollis looked at him. "I don't know why I didn't see that word before, because it's here. His neck was broken, all right. Between two vertebra that weren't damaged. The spinal cord was very neatly and cleanly severed. As if . . . as if a razor-sharp knife slipped in between the vertebra and severed his spinal cord just below the base of his brain."

"Without cutting his skin," Trinity said slowly.

"Yeah. Without cutting his skin."

"Which makes it more than possible," DeMarco said, "that we're dealing with a killer in possession of some kind of psychic ability."

"Someone able to . . . slip a psychic knife into someone else's brain?" Trinity asked, not quite incredulous.

Hollis nodded slowly. "It's all about energy. And energy can be a force that dances, that swirls, that pushes or pulls . . . or forms an edge as sharp as a scalpel to neatly sever a spine."

Deacon ran his fingers through his hair and took a long drink of his coffee, but his eyes still appeared a little bleary when he looked at the others. "So, the mysteriously broken neck is even more mysterious than we first thought."

"Yeah." DeMarco eyed him. "Late night?"

"Late, yes. Fun, no."

Trinity murmured, "How is Melanie?"

"A bundle of nerves," he replied cordially. "And so are at least two of her friends. I know that because she got one call while we were having dinner, which sounded very enigmatic on my end, and then when I was about to leave her apartment after enough wine, I hoped, to settle her nerves, another friend showed up. Annabel. And she'd already had wine."

"Still nervous?" DeMarco murmured.

"Scared half out of her wits."

Hollis sat forward in her chair at the conference table. "What had scared her?"

"Her television."

He realized he was being stared at, and grimaced. "Yeah, I know. But she was genuinely terrified, I felt that. And when Melanie managed to calm her down enough to get some sense out of her, I have to admit it creeped me out more than a little." He explained what Annabel Hunter had experienced in her apartment.

Hollis rubbed her forehead, wishing the remnants of the previous day's pounding headache would finally leave her in peace. "Spiritual energy has been known to affect electronics, even control them. It's actually fairly common. If there's no medium nearby, it's one way they can try to make contact with the living, using as a conduit something electronic."

"Annabel didn't want to make contact," Deacon informed her politely. "In fact, I got the sense her response of choice would have been to get the hell out of Dodge."

"But not alone," Trinity said. "Annabel's family has lived in Sociable for generations, and she's the last of the line. She sold the very large family home years back and netted enough to live comfortably for the rest of her life. Bought some investment property here because her roots are here. Occupies herself with volunteer and charity work. Everybody genuinely loves Annabel. She's that sort. Has lots of friends, remembers birthdays and anniversaries, gives clever little gifts, sometimes for no reason, and if anybody needs to crash on her couch, they're welcome—and get treated to home-cooked meals for the duration.

"Far as I know, Annabel never made an enemy in her life. And she'd never leave Sociable and strike out on her own, even to run away from something that scared her. Maybe especially not then. She'd run to friends, but not run away."

"That was my impression," Deacon said. "And Melanie obviously knew Annabel didn't need to be alone last night."

DeMarco said, "I gather you took the couch?"

"Yeah. I think Melanie would have been okay locked in, even alone, but Annabel was shaking like a leaf and still talking nervously at three this morning. They finally went to bed, and I caught a nap on the couch. Everybody was up early. Melanie insisted on going to work, and since Annabel was still too frightened to be alone, I escorted them both to the bank. Then I went to my room, showered, shaved, dressed, and got my gun—consider that official notice, Sheriff, that I'm now armed." He had returned DeMarco's second gun to him before leaving the sheriff's department the previous day.

"Noted." Trinity clearly wasn't surprised.

"I plan to stay armed from now on."

"I'll make sure your boss knows you're officially on the investigation, at my request."

Deacon shook his head slightly. "You can call. I doubt he'll be surprised. He's probably already taken me off the leave list and put me back to active duty. Whatever you want to say about Bishop, he's scrupulously fair about stuff like that. If I'm working a case, it's not taking up any of my leave time."

"Sounds like a good man to work for." Almost absently, Trinity added, "If you want to see Scott's apartment later on, it's no problem. But Hollis and Reese didn't see or sense anything I missed. Unless they're holding out on me."

"We aren't," Hollis told her. "Where does Annabel live? I mean, does she live here in town?"

Trinity met her gaze. "She lives in a duplex, one of those conversions from what was once a very large single-family home. About seven streets down from the church."

Deacon said, "So that weird energy up there might have affected her electronics? Look, I'd buy that for the channel-scanning thing, but she said it had never happened before, and from what you say, Trinity, if it *had* happened before, it isn't likely she'd still be living there."

"True enough."

"Besides, what about the direct threat to her? 'I'm coming for you next, Annabel'?"

"She could have imagined it," Trinity said slowly. "All those scenes from horror movies and her own nerves on top of losing two friends in the last week? Plus wine? Possible, at least."

Hollis chewed on a thumbnail absently until she caught DeMarco watching her, then reached out for her coffee, frowning. "With a killer on the loose, I say we err on the side of believing her. She was friends with the two victims, a friend of Melanie's—I take it she's in the right age bracket to be a potential target?"

Deacon nodded. "So is the other friend, the one who called Melanie last night while we were having dinner, also shaken, though I didn't get details. Toby Gilmore?"

"Shit," Trinity said, her tone both resigned and, curiously, almost angry.

"What is it?" Hollis asked.

"Two things," the sheriff replied readily. "First,

Toby plays at being a fortune-teller. Tarot cards, mostly. Except that she can be uncannily accurate, and I've suspected more than once that she has some precognitive or clairvoyant ability."

In a slightly accusing tone, Deacon said, "Yeah, about that. Telling me about Melanie sort of shoved everything else out of my mind yesterday, but when we met, you told me you hadn't experienced anything paranormal." He jerked a thumb to indicate the chair across from him at the table, a chair occupied by Braden. "Just before you introduced him, as a matter of fact."

"I lied," she responded, calm. "Besides, whatever I've seen in Toby is completely normal. For her."

"And Braden?"

"What about him?"

"Oh, come on," Deacon said. "He's led you to two murder victims. And I was in the Jeep with you yesterday, so I can state with fair certainty that he was *guiding* you. Very specifically. He knew exactly where he was going, and he knew exactly how to direct you where he wanted you to go."

"He's a dog, Deacon. A very smart dog, admittedly. An unusual dog. And I haven't yet figured out how he knew about the victims before any alarm was raised. But unless and until someone tells me different, Braden has remarkable faculties for a dog, and a remarkable sense of . . . duty. And that's all."

Deacon knew she was daring him to question that. He could feel her daring him to—with his shields up. He decided not to question, at least for now.

Hollis waited him out for a moment, then said to Trinity, "There were two things?"

"Yeah. I honestly didn't think much about it when the idea first occurred, but with Deacon adding in Melanie, Annabel, and Toby . . ." She pushed a couple of folders out of the way, drew a legal pad and a pen within reach, and began to write quickly. When she was finished, she pushed the legal pad to Hollis, who was sitting nearest her. "Meet The Group," she said.

It was a list. Fifteen names. Two of them neatly crossed out.

~~Scott Abernathy~~
Cathy Simmons
~~Barry Torrance~~
Melanie James
Jeff Stamey
Toby Gilmore
Dana Durrell
Trinity Nichols
Xander Roth
Caleb Lee
Annabel Hunter
Patrick Collins
Rusty Douglas

Skylar Pope
Jackson Ruppe

Steadily, Trinity said, "We were all in high school together, same graduating class. Some of us moved away for college or even jobs for a while, but we all either stayed here or came back to work and live within the last few years. And we were the last graduating class to have so many to settle in Sociable. Oh, there are a few adults in town not many years older and younger than us, but we've always been a kind of unit.

"Cathy dubbed us The Group because we tended to hang out together, use the same gym, have the same or similar hobbies, invite each other to parties, stuff like that. Some of us were even in relationships at one point or another, and still managed to stay friends when they were over. More or less.

"It started out as a joke, that name. After a while, it was just something that stuck." Trinity drew a breath and let it out slowly. "And now it seems The Group is unique in another way. Looks like it's quite possible we're the killer's hit list."

After a long moment, Hollis pushed the legal pad toward her partner and said, "That's not all it means, Trinity. If The Group is that specific in age and interests, and these are the people the killer is targeting, then the victim pool is a lot smaller than we first believed. And if that's the case . . ."

"If that's the case," Trinity finished, her voice still steady, "then it's likely that the killer's name is on that list as well."

FIFTEEN

Melanie went into the bank's employee lounge, carrying two hot lattes, and as soon as she saw two of her friends instead of the one she'd left there, her uneasiness climbed. Especially when she saw what one friend was doing.

"Toby, the tarot cards? Here?"

"I didn't think anybody would mind. Everybody knows me, Melanie, they know I read tarot for fun. Besides, I didn't want to be at the office alone, and Annabel wanted me to read them."

"I thought it might help, Melanie," Annabel confessed. She sat very still across from Toby, but her hands were writhing in her lap, betraying her nerves.

Sitting down at the end of the table, Melanie handed one of the cardboard cups across to Annabel. "I didn't know you were here, Toby, or I would have got one for you."

"I'm okay," Toby replied, her gaze on the cards she was dealing. "I had coffee earlier."

"But again—tarot, Toby? Here?"

"Why not here?"

Melanie tried to hold her voice steady. "Look, we all know you do this for fun. But in case you hadn't noticed, most everybody is more than a little anxious, even creeped out, today. However badly Barry was . . . mutilated . . . gossip has it even worse." She frowned. "At least, I hope gossip has it worse. Anyway, everyone I've seen today has been really shaken up. I wouldn't be surprised if whispers about demons or shit like that aren't already spreading."

Annabel made a little inarticulate sound, but Toby looked at Melanie with a frown. "Seriously?"

"Toby, which would you rather believe? That someone you know and possibly speak to every day is an insane killer, or that something evil that doesn't belong here is doing these horrible things?"

"Neither," Toby said, serious.

Annabel made another little sound, and Melanie absently reached over to briefly grasp her knotted hands.

"Toby, trust me when I tell you that when things get as bad as they are right now in Sociable, people start looking for someone or something to blame. I was the prime suspect for a while there, being a relative newcomer, but since I was highly visible in town all day yesterday during the time Barry was murdered, I seem to have lost favor as a possible killer. Thank God."

"I never thought you were that, Melanie."

"Neither did I," Annabel murmured.

"Yeah, you two, my brother, and possibly Trinity." Melanie sighed again. "The point is that how Barry was killed seems to any sane person to be either absolutely *in*sane or purely evil, and nobody really wants to deal with that. They want something to blame, and the wilder the stories get, the wilder the speculation will be. Tarot for fun is all well and good, Toby, but some people still look at those images on the cards and think witchcraft."

Toby blinked. "I sing in the church choir," she objected.

Melanie almost laughed, except that what she felt was too grim to allow for humor. "And the devil can quote scripture for his own uses. Fear makes people look in unusual places for answers. It's not rational, it just *is*."

"But—"

"Listen, just put away the cards for a while, okay? You two can do something else to occupy your time. I'll get my tablet, and you can play mahjong or solitaire or something."

Annabel's glance sort of skittered over the partial tarot card layout, then away nervously.

Toby bit her bottom lip, then said, "Never mind the cards. I didn't tell you this last night, but . . . I saw Scott. Yesterday."

Melanie shook her head. "We both know you can see what you want in the cards—"

"He wasn't in the cards. He was standing in my office, not three feet away from me. Melanie, he was trying to tell me something."

Annabel was staring at Toby, her eyes huge.

Melanie studied her friend for a long moment, hoping her inner struggle wasn't visible. Then she said calmly, "Ask me, you two had some unresolved issues when he died. Guilt and regret can manifest itself in a lot of ways, Toby."

"So you don't believe me."

"I believe *you* believe you saw Scott."

Annabel spoke up then, her sweet voice not as steady as it normally was. "Melanie, do you believe what I told you and Deacon about what happened at my house last night?"

"I believe something scared you."

Toby gathered up her cards, her face still but her lips pressed together firmly.

Annabel bowed her head.

Melanie felt like she had kicked a puppy. And guilty as hell, because she had seen Scott—and didn't want to admit it even to herself, much less out loud.

Toby said, "She told me about what happened, Melanie. I'm the one who has the weird experiences, remember? Not Annabel. I know odd things happen on her street, but nothing like that has ever happened in *her* house."

"There's a storm coming," Melanie said slowly. "Just saw the weather. Maybe that was it."

"An approaching storm told Annabel she was next?"

Melanie really wished Toby hadn't brought that up, because she could see Annabel's pale face lose even more color.

"Toby, we're all having it rough right now. Our friends have been horribly murdered. And I think we're all afraid that the killer is probably somebody we know. It's natural for us to try to cope with all that the best way we can."

"So Annabel scares herself with scenes from horror movies and *imagines* a threat against her specifically, while my way is seeing the spirit of my murdered ex-lover."

"Maybe it is." Trying to keep her voice calm, Melanie said, "Maybe we all see what we need to see—"

"So what do you see, Melanie?" Toby's face was uncharacteristically hard. "What nonexistent ghost haunts *you* these days? Did you see Scott, too? Or were you still his lover when he died?"

"Melanie wasn't born here," Deacon objected. "She didn't go to school here."

Trinity nodded. "Yeah, Cathy brought her into The Group after the thing in Atlanta. There really was a job opening, and Melanie really did get the job. She was here, and . . . I mean, it's not like we were some kind of exclusive club or anything. There weren't rules to exclude—or include—

anybody. Nobody voted or even said anything. Cathy brought her along one day when most of us were going horseback riding. And . . . she fit right in."

DeMarco glanced at Deacon, then said to Trinity, "Are there other members of The Group like Melanie? Not born and raised here?"

Trinity hesitated, then shook her head. "No. The rest of us were born and raised here. Like I said, a few of us were away for anywhere up to ten years but chose to come back here to settle down."

Deacon sighed. "Well, cross off the victims, you, and I hope Melanie, and that leaves us with eleven names."

Hollis said, "We can't automatically eliminate the women of The Group, not on the basis of two victims. I agree Trinity's unlikely for two major reasons: because she's the sheriff and because Braden is always with her. And Melanie wasn't born here, so she's off. The rest of the women have to be considered potential targets. So the women, plus six men. Trinity, isn't Jeff Stamey one of your deputies?"

"Yeah."

"Could he kill?"

"As a cop, sure, I think so, if he had reason. Like this?" She gestured toward the evidence boards. "I can't see it."

"How about the other names?" He leaned

forward so he could see the legal pad that had made the rounds and settled in front of Hollis. "Xander Roth, Caleb Lee, Patrick Collins, Rusty Douglas, and Jackson Ruppe. What about them?"

Trinity shook her head again. "Honestly, I'm probably not the one to ask. I can't be objective. Xander has a temper, but I've never known him to harm anyone. Caleb is . . . an old soul. Very Zen—and a vegan. Pat is cheerful and likes jokes; he has an antiques shop, but really supports himself by restoring and selling antique cars—they're his obsession. Rusty is . . . Well, he drinks too much too often, but he's a charming drunk, not a mean one. Usually either goes home with a woman and passes out on her couch, or one of us sees him safely home to his own couch."

"He's an alcoholic?" Hollis asked.

Trinity sighed. "I don't know if he'd ever admit it, but yeah. His father was pretty much the same. Ended up missing a curve between here and the highway one rainy night about eight years ago and going off the side. Didn't kill anyone else, thank God. Rusty's mom died when he was a teenager. Cancer."

DeMarco said, "That's a lot of pain for a young man."

"Yeah. And he coped by drinking more. Several of us tried to help, even got him into programs a couple of times over the years. He'd come back sober. And then fall off the wagon. If self-destructiveness is in the genes, it's in his. But he's no killer."

"And this last one, Jackson Ruppe?" Hollis asked.

"Jackson works down in the valley, on his family's ranch. They're one of two big outfits that breed and raise horses. Jackson's family specializes in Arabians." Trinity shrugged rather helplessly. "He's always seemed like a nice guy. Pleasant, friendly, sort of the big-brother type. He's big, always was, and when we were in school he tended to stand up for smaller boys who were bullied. The horses seem to respond to him really well; all animals seem to. He's an excellent trainer, by all accounts."

Deacon said, "Nobody sticks out as a killer."

"No, they usually don't," Hollis murmured. "We'll need complete background checks on all of them. We'll start with the men, see what if anything we find. Try to establish habits, routines. See where everyone was around the times of the two murders. And go from there."

Trinity said, "If we focus on just these men, it won't take long for people to connect the dots."

"I know. And I'd rather not give our killer a heads-up if he's on this list—or too much complacency if he isn't. So we shake things up a bit." She looked at Trinity. "Even the most peaceful town has troublemakers. The usual suspects whenever anything goes wrong. Guys you may bust once or twice for doing something illegal but not violent. That guy everybody whispers beats his wife, even if she *did* swear she just ran into something when she wasn't looking. And other men gossip has labeled as trouble—for whatever reason."

"Yeah, we have a few in each category."

Hollis nodded. "Add them to the list. Have your people run backgrounds and then do preliminary interviews. As far as your deputies *and* the townspeople of Sociable know, we're checking out known troublemakers, men who were friends of the victims and might know about enemies and such, and anyone else you can reasonably use to pad that list."

Trinity found a fresh legal pad and began jotting down names, this time mixing those from The Group with other names. "We're going to end up with a lot of extraneous information," she said. "And at least a few offended but innocent-of-this citizens."

"I know. Can't be helped." Hollis hesitated, then said, "Is there a deputy you trust to quietly run a background on Jeff Stamey—and tactful enough to ask a few innocent questions without getting caught at it?"

With a sigh, Trinity said, "Yeah, I know just the one. She's smart, ambitious, keeps her wits about her even under pressure—and Jeff's had his eye on her. She's pretending not to notice, mostly because she's gay. Not really something you talk about in a town like Sociable, but even so, Jeff seems to be the only one unaware of it. Amy Frost."

DeMarco lifted an eyebrow. "Seriously?"

"Yeah. Jeff jokes about it, says that's why he can't talk her into going out with him. Says he gets his fingers frostbitten."

Hollis winced.

Trinity, noting the reaction, said, "It'd probably be kinder to put him out of his misery. Maybe I'll do that once we get all this behind us. In the meantime, I think Amy'll be willing to . . . thaw a bit in the pursuit of truth and knowledge."

"Sorry the deception is necessary," Hollis said.

"Listen, if I've got a killer in my department, I'd rather know about it—even if he hadn't already killed two of my friends." She shook her head. "And if one of my friends is a killer, same thing. Any way you look at it, we have to get at the truth. Preferably before anybody else dies."

She picked up the legal pad and got to her feet. "I'll brief everybody. The background checks of the victims were going on all night, and we've already accumulated a lot of paper. I'll have that brought in so you can start going over it, maybe get a timeline for each victim at least roughed out. Then I'll add these names to the list for the first shift to start working on. And start sending select deputies out to do interviews."

"Select?" DeMarco asked.

"Some are better at it than others. I'd rather have the ones who can ask polite questions, soothe any ruffled feathers, and still pick up on the subtleties."

Hollis smiled wryly. "I'm glad you have a few."

"So am I. I'll have them question people around the areas of the crime scenes as well." Rather grimly, she added, "Do my best to get us as much useful information as possible and muddy the waters at the same time."

"Good luck," Deacon said.

Trinity eyed him. "Don't go far. With the women still on the list, we have potential victims, a few witnesses, and quite a few women who knew the murder victims. I'd like you with me when I go talk to them."

"Because of my charming smile?"

"Because you're Melanie's brother—and by now, everyone in town knows it. I want them thinking about that and not thinking so much about the questions I need to ask them."

"Smart," DeMarco murmured.

"Well, we'll see."

Hollis was looking at the original list Trinity had given them, frowning. "What about people who didn't come back?" she asked suddenly.

"What do you mean?"

"I mean, are there any names not on this list who *were* once upon a time? Who were raised here, went to school here as part of the same class as the rest of you, maybe even lived here for years as adults and were part of The Group—but aren't here any longer?"

"Yeah, a few," Trinity admitted after thinking about it. "Matt Reeves took a construction job on a crew working out in the Gulf area. It was meant to be temporary; he didn't even sublet his apartment. But there was an accident, not so uncommon in construction. A cable snapped, and a steel I-beam fell on him. Killed him instantly."

"How long ago?"

"Last summer."

"Who else?"

"Well, we've been at war. Half a dozen from our graduating class entered the service. I know of two who were killed: Sam Eliot and Bruce King. No idea what happened to Wayne Morrow, I just know he didn't come back here. Neither did Kendra Logan. Let's see . . . Sonny Lenox. He and Toby were an item for a while, but they broke up. Must have been three years ago, just before I came back, so I hadn't even seen him since graduation. Gossip had him heartbroken, but I wouldn't have said he was the type. More the type to do what he did. Big dramatic gesture. Packed all his belongings in the back of his pickup and left Sociable, swearing he'd never come back. And there was no family left here for him to come back to, if he'd wanted that excuse." She frowned. "You know, I'm not positive, but I have a vague memory of someone commenting that he'd been in a car accident and was left a vegetable, then later died. Not here in Georgia, somewhere north. He was never really a friend, so I didn't follow up and find out for sure.

"There were a couple of women who came back here for a while after college, then married men they'd met in college and moved away. The only other man I can think of from our class who was here for some years and then left was Andrew Ware. He and Dana Durrell had been sweethearts since high school, so everybody expected them to marry, have kids, the whole happily-ever-after deal."

"What happened?" Hollis asked.

"Amy Frost joined the department."

"Ah."

"Yeah. It took Andrew a bit longer than it did most of the rest of us to see which way the wind blew, and even then he got it wrong. I mean, Amy and Dana were discreet, didn't even go out together in public—but the breakup with Andrew was anything but. He suspected another man and told everybody he could get to stand still long enough everything he suspected. Far as I know, nobody ever corrected his assumption."

"So he left town?"

"Yeah. He kept in touch with Rusty for a while.

They'd been good friends when they were kids, though not so much later on. Still, once or twice when Rusty was sober, he said he'd gotten a few e-mails. Andrew was out west somewhere, taking flying lessons, wanted to be a commercial pilot."

DeMarco said, "Why do I get the feeling any of The Group leaving Sociable just never ended well? He died, didn't he?"

Trinity nodded. "Made the news, which is the only reason I knew about it. First solo flight, his small plane went down in the mountains near his flight school. Exploded on impact. They never found enough of him to bury."

Deacon settled down in a chair across the table from Toby Gilmore and Annabel Hunter, glanced around at the almost deserted employee lounge of the bank, and said, "I guess we missed lunch."

Trinity, sitting down one chair over from him and opening her notebook, said absently, "Nearly done, for now. We'll stop for takeout on the way back to the station."

Braden was, as usual, sitting beside her, silent and attentive. Deacon had found it interesting that everyone they had spoken to all morning long had accepted the dog's presence without comment, a few even greeting him pleasantly.

Melanie, sitting at one end of the table, said to her brother, "Hope you still like Chinese. That's the only restaurant between here and the station."

"It's a small town, Mel. Half a block in either direction, and I have more choices."

"What do your friends prefer?"

"We've never worked together before, so I have no idea."

"Then you *are* working here? You haven't been talking to possible witnesses with Trinity just to keep her company?"

"What, I can't be good company?"

"You can't stop being a cop."

Before he could respond, Trinity said, "I requested his help, Melanie. If you want to pick a fight about it, pick it with me."

Deacon looked at her with a faint grin. "Oh, I can tell you were an only child."

She looked slightly disconcerted.

Even Melanie had to laugh. "Sorry, Trinity. The default age for siblings tends to be about twelve. And a brother and sister can get into an argument about the weather. There's a storm coming, by the way, in case you two didn't know."

"I didn't know," Deacon said. "No chance to catch the weather so far today."

"Snow by tonight," Melanie told him. Then she looked at Trinity, brows lifting. "Is that going to make things easier or harder?"

"I have no idea," Trinity answered. "I'm hoping it keeps everybody, including the killer, inside. But we'll see."

Melanie's expression darkened. "I wish I knew

who it was. They didn't deserve to die. Not Scott, and not Barry. They were good people, Trinity, you know that."

"Yeah."

"Then why *them?* Why did this sadistic killer pick them?"

Deacon said, "If you try to find your kind of sense in the mind of a madman, you'll drive yourself crazy, Melanie. Even trained profilers know better than that." He still wasn't sure he agreed with Trinity's determination to not warn the members of The Group that they were likely targets and that the killer likely lurked among them, but it was her town—and her case.

They were just here to advise and offer their expertise.

And, so far at least, neither Hollis nor DeMarco had argued with the sheriff about this particular decision.

Trinity said, "Deacon's right. There's no sense in this. Maybe, when we catch him and if we catch him alive, he'll have a reason. It won't be a good reason, and to us it probably won't be a sane reason. But it'll be his. And who he kills will make sense according to his reasons."

SIXTEEN

"You're rubbing your forehead hard enough to make a dent," DeMarco told his partner.

They were in the conference room, alone since Trinity and Deacon had been gone for several hours interviewing people, and they were still only about halfway through all the paperwork the sheriff's really well trained staff had, overnight and through the morning hours, accumulated on the two victims and a *lot* of potential targets and the potential killer.

Hollis straightened and flexed her shoulders, sighing. "Something's bugging me," she said.

"Clearly. What is it?"

She pointed to the small evidence bag containing the silver cross. "That."

"What about it?"

"I think we both missed an obvious question. And I think Trinity ambushed us with the information about Melanie *and* her past connection to Bishop very deliberately, so we wouldn't think to ask about it."

"You've thought she was holding back on us. Even after telling us all that, you still thought it."

"If you don't stop reading me—"

Sighing, he said, "You were very tired last night. And bothered. And I was tired, so my shield

257

wasn't as solid as usual. So I picked up a few things. Without trying, Hollis."

"I wish that made it better," she murmured.

"And I wish it didn't bother you so much."

She avoided his gaze. "I told you months ago. I have a lot of baggage."

"And I told you everybody has baggage."

"Reese—"

"Hollis, I went to war." His voice was very steady. "And I was an officer. I saw a lot of people get killed, a few blown to bits right in front of me, and they were there because of my orders."

"You were following orders, too," she managed.

"That didn't make it easier."

"I get that. I do, really. I'm not trying to minimize what you went through. I know it had to be hell, a desert hell a long way from home."

"But I came home whole."

She chose her words carefully. "I'm betting you left pieces of yourself over there, just not literally. Not limbs or—or bits of flesh, maybe. But still pieces of yourself. I don't think anyone can go through war and come back whole."

After a long moment, he said, "Okay. We both went through trauma of a kind nobody should have to endure. But what happened to you—"

"Is something I really don't want to talk about." She looked at him with a hard, bright smile. "Baggage, that's what it is. Everybody has baggage, as you said. Mine may bump against my heels more than most, but that doesn't mean it's . . . hindering me."

"I never said it was."

Hollis shook her head. "And you've never believed it hindered me—from doing my job. I don't think anybody has any doubts about that; Bishop would never have put me in the field if he had. Hell, maybe that's what . . . shaped me to do this job, and in ways I haven't even figured out yet. But, personally, as a woman . . ."

"Baggage," he murmured.

"I warned you. I don't think about it because I don't want to think about it. Because I'm not ready to think about it. Because I *know* what kind of pain thinking about it and talking about it will cause, and I'm . . . just not ready for that."

After a moment, he said, "There are some decisions that get made for us. I hope, for your sake, this isn't one of them."

Hollis shook her head again, already dismissing the subject, shoving it aside, refusing to open a door locked securely deep, deep inside her. "In the meantime, we have this case."

DeMarco accepted the change in subject because it was all he could do. For the moment.

"We have this case. What do you think Trinity distracted us from seeing?"

Hollis chewed on a thumbnail for a bit, frowning at the evidence board. And then she muttered, "Shit. She said it. She *said* it. And then with everything that came after, I just forgot. Jesus, how could she not think it's important to the investigation?"

"Hollis—"

"Except . . . maybe she doesn't know how it ended. Maybe she thinks Samuel's cult is still alive and well. Maybe when she found the first cross and called Bishop—and I know she did—maybe he didn't tell her. Maybe he just sent us down here knowing there were two connections we'd have to make. The first to the mountain serial, and the second to Samuel. Or maybe . . . he really didn't know if a connection existed. Because it wasn't a part of what we had to deal with then, facing Samuel in North Carolina."

Slowly, DeMarco said, "The cross reminded her of getting Melanie out of the cult more than three years ago. But there were no crosses specially made at the church in North Carolina."

"No, there weren't. But afterward, when it was all over with, I went back and read *all* the reports on the church, everything that had been sent in from all the different organizations that had been investigating Samuel and his churches."

"Why?"

"Because . . . because even though he was dead, only Galen and I got the full force of one of those energy blasts of his. I mean, without being able to repel it. I don't think it meant anything special to Galen."

"No. Galen is a watchdog, a guardian in the unit. And not even technically a psychic. Or, at least, he wasn't then. Energy wasn't something he could have . . . interpreted."

"No. But I could. Even then, I knew how dark Samuel's power was. And how strong. I had this nagging feeling it wasn't over, even though I kept telling myself that he was destroyed, all of him. I don't think I was all that surprised when he kept the fight going from his grave, when he sent more of his minions after us months later."[5]

DeMarco was frowning. "When Diana was hurt and you healed her, when you were so exhausted, you said something later. I thought it was the exhaustion talking. But you said something about hoping he hadn't escaped. Hoping Samuel hadn't found the door."

Hollis nodded. "In Diana's gray time, that corridor between this world and the next, that was where Samuel's spirit was, where it had been trapped since he died. I don't know if it was another place, another time—another dimension. I don't think Diana knows. But she was so worried then that he'd escape. She was weakening, dying because of her physical injuries, and yet she was willing to stay there to avoid making a door so he could escape."

"Because he wanted to *live* again."

------

[5]*Blood Ties*

"You think the mountain serial . . . is Samuel?"

"I think he wanted to *live*," Hollis replied. "And if there was any way, any possibility that he could have, he would have figured it out. And planned for it."

"Possession?"

Steadily, she said, "If anyone could have pulled it off, it would have been him. He had the will, he had the strength. He'd been stockpiling energy, stealing nearly every psychic ability he could. All he would have needed was a weakened body, someone unable to prevent him from taking over their mind. And we were in a hospital, Reese. An intensive care unit in a hospital. That's where Diana and I came back. If he came back with us, if he slipped through, he could have found a vessel. None of us were in any kind of shape to notice anything odd about the energy in the ICU, not then. He could easily have slipped past us."

"Assuming that's so," DeMarco said, still slow, considering, "and Samuel did find someone to possess physically, then it's also possible that his new . . . vessel . . . lacked the capability to absorb energy the way Samuel could. He'd spent his life learning how to collect, store, and channel energy, but that's as much a physical thing as it is a psychic one."

"Don't I know it," she murmured.

"So maybe he can't get power that way now. Maybe he has to . . . build up to it."

"By committing evil acts," Hollis suggested. "Like abducting and brutalizing young women. The darkest acts create the darkest and most powerful energy. Reese, maybe there is no team. Maybe there's just whoever and whatever Samuel has become."

"The energy you felt at the church up the mountain," DeMarco said slowly.

She nodded. "It was familiar. There was something almost . . . gleeful in it. As if he wanted me to know who he was. Maybe that's why he left the crosses with some of his victims. Not a huge red flag, not unless one of us had studied *all* the reports and knew that his church in Atlanta made crosses just like those to sell at flea markets and festivals."

"And that was what Trinity recognized," DeMarco said.

"I think so. I think that's what she reported to Bishop, how he knew whatever was happening here was at least possibly connected to Samuel."

"Because Bishop would have read all the reports, too," DeMarco said.

"Of course. The big picture. It's what Bishop always has his eye on. It's why he wasn't surprised when Samuel had killers hunting us even after he was dead and supposedly gone. And I'll bet anything you like that he's been suspicious that somehow Samuel would turn up again. And draw us in to another of his deadly games of cat and mouse. Because we beat him. And he'd haunt us forever, trying to get even for that."

"You'd make a fair profiler," Deacon told Trinity.

"No, thanks. If I wanted to chase scum and monsters for a living, I would have stayed in Atlanta."

"Well, the monsters we chase tend to be somewhat out of the ordinary, but it does lend itself to some sleepless nights."

Trinity looked as if she would have questioned that, then obviously remembered why she was here. "Melanie, we have your statement taken after Scott was found, and since you were in town and very visible when Barry was killed, I don't think there's any need for a second statement."

"Thank you," Melanie said. And it wasn't sarcastic.

"Toby—"

"I didn't kill anybody, Trinity. And I've already checked my books; I was with clients all day when Scott was killed, didn't even hear about it 'til I got back there."

"And Barry?"

Toby shook her head. "I was in my office, mostly catching up with paperwork. I'm sure you can find somebody who walked by the storefront and saw me there. I didn't leave until—until someone came in and told me about Barry."

Trinity made a few notes, nodding, then looked at Annabel.

Her eyes were huge.

"Annabel, I don't suspect you of murder," Trinity told her calmly. "I don't think you have it in you to kill anyone."

A little gasp escaped Annabel. "I didn't. Honest, I didn't."

"I never thought you did. I just wanted to talk to you about what happened in your apartment last night."

She looked slightly confused. "Why? I mean, it scared me half to death, but Melanie reminded me that electronics do weird things all along my street. Always have. It was just my turn, I guess."

"And the warning?" Deacon had to ask. "That you were next?"

"I'd had a lot of wine." Annabel still looked frightened despite the reasonable words. "And two of my friends had been horribly murdered. I just . . . I just scared myself, I think. In the daylight, with people around me . . . I don't know what I heard. If I even heard anything at all."

Trinity turned her gaze to Toby. "What about you, Toby? You called Melanie last night, didn't you?"

"Traitor," Melanie said to her brother.

"It's a murder investigation, Mel. We don't yet know what facts might be important. And I overheard enough to know that Toby was . . . shaken up. By something."

"What was that, Toby?" Trinity asked. "What shook you up enough to call Melanie?"

"I was just upset. After hearing about Barry . . . I was just upset."

Annabel was looking at her. "They need to know, Toby. It might be important. I mean—what you saw."

"I didn't tell Melanie about that last night. Besides, she didn't believe me," Toby said. "Why would they?"

Trinity's voice was matter-of-fact. "There are a lot of odd things about this investigation, Toby. About these murders. So whatever it is you saw, I need to know about it."

"I saw Scott," Toby said defiantly. "In my office, nearly as clear as I'm seeing you now. And he was trying to tell me something."

Melanie moved restlessly, as if she would have objected, but remained silent.

Trinity sent her a glance, then looked back at Toby. "Could you tell what he was trying to say?"

"You believe me?" Toby asked warily.

"Like I said, plenty of odd things happening. Could you tell what he was trying to say?"

"No. He just looked . . . upset. Worried. It only lasted a few seconds, and then he was gone."

Deacon said, "What were you doing just before he appeared?"

Toby frowned at him. "What do you mean?"

Deacon knew Trinity was looking at him as well, but he also knew that questions would occur to him—because he used psychic tools in investigations—that wouldn't necessarily occur to Trinity or any other standard law enforcement officer.

"I mean, what were you doing? A spirit . . . visitation . . . isn't exactly a common thing, unless you're a medium or the spirit was a blood relative. So he must have wanted to come through badly, and something you were doing helped him to do that."

The dark, almost absurdly exotic-looking woman was clearly both uneasy and uncertain. She avoided Trinity's steady gaze. And was rather stubbornly silent.

Trinity spoke up then, her voice still utterly calm. "Toby? Was it the cards? Or the Ouija board?"

Deacon sat up straighter before he could catch himself. "You use a Ouija board?"

"Well, just for fun." Toby was looking at him now, clearly startled. "At parties sometimes. But I haven't even opened the box since Scott was killed. I . . . I just couldn't."

"Good," Deacon said. "Don't." *Ever,* he almost added.

Trinity glanced at him, and then spoke to Toby before she could even try to express the confusion on her face.

"But you did use the tarot cards yesterday or

last night, didn't you? That's why you called Melanie. And probably what you were doing just before you saw Scott. Why you were upset."

"Everybody keeps telling me they're just for fun," Toby muttered. "So what does it matter? I might as well be playing solitaire."

"Not quite," Deacon murmured. He intercepted another glance from Trinity and reminded himself that this was not his interview. And that she hadn't exactly been open with anyone other than the feds about anything even vaguely smacking of the paranormal. Until now, at least.

She said, "Toby, did you see anything in the cards? Anything that shook you?"

Melanie said, "Tell her, Toby."

"Well . . . I saw The Group. Every time I dealt the cards, no matter which layout I used, I saw The Group." She sent Deacon a sidelong glance. "I don't know if you know about—"

"I know about The Group. Trinity told me." He decided in the moment not to mention that the other federal agents knew about it as well. Not that it really mattered, as far as he could see.

"Did you see anything else?" Trinity asked calmly. "Feel anything else?"

"I . . . felt . . . we're all involved somehow. All tangled up with the killer. And I knew Melanie's brother was coming to Sociable, that he was some kind of cop. And—"

"And?" Trinity prompted.

"It's just what I felt," Toby said, her anxiety obvious now. "I could be wrong. I'm probably wrong."

"Wrong about what? What else did you see or feel, Toby?"

Toby stole another glance at Deacon's face, then returned her worried gaze to Trinity. "I saw the other two coming. Them and Deacon, all monster hunters. Come to help us."

Trinity waited a moment, then prompted again, "And?"

"And I knew . . . I *felt* . . . one of them would be destroyed."

Hollis was sitting on the conference table, staring at the preliminary timeline they'd been able to assemble, still brooding.

"You think they know? Bishop and Miranda?" DeMarco asked, but not really.

"I'll give them the benefit of the doubt and say they probably didn't know for sure until that first cross turned up. Until Bishop remembered what I did, from the reports on Samuel's churches. And even then, I doubt even Bishop could have worked out exactly what was going on, much less figured on two separate *serial killers* operating just far enough apart to demand that he split the investi-gating team.

"Trinity had a weird murder here, found the cross—and recognized it, or thought it might be what she remembered. Whether or not she knew Samuel was supposed to be dead, any connection to a cult that had preyed on psychics would have had to worry her, especially with Melanie here. And if Toby's psychic, too . . ."

"Bishop had probably kept in touch," DeMarco offered. "We know he keeps tabs on psychics outside the SCU, outside Haven. Trinity already trusted him because he helped her get Melanie out in Atlanta. For all we know, they talked regularly."

Hollis nodded. "So she called Bishop. He knew that at the very least those murders and the murder here could have been connected. Maybe not, because crosses are really common, especially in the South, and word about the victims having them *could* have leaked out somehow. But reason enough to send us."

"Without warning us."

"You know," Hollis said, "as pissed off as I get just about every time something like this happens, I think I'm beginning to get why he does it. He doesn't send us in blind just so we can stumble around in the dark; he sends us in with what information he believes will be useful partly because he really doesn't know the specifics beforehand.

"And because he doesn't want us coming in with preconceived ideas. If we'd had even a hint that Samuel might somehow be behind the mountain serial and what was happening here, we would have focused on that; it would have colored every decision and choice we made."

She looked at DeMarco wryly. "It's how a profiler is trained to think. Don't listen to what people tell you; look for yourself. Don't try to bend the facts to fit your pet theory; let the facts *lead* you to a theory. Notice details, notice behavior. Look for a signature."

"So the cross is his signature."

Hollis shrugged. "It's the only thing he's done so far that was both consistent and not necessary to the murders. It's also the only thing he's done that even *hinted* at who the killer might be. Or . . . might be working for."

"So you think Samuel could have arranged, before his death, for a second team of killers to draw out the SCU and, hopefully, Bishop? To destroy it all?"

"It's more likely than possession."

DeMarco shook his head. "You don't believe that."

"No. When we faced that team of killers he sent to destroy us, I didn't . . . *feel* Samuel. Ever. Even in Diana's gray time, I didn't *feel* him. I don't think he wanted me to. He was always weird about mediums, and I'm sure he hated having to depend on one—or two of us—to set him free."

"But you feel him here?"

"It was that gleefulness I sensed up at the church. The girls killed north of here, that was deadly serious, and I don't think he wasted a thought on games. He was too busy building up his strength. I bet when all's said and done, we'll find out that he's killed a lot more these last months than we ever knew."

"And now?"

"Think about it. If he's spent all these months gaining strength every way he could, committing the darkest of acts both openly and in secret, by now he's probably strong enough that distances don't matter to him. Time doesn't matter. He could be killing in the mountains and killing here in Sociable."

"Seriously?"

Wryly, she said, "I'm not saying he can fly or—or teleport." She reflected. "On the other hand, I'm not saying he can't. I don't think we know his limits now any more than we did then."

"Just that he's filled with dark energy, an eternal hatred for Bishop and the SCU, and the bastard just won't die."

"That's about the size of it."

SEVENTEEN

"Did you know it was Samuel?" Hollis asked.

Miranda's voice came clearly and calmly from the speaker in the conference room. "We didn't know, not for certain. When you kill an enemy, you expect him to be dead. But Diana has been uneasy since you went into the gray time and pulled her out, healed her."

"She didn't tell me that."

"She didn't tell anybody except us and Quentin. Not that she actually has to tell him anything."

Diana and Quentin Hayes had been married for nearly three months, and their connection was . . . rather special.

"She believed Samuel had slipped out with us? Escaped the gray time?"

"She thought it was possible. And no one knows that place or time or dimension or realm—whatever it is—better than Diana. She thought he could have escaped, so we had to consider it. We suspected he might be behind all the dark energy you had to channel at Alexander House a few months ago."

"That wasn't him?"

"You would have felt it if it had been him. Did you?"

"No. Not a hint."

"That was what we thought. Noah was suspicious, but . . . When that vortex was closed, the dark energy was trapped again, rendered more or less harmless."

"More or less?" DeMarco asked wryly.

"You both know energy can't be destroyed. It can be transformed, it can be channeled—and it can be trapped. But it can't be destroyed."

"Well, that's comforting," Hollis said with a sigh. "And what's going on there? The fourth pair of girls, have they been found yet?"

"No. But there's an army searching these mountains, on foot, on horseback, by ATV, and by chopper. He hasn't tried to hide any of the other girls. We believe if the last two are dead, they'll be found like the others."

"If?"

Miranda hesitated, then said, "It's at least possible that Samuel—whoever or whatever he is now—does have a disciple, an apprentice. The former is probably more likely; being worshipped was part of what made him powerful. At any rate, if that is the situation, then once Samuel fixed his attention on Sociable—for whatever reasons—he could have left his disciple here to continue this part of his plan. Gathering more dark energy."

It was DeMarco who said, "But that would only work if he and his disciple were connected in some way, probably psychically."

"Yes."

"Then it's a woman," he said definitely. "That's the way his connections worked, the way he drew power."

"It's something we've considered. And it's entirely possible that if Samuel *is* at the heart of this, he does have a woman here in the mountains doing his bidding." Her voice changed, became more brisk. "But that's our worry, at least for now. You two have the greater worry."

"Understatement," Hollis muttered.

"Hollis, the two of you are there because you're the best team for the situation."

"Why?" Hollis demanded baldly.

"Because he's about energy, about power. He thinks of it as a weapon, so he hoards it, builds on it, covets it."

"Uses it," DeMarco reminded.

"Yes, he uses it. Or at least he did. We aren't at all sure he can do anything now the same way he could before."

"But if he can?" Hollis held her voice steady. "I felt the force of his energy, Miranda, and it nearly killed me. Would have killed me, if I hadn't been able to heal myself."

"You're stronger now," Miranda said.

"Am I strong enough?"

"I don't know. And neither do you. Until you find him. Until you face him."

"And then? Am I supposed to throw rocks? I have a feeling bullets won't even slow him down."

"Hollis. He's about energy."

She opened her mouth and then closed it, thoughtful.

"I don't like this," DeMarco announced.

"No," Miranda murmured. "I didn't expect you would. But you're there, too, Reese. Even if she doesn't like to admit it, Hollis knows as well as you do that the two of you forged a very unusual connection when she was channeling all that energy—and you were her lifeline."

"Dammit," Hollis said.

"Connections are also a tool we can use, Hollis. Believe me, I know," Miranda said.

Hollis avoided any glance at her partner. "I get that. It's just . . . I feel a connection to Samuel I don't like at all. It's as if he's gotten inside my head somehow."

DeMarco said, "You haven't mentioned that."

She still refused to look at him. "The headache. The nosebleed. What I felt up there at the church and the parsonage. The . . . *unnatural* way it all felt. It was him. I wasn't sure what it was at the time. But I'm sure now."

"He thinks he knows you," Miranda said. "But you've grown incredibly since you faced him in North Carolina. Among so many other things, he's an utter narcissist, Hollis. He doesn't really think about anyone but himself. And I'm betting—we're betting—that you're going to surprise the hell out of him."

Melanie rubbed her forehead between her brows and said, "Well, that was weird. Still weird."

"You still have the headache?" Annabel asked.

"No, the pain's gone. But I feel kind of light-headed."

"Toby?"

"Yeah, me, too."

Practically, Annabel said, "None of us ate much for lunch. Melanie, you said you didn't have any more appointments today, and most everybody is getting ready for the storm. Why don't we go get something to eat and—and then decide where we want to ride out the storm."

Melanie eyed her. "Is this you not wanting to be alone, Annabel? Because if that's what it is—"

"No, this is me thinking we all belong to The Group, and it wouldn't be a bad idea for us to stick together until Trinity and your brother and the other agents figure out who the killer is."

Toby said, "I agree. Look, why don't we take that other two-bedroom suite at the hotel? I know the agents have one of them, but the other's empty, and Bill would probably cut the price in half just to have somebody there this time of year."

Bill Moss was the hotel owner and manager.

"Toby—"

"It's right in the center of town, above a good restaurant, and it almost never loses power during storms. Melanie, I don't think even you want to go home alone. Not now, with all this happening. Why don't we go together, and each pack a bag at home, leave a couple of lights on, and come back down here to stay at the hotel."

Melanie studied her for a long moment. "You

know, you kept it pretty calm, and you haven't mentioned it since, but you did say you believed one of the agents would be destroyed."

"Do we have to talk about that now?"

"Well, why not?"

"Because . . . it's all shifted. Storms always change things. Energy shifts and things change. Trinity and the agents have to get ready for the storm just like we do; we'll all be stuck inside. At least they'll have files and things to go over, and I wouldn't put it past Trinity to ask at least a couple of the guys she may be suspicious of to come to the station to answer some questions. Good time, with everybody preoccupied by the storm."

Melanie shook her head. "You're avoiding, Toby. What do you mean, it's all shifted?"

Toby frowned. "I don't know. It's . . . fuzzy."

"You don't still believe one of the agents will be destroyed?"

"I think . . . I feel . . . that somebody is going to suffer. Be in a lot of pain."

"There's this killer," Melanie reminded her, not as dryly as she had intended.

"Not that kind of pain. Not physical injury. Not torture, the way Barry was . . . Something else. Something deeper, in a dark place. From a dark place. An old agony exploding." Toby shook her head. "Look, I know that sounds like the worst kind of carnival bullshit, but I can't explain it any better."

"And in the meantime, you believe we should stay together."

"Yes. I do."

"So do I," Annabel said. "Because I didn't imagine that voice last night, Melanie. I hadn't had too much wine. And because we both know Toby *saw* Scott, just like she said she did."

"Annabel—"

"We need to stay together, Melanie. It's important."

Melanie could have thought of several reasons to disagree, but none of them convinced even herself. The truth was that two of her friends had been horribly murdered in the last week, that their killer remained unidentified but was being pursued by another of her friends *and* her brother, that a storm of unknown severity and duration was approaching—and she didn't want to spend any more time alone than she had to.

And because Toby wasn't the only one who had seen the spirit of a murdered ex-lover trying desperately to tell her something.

"Hollis?"

She was alone in the closed conference room, since DeMarco had gone to get coffee, and Hollis hadn't heard the door opening. She wasn't surprised she hadn't.

She was surprised at the stab of relief she felt when she pushed back her sleeve to watch gooseflesh rise on her arm, when she felt the odd chill, the change in the very air around her.

When she looked up slowly and saw a grave girl of about twelve standing at the end of the conference table.

Hollis could, just barely, see the closed door behind the girl. Through her. Because she had died violently at the hands of Samuel many months before.

"Brooke," she said.

The spirit of a little girl who was lifetimes older than she appeared smiled at Hollis. "We thought we'd give you a break," she said.

Hollis blinked. "What? You mean it wasn't my fault all these months that I couldn't see spirits?"

"You needed to rest," Brooke said seriously. "Clear your head, so to speak. You've been through a lot."

"I thought I was broken," Hollis told her indignantly.

"You've never been broken, Hollis. Even when you thought you were."

That silenced Hollis, but only for a moment. "You've appeared to me even though you're one of Diana's guides. But the stakes were high then. Are they now? Is Samuel here?"

"He wanted to live. He found a way. But . . ."

"But?" Hollis was so accustomed to uninformative spirit "guides" that she was honestly surprised when Brooke answered.

"Reese was right. Samuel had spent a lifetime learning how to collect and contain energies. How to use them. How to keep them from destroying him. Even though he was weak when he crossed back over, he still had the ability to collect energy. The dark energy he wanted and needed. What he hadn't counted on was that his new vessel lacked all those years of building control."

"So he's burning out his vessel?" Hollis asked directly, digging for information while she could get it.

"He will, if he expends too much energy. But that isn't his main problem."

"What is?"

"His vessel still has . . . the original personality."

"What? I thought he'd probably choose someone who was brain-dead, no personality of their own left. That must have been an easier thing to do."

"He thought he had done just that. As it turned out, the doctors and machines didn't know everything. And Samuel wasn't strong enough to totally overwhelm the personality he found there."

Hollis frowned at her. "You're being awfully forthcoming. Why?"

"I can't be helpful?"

"Is that sarcasm? You're actually being sarcastic with me?"

Brooke smiled, but then sobered and said, "I wanted to warn you. There's still some of the original person left, and he can . . . surface now and then. He's confused. Sometimes he's weak. Sometimes he thinks he's in the middle of a very vivid nightmare where people who wronged him, often only in his own mind, are punished. Other times . . . he knows what's happening."

Sober herself, Hollis said, "Oh, man, that's gotta be hell."

Brooke nodded. "Poor man. You have to understand . . . his only release is death."

"Shit. I knew you were going to say that."

"I just didn't want you to feel guilty. He wouldn't have survived physically if Samuel hadn't taken him. And he won't survive much longer no matter what you do or don't do."

"What about Samuel? We can't seem to kill the bastard."

Brooke seemed to hesitate, as though listening to a voice only she could hear, and then she said, "He knows the weakness of his vessel, and he's beginning to get desperate. He's tried more than once to invade someone else's mind."

"My headache? The nosebleed?"

"You have a kind of shield he didn't expect."

"I don't have a shield at all."

Brooke smiled faintly, but said only, "He's tried others. He'll go on trying. Sooner or later, he'll find a vessel he can possess that's strong enough to hold him indefinitely. Or else you'll destroy him. There is no in-between."

"*I'll* destroy him? Brooke—"

The spirit guide was fading.

"When the time comes," she said in a voice already growing distant, "you'll know what to do. Don't be afraid to use your connection with Reese. He's still your lifeline, Hollis. He always will be."

Hollis opened her mouth to speak, but Brooke was gone. And before she could gather her thoughts together, a wave of intense dizziness swept over Hollis, she felt icy cold—and then everything went black.

Hollis was standing in front of the small grave-yard between the church and the parsonage when DeMarco joined her.

"The negative energy has lessened, hasn't it?"

"Reading me?"

"Your shoulders are more relaxed," he said, maybe answering.

Or not.

Hollis glanced at him, then returned her gaze to the graveyard. "I thought maybe if I stood here long enough, I might sense a different kind of energy. But these are old graves. If anybody waited around long enough for me to get here, I guess they don't have anything much to say."

"And Barry Torrance? He died here."

"Not a peep from him, either. Have to say, I'm relieved by that. I generally don't see them with

the injuries that killed them. Really hoping that holds true here. Assuming I see anything at all, of course. Or hear. Whatever. Right now I barely have five senses."

DeMarco frowned. "Barely?"

"Yeah. My eyes are . . . acting up."

"What do you mean?"

Hollis kept her gaze on the graveyard. "The church is white. The parsonage is white, too."

"Yeah. So?"

"When I look at the church now, there's a . . . there's something almost like an aura around it. Red."

He waited a moment, and then said, "And the parsonage?"

"It's just . . . All red. The siding, the front door. Even the roof. Sort of white trim here and there, but there's red dripping or smeared on that. Other places still white, like someone was in a hurry and missed spots, or were on a ladder that didn't reach far enough. In some places things look . . . distorted, as if I'm seeing just those places through a magnifying glass held at the wrong angle or something. Everything I see is wrong. It's a house of blood, Reese. So it has to be my eyes, right?"

"Hollis—"

"It has to be my eyes. Maybe the energy up here. Because I've never seen anything like this before. Or maybe, hopefully, just because I'm asleep and dreaming all this."

"I'm in your dream?"

"Of course." Her voice was abruptly calm and certain when she told him that. "You've always been able to hear the whispers of my dreams. The next step was always this one."

"This one?"

"Walking with me in my dreams. Or in yours, I suppose. We'll have to figure that out. If there's time. Later."

He tried again. "Hollis—"

"Is Braden still on the steps?"

DeMarco turned his head and saw that the black dog was at the steps leading to the front door of the parsonage. His front paws were up a step or two, and his head was turned, his gaze fixed on them.

"I'm not going back in there," Hollis said.

"Is that what you believe he wants you to do?"

"Don't you? I'm the only one here who's supposed to be able to talk to the dead. And I'm pretty sure Braden knows there's nothing alive in that parsonage."

"But something you—we—need to know about?"

"I'm not sure. Maybe. Maybe he thinks so."

DeMarco was as certain as he'd ever been that he knew exactly what Hollis was feeling, and despite the lessening of tension in her posture, what his certainty told him was that she was afraid.

He couldn't remember Hollis ever being afraid.

Not like this.

He put his hands on her shoulders and turned her to face him. But she didn't look up at him. She kept her eyes fixed on the center of his chest. And he could see for himself that her eyes were . . . different. The pupils were enormous. And around them was a thin rim of bright, bright blue.

"Hollis, what are you afraid of?"

An odd little smile made an attempt to shape her lips, but it was unsteady. "Ghosties and ghoulies and things that go bump in the night. We deal with those."

"Yes. Is this something new? Something we haven't dealt with before? Isn't it Samuel?"

She gave a little nod. "It is . . . and it isn't. Not the man you knew. Not even the madman we knew. I know . . . what's been watching us. All this time, ever since we got here."

"What? Not who?"

"It's . . . a what. Maybe they all start out as whos, and then they get darker . . . and darker . . . and darker. From evil. From soaking it up. Until they're black. Until there's nothing left of them that's human anymore."

She raised her eyes to meet his at last. "The parsonage. Second-floor window on the left. It's standing there. Watching us. Not a spirit. Not a shadow. Something . . . old. Something ancient.

Something he thinks he created. Something that wants us to go away."

DeMarco hesitated only an instant, then quickly turned his head and found the window.

And for a split second, he saw a shape in that window.

A featureless bit of utter darkness with the outline of a man.

For a split second.

And then it was gone.

EIGHTEEN

Melanie made sure her apartment door was locked behind her, then made her way downstairs to the lobby where Toby and Annabel were waiting for her. Of their three homes, her apartment was the only one with a lobby, and the other two women had remained there to watch weather reports on the flat screen in a nice little seating area across from the security desk.

Annabel was sitting on the arm of a chair, and as soon as Melanie reached her, she said, "The weather people don't seem to know what the storm's going to do. Far as I can tell, on their maps we're in the colored area that's somewhere between a dusting of snow—and a blizzard."

"Figures. Where's Toby?"

"Restroom."

Melanie stood there for a few minutes half listening to weather people discussing low-pressure areas and elevations and the abrupt and unusual dip of the jet stream, then felt a sudden jab of uneasiness. "How long's she been gone?"

Annabel frowned at her. "She went . . . right after you went upstairs," she said slowly.

Melanie left her bag at her feet and immediately crossed the lobby toward the restrooms, gesturing toward the rather confused-looking security man behind the desk.

"Carl, there's an emergency exit just past the restrooms, isn't there?"

"Yes, Miss James, but—"

Melanie didn't wait. She checked the ladies' room quickly, coming out before either the guard or Annabel got there, then turned down the hall to the emergency exit.

Even from several feet away, she could see that a brick held one of the doors just slightly ajar.

"The alarm," Carl said, somewhere between angry and bewildered. "The alarm is supposed to sound unless we buzz somebody through at the desk. With parking at the side, so many people come in and out that way—"

Annabel said, "Toby wouldn't have left, Melanie. We both know she wouldn't have left. Not alone. Not unless . . ."

Melanie pushed the heavy door open and

looked outside anyway, but she didn't expect to see Toby, and she didn't see her.

"Call the sheriff's office," she told Carl.

"But, Miss James—"

"Two people are dead, Carl. Call the sheriff's office and report that Miss Gilmore is missing." She turned back to Annabel. "We can check the hotel on the way, just in case."

"We both know she won't be there," Annabel said, her voice hollow. "But I thought it was me. That voice I heard . . . saying he was coming for me next . . ."

"Come on." Melanie grabbed her bag. "With this storm coming, there won't be much time to search. We have to hurry."

When Hollis opened her eyes, she was utterly unsurprised to find DeMarco bending over her.

"That was a first for me," he said. "How about you?"

Hollis realized she was lying back on the conference table. On top of files. And on at least two or three pens or markers, because she could feel them pressing into her.

"I had a dream," she said.

"I know. I was there."

She frowned up at him. "I thought I dreamed that part, too. It hit me all of a sudden, so I can see how I could have just fallen back on the table when I apparently passed out. Where were you?"

"Luckily, on my way back from getting coffee, I stopped by Trinity's office, looking for those old maps of the town she said she had in there. Her couch kept me from hitting the floor. I've never gone out so fast in my life."

"Yeah, it was quick. One minute I was talking to Brooke, and the next—"

"You saw Brooke?" Since DeMarco had been undercover in Samuel's cult, he had actually known Brooke when she had lived as a frightened and traumatized little girl.

"Uh-huh. Apparently, the spirits were being considerate and giving me some time off."

"They might have warned you."

"Yeah, I said something along those lines." Hollis stared at him a moment, suddenly became aware of their positions relative to each other, and said, "Um . . . I think I'd better sit up."

His faint smile told her that he knew very well why she was uncomfortable.

Damn telepaths.

He straightened, offering her a helping hand.

She accepted it.

"We need to get up to the parsonage," she said.

DeMarco frowned at her. "Everything I felt in your dream says that's a bad idea."

Bluntly, Hollis said, "So is possession. According to Brooke, Samuel picked a weak vessel—but one that still had his own personality. One with a few old grudges against some members of The Group, I think, which is why they're being killed. The original personality was drawn back here for that, and then when we showed up, Samuel decided to stay."

DeMarco frowned. "Somebody from Sociable had a grudge bad enough to disembowel a man?"

"I'm making an assumption here, but the *degree* of torture, at least with Torrance, that was all Samuel. I don't know what the vessel planned to do, but I doubt it was all that. I'm guessing Samuel took control for the sick and showy bits. To gather more negative energy—and for us."

"It could explain why Abernathy's neck was severed so quickly and cleanly. No torture at all. He could easily have been killed by someone else."

"And was, I think. The vessel. I think he's mad at people, and I think that's pretty much all that's left of his personality."

"So that part is disintegrating."

"With every evil act Samuel commits, the original personality gets weaker, loses his grip. Because Samuel gets stronger. The original personality can surface now and then, but probably for briefer and briefer periods. Pretty soon, he'll be gone for good."

"Why do I feel there's more?"

"It's what Brooke said. Samuel picked a weak vessel. Or maybe any human vessel would have been weak when subjected to Samuel's needs.

Either way, the vessel can't handle what Samuel spent his life learning to handle: all that raw energy. All the power he's been trying to collect and hold is slowly destroying the other man's body."

"I hope you're not about to say what I think you're about to say."

"Yeah, apparently he's tried more than once to get himself a new vessel. I don't know who else he tried to invade, but that was the cause of my pounding headache and nosebleed."

"And yet . . . you kept him out."

Hollis shook her head. "No idea how. Brooke said he discovered I had my own kind of shield. But that was as far as her helpful streak extended, because she didn't explain what that meant."

"All that, and you still want to go back to the parsonage?"

"We have to, Reese. This is going to end one of two ways. Either Samuel finds himself a new vessel and slips away from us again—to fight another damned day—or else we stop him. Here and now."

"There's a storm coming," DeMarco said.

"I know. And we need to get this done before. I have an awful feeling that, if we don't, when the storm is over there won't be anything but wreckage in its wake."

"You were scared up there. In the dream."

"I'm scared now. But more scared of not going

up there. Everything in me says we have to go, and we have to go now."

DeMarco studied her for just a moment, then nodded. "Okay. Here, take your coffee. It's going to be cold up there."

He was right. It was freezing.

"Are you sure about this?" DeMarco asked nearly ten minutes later as he came around the front of their vehicle to join his partner. He had parked on the topmost cross street in front of the church and parsonage, at a break in the overgrown hedge where a path meandered toward the graveyard.

"Of course I'm not sure about it." Hollis didn't budge from her side of the SUV, just stood there outside the closed door, her hands in her pockets, and stared at the graveyard right in front of them.

To their left was the church.

To their right, the parsonage.

"Trinity wasn't kidding about freakish weather. That front popped up out of nowhere. Even the weather guy was baffled by it. We'll have snow starting within a couple of hours, before nightfall, and by this time tomorrow, the only way we'll get up here is to hike it. No telling how long this area will be all but inaccessible."

"You really don't want to go in there," DeMarco said.

"Like Bishop, you have an annoying habit of usually being right," she muttered, her gaze fixed on the graveyard. Before he could respond, she said, "One thing I checked on earlier. That preacher who murdered his wife and baby and then killed himself, he isn't buried here. None of them are."

"Because it's sanctified ground?"

"Be a good reason to deny him burial. But according to the newspaper account I read, his parents wanted them all buried back in the family cemetery in Kentucky. I gather it was a very, very private service."

DeMarco waited a moment, then said, "We both know that where the dead are buried doesn't have a lot to do with where their spirits end up if they don't move on."

"You think I was worried about bumping into them here?"

"Are you?"

Hollis shook her head. "Not really. That is . . . not unless he's that shadow man who was standing in the window."

"You seemed to believe that the shadow man isn't anything human. Not anymore, at least."

She hunched her shoulders against the growing cold, inside as well as out.

"Hollis?"

"I don't know what it is. If I had to guess, and I do, I'd guess what I saw in that weird dream was the representation of Samuel. All dark evil. And since we don't yet know who his vessel is, I couldn't see him as a person. Maybe it was just that. Or maybe it wasn't a representation at all. Maybe it was just evil."

Quite deliberately, DeMarco said, "Even in the dream I caught a glimpse only because I was touching you."

She didn't look at him. Rather fiercely. "Well, we knew all that energy at Alexander House would . . . intensify connections. Miranda said as much. So that makes sense."

"Does it?"

"Sure."

"She also said that connections were tools we could use."

Hollis thought that sounded . . . odd. But she didn't say so. Instead, she said, "Maybe that shadow man was from my imagination."

"I don't think our connection is quite that deep," DeMarco said in a thoughtful tone.

Hollis felt her cheeks growing warm and hoped he'd think the cold, fitful breeze was chapping her skin.

Then she remembered he was a telepath.

Damn telepaths.

"Hollis, you don't have to go into the parsonage. We've already been through it. And, so far, nothing about these murders indicates any connection. You saw a shadow in a window—in a dream."

"Yeah, right after talking to a spirit. A spirit who as good as told me I'd have to fight the devil."

"Samuel is the devil?"

"Isn't he? I think he's up here, Reese. I think he's been up here most of the time, maybe because of all the weird energy up here. And I think he killed Barry Torrance up here, the way he did, posed him like that, to make sure we'd have to come back. Because . . . he needs a vessel."

"He's not getting you," DeMarco said. "And he's not getting me."

"I hope you're right." With both hands in her pockets, she chewed on her bottom lip. "That dream. Didn't you find it odd that Trinity's dog was in it?"

"I found the whole thing odd," he retorted.

"Look, I can't explain it. All I know, all I *feel,* is that what he was trying to tell me in that dream was that I need to go inside the parsonage again."

"It was your dream," DeMarco pointed out. "Sparked, you believe, by the encounter with Brooke. Right?"

"Yeah. I guess."

"So why would Braden be included?"

"You want logic from a dream?"

DeMarco raised his brows at her.

"I think Braden is important. That he's here, like we're here, for a reason. Maybe it's to lead Trinity to murder victims. Or maybe it's something else."

"Do you want to go get him?"

"I think he'll be coming." Hollis frowned

296

slightly. "I am not a precog, so I don't know where these hunches are coming from. But they feel awfully certain."

After a long moment, DeMarco said, "Okay." He held his hand out and waited for her to take hers out of her pocket and slowly place it in his. "Then let's go see what's in there."

Deacon said, "I have a headache."

They were standing outside one of the small cafés in town, where they'd had coffee and talked to another of The Group, this time one of the men. Caleb Lee, who was definitely no killer.

Deacon still felt oddly calm from that encounter; the guy really *was* Zen.

Even so, Deacon also had a headache growing worse by the second.

Trinity looked at him in some surprise, because his tone wasn't one of complaint or even of someone wishing to convey information. What he was saying meant more than the words.

"Okay," she said.

"It's not my headache," he said.

It took several seconds of bafflement before Trinity remembered that he was an empath. He could feel what others felt.

"I thought that was just emotions," she said, because it was the first thing she thought of.

"Usually. For it to be pain . . ."

"What?"

"It has to be bad. It pretty much has to be from another psychic. A psychic not capable of shielding."

"Hollis?"

"I think . . . yeah. Hollis."

She turned and looked back toward the sheriff's office, only a few doors down. "Their SUV is gone."

Deacon rubbed his face with both hands. "Damn. I'm surprised she can even see. It's getting really bad. I feel like my head's going to fall off."

"Women have a higher pain tolerance than men." Trinity reached for the walkie clipped to the shoulder of her jacket. "Base, this is the sheriff. Where are our federal friends?"

The response, a female voice, came almost instantly from the other part of the device clipped to Trinity's belt, crackling with static. "They . . . left a while . . . ago, Sheriff."

"They say where they were going, Sadie?"

"Said if . . . came back . . . asked, I was . . . tell you . . . up the mountain."

"What's wrong with the radios?"

More static, and then, very clear, ". . . acting up like this for the last hour. Storm . . . probably."

"Thanks, Sadie." Trinity looked at Deacon, her expression grim. "The parsonage. I could tell Hollis was . . . drawn to that place. That's not a good place, Deacon. Especially not for a medium. I thought I'd told her enough to keep her away."

"Crime scene," he reminded her.

"One we've already checked out. Thoroughly."

"It's probably because she's a medium that she's there. They're drawn to the sort of places that would keep you and me away."

"Great, that's just great. But why now?"

Deacon glanced up at the sky, one hand rubbing his temple. "The weather? If they know about that storm moving in, maybe Hollis thought it'd be her last chance for at least a few days. And maybe she knows or feels we can't afford a few days."

Trinity's Jeep was parked right outside the bank, and she took a step toward it before halting to frown at Deacon. "If you're in this much pain down here, what's it going to do to you to be exposed to all that energy up there?"

"I have a shield. What I'm feeling is Hollis's pain, not mine. She doesn't have a shield. She's got Reese, but too much baggage to let him help her the way I think he can." Deacon was reasonably sure he was talking way too much, but the pounding in his head made clear thought a tricky proposition.

"Let's go." As soon as Trinity opened the driver's-side door, Braden was in and hopping over the console to get into the back seat.

Deacon got in the front passenger seat. "So he knows you don't need guiding this time, huh?"

"Guess so." Trinity lost no time in backing out

of the parking place and heading for the climbing side street that would take them straight up to the church.

Deacon clutched his head with both hands.

"Shield or no shield, it's getting worse, isn't it? We're getting closer to that energy bubble."

"You mean the one Hollis and Reese are in?" He gritted his teeth. "Yeah."

"Why won't she let him help her?"

"Not my story."

Trinity glanced at him, then repeated, "Why won't she let him help her?"

"Not fair," he managed.

"Why won't she let him help her?" Trinity repeated inexorably.

"Because . . . she thinks she's . . . damaged goods. Way down inside, buried, that's how she feels. Damaged. Broken. Never be the same person she was. Doesn't even realize it consciously most of the time. When she does . . . she thinks it's why she keeps getting new abilities. To make up for . . . what he took from her. Balance. It's all about balance. Evil did its best to . . . break her. And she survived. But she . . . was hurt. So badly hurt."

"When she first became psychic?"

"Yeah. Her trigger. It was . . . horrific. The worst psychic awakening we have on record. It was a miracle she even survived that attack. I only heard a few details, but . . . what I've felt from Hollis once or twice is . . . beyond pain. Something there isn't a word for. She's buried it deep, and maybe she even believes she's healed, but . . . it's still there. Still . . . unfinished business. Reese knows it's there. It's why he hasn't . . . pushed her."

Deacon wanted to yell, because the pain in his head was almost beyond bearing. But then, suddenly, it was gone.

For a moment, he had no idea what had happened. The Jeep was climbing the side street at a faster-than-posted clip, getting closer to the energy rather than retreating, so he should have been feeling worse instead of better.

Then he realized.

He turned his head slightly to see the black muzzle resting on his shoulder. Heard a soft whine.

"I'll be damned," he said.

The headache started abruptly just about the time they moved past the graveyard and stepped onto the walkway that led to the front door of the parsonage.

Hollis stopped because she had to, drawing a deep breath and letting it out slowly, telling herself she could handle this. She had a very high pain threshold, for one thing, something that had come in very handy several times. She and pain were friends of a sort, she had thought from time to time with dark humor.

"Hollis?"

"I'm okay."

"No, you're not okay. You're in pain."

"Stay out of my head."

"I'm not in your head." He took her arm and turned her to face him, frowning. "What is?"

Hollis realized her eyes were closed, and opened them slowly to look up at him. His aura was . . . very bright. It made her head hurt even more. It also made her squint.

"Hey, keep a lid on it," she said.

"What?"

"Double shield. Top one's wide open."

After a moment, he said, "No, Hollis, it isn't. Because of the energy up here, I'm closed up tight. Both shields."

"Reading me."

"Only your expression and posture."

That surprised her. "I'm not broadcasting?"

"Not exactly."

She wished her head would stop hurting; just because she could handle it didn't mean it wasn't a hell of a distraction. "Then what? Exactly?"

DeMarco hesitated, frowning. "Whispers. I can just barely hear them. Fading in and out, like a radio station almost out of range. Coming from you. But not you."

Even with all the pain, Hollis felt a chill that didn't owe anything at all to the cold wind picking up all around them. "Not me? You mean that bastard's in here?"

"No, I don't think so. Not yet. But trying."

"What's stopping it? I don't have a shield, no matter what Brooke said. I don't know . . . if I can keep the bastard out."

DeMarco put both his hands on her shoulders. "We know what happens when I try to pull you into mine,"[6] he said. "It muffles all your senses and makes it nearly impossible for you to use them the way you have to use them. You said the dead seemed more alive than the living."

Hollis was doing her best to think clearly. "That was in a hospital. With lots of spirits. I haven't seen any spirits up here. Give it a shot, will you?"

"I don't like taking chances that might harm you, Hollis."

"Listen, my head's gonna explode if we don't try something. And if Samuel is trying to get in, I'd really rather he didn't. Try that dampening field of yours, and let's hope it keeps that son of a bitch out. Please."

There was no way he could deny that plea, especially when he knew better than most the sort of threat Samuel was capable of, the sort of damage he could do, so DeMarco closed his eyes and concentrated. Because he had done something like this before, and to protect Hollis—or try to—it was much easier than other times when he had been intent on preventing a very powerful

---

[6] *Blood Ties*

psychic from using the full strength of his abilities.

He simply visualized a kind of bubble surrounding them both, protecting them.

He felt a sharp jab of pain in his head, just that one quick burst, and then, as he opened his eyes, he saw Hollis relax.

"Okay," she said. "Better, much better." She squinted a bit as she looked up at him. "But you still seem awfully bright. Your aura is like a hundred watts or something."

"Your pupils are contracted," he told her. "All the way."

"Are they? Well, that would explain it. I wonder why they are."

DeMarco didn't let go of her shoulders. "What do you see when you look at the house."

"The parsonage?" She turned her head, squinted again, then muttered, "Damn, I'd hoped it wouldn't be red. It wouldn't happen to be red to you, would it?"

"Actually, yes, it is." Part of DeMarco was deeply relieved that he saw what she saw, because it told him the connection between them still existed—no matter how much Hollis would wave aside or even deny its existence.

But part of him, the trained investigator with a great deal of psychic ability and experience, was more than a little wary. Because he had no idea what this was. And he understood now why

Hollis had found the experience of her dream so . . . creepy. Because it wasn't like looking at a building painted red. It was looking at something . . . unnaturally coated in red.

"Well, I'm glad I'm not alone in seeing it," she said and heard the relief in her own voice.

"I can see how you would be. Odd doesn't begin to describe it." He studied the parsonage. "And it seems a bit wavery."

Since that was more the sort of word Hollis would use, she found it odd coming from him. "Wavery? What does that mean?"

"There's a shimmer. Like heat off pavement. But not the whole building. Just places here and there."

"But still a red building?"

"Still red."

"And still red to me, more or less." She looked at the second-floor window on the left and was relieved not to see the shadow man watching them.

Of course, that hardly meant he—or it—wasn't waiting for them in the house.

"Still feel you need to go in there?"

"Yeah. More than ever. I don't want to, but . . . It has to end here."

"And you have to end it."

She nodded.

"Do you know how you're going to end it?"

"No idea. Brooke said I'd know when I had to know. Or something like that."

"Not sure I like putting so much faith in a spirit." He had seen her once himself, through that deeper connection with Hollis that had come from her channeling an enormous amount of energy while literally holding on to him as her anchor.

But he hadn't seen any spirits since then, whether because Hollis hadn't either or because that had been a temporary thing.

"Everything's connected," she said suddenly, as though answering a question he had asked.

"Yeah. Including us." He shifted his hold so that their hands were linked. "Extending my shield seems to come easy when it's you, but let's not tempt fate, okay? Don't let go."

As they resumed walking toward the parsonage's front door, she murmured, "You always seem to be protecting me or anchoring me or connecting to me."

"I wondered when you'd notice."

"Oh, I noticed. You know damned well I noticed." She didn't look at him. And changed the subject. "I wonder if the key is still under the flowerpot."

"Bound to be. Small town."

"And predictable."

"Habits. Same thing, I guess."

DeMarco was perfectly aware that they were talking the way kids whistled in a graveyard: because their surroundings made them uneasy. His inner shield tended to guard his thoughts and shut out the thoughts of others, but that had never been easy with Hollis; in fact, it had been all but impossible.

If he wasn't careful, even her dreams seeped into his own sleep.

And the nightmares he was pretty sure she never remembered and he could never forget.

Something he wasn't about to tell her.

NINETEEN

Just as Melanie and Annabel burst into the door of the sheriff's department, the whole place went dark. They froze instinctively, hearing several confused voices call out. And then the emergency generator kicked on, and the lights came on, flickering for several seconds.

Deputies and other staff settled back at their desks, frowning over equipment as various pieces rebooted. Or not.

"What the hell?" Melanie said.

The receptionist, a woman no more than a few years older than Melanie, stood at her desk instead of sitting and ran fingers through short, spiky hair that looked as if she'd been clutching it. A lot.

"Dammit, the whole place is going haywire," she said. "Phones ringing with nobody on the other end, computers crashing—and now the power. And the storm isn't even here yet."

"Did Carl call you? The security guard from my building?"

Sadie shook her head. "If he did, he didn't get through. I was barely able to talk to the sheriff before she and Agent James took off."

"Took off where?"

"Up the mountain, I gather. After the other two agents."

"Why? I mean, why are they all going up there?"

"I don't know," Sadie replied, her tone the sharp one of someone pushed beyond normal limits. "Nobody was telling me anything even *before* the power went."

Melanie leaned on the reception counter. "Listen, we have to start a search. Toby Gilmore vanished at least half an hour ago, maybe a bit longer."

"What do you mean, vanished?"

"I mean she's *gone*. She could be the murderer's next target."

"Miss James—"

"You have to get word to Trinity and Deacon, and the others. They have to know Toby is missing."

Sadie stared at her for a moment, looked past her at Annabel's frightened white face, then sat down and began trying to raise the sheriff.

Nothing except static greeted her efforts. The radio, the phone, every channel, every line—static.

"Hank, Joey," Sadie said, turning to summon

two of the deputies in the bullpen, "you two head up the mountain to the old church and tell the sheriff Miss Gilmore's missing. Move it."

She might not have been one of the deputies, but clearly Sadie's word was law, because the two deputies lost no time in hurrying out the front door.

Melanie was about to say something else, but a sudden bolt of pain made her instinctively grab for her head. "Damn. Oh—*damn*."

"Melanie?" Annabel was beside her, worried.

It felt like someone was trying to ram a spear through Melanie's head. A hot spear. She bit back a groan and pressed her hands harder to each side of her head. What could be—

Melanie. Let me in, Melanie.

She hadn't realized her eyes were closed until that inner whisper, oozing darkness, made her stare wildly around the room. Too familiar. That horrible slimy voice was too familiar.

But it couldn't be. Because he was dead. She knew he was dead because she had felt it happen, months before. Samuel was dead.

"Melanie, what's wrong?"

She looked at her friend almost blindly for a long moment, and then it was as if something clicked in her head, like a door quietly closing.

The pain was gone. And so was the voice. Thank God.

"Melanie?"

Annabel's face came into focus, and Melanie heard herself saying calmly, "I'm fine. Really."

And she felt fine, actually better than she had in at least a week. For about another minute and a half. And then the front doors opened, and two deputies with bewildered faces came in.

Sadie said, "I told you two to go—"

"We can't go anywhere," the older deputy said. "Two Jeeps outside and neither one will start. Dead as doornails, both of 'em. And that's not all. There are a dozen people along the street standing beside their cars saying they won't start, either."

Annabel looked at Melanie, her face even whiter. "This feels like with the TV," she whispered. "Like something else is in control."

"Or trying to be," Melanie said grimly.

"What?" Trinity asked her passenger.

"The pain's gone. My headache. Gone."

She sent him a glance, noted her dog's position, then said, "You think it was Braden?"

Deacon reached up a hand to scratch the dog gently behind one ear. "Well, you said he wants to help. If he stopped the pain, he sure as hell helped me."

The black dog made a soft little murmur of a sound, then lifted his head off Deacon's shoulder.

Deacon instinctively braced himself, but the pain did not return.

"Well?" Trinity asked.

"Gone. If Braden didn't do it, he has a wonderful sense of timing—and I have a different question. It could be that I'm just not feeling Hollis's headache anymore. Which worries me a bit."

"We're almost at the church," she said.

Only a few seconds later, they were there. Trinity parked her Jeep beside the black SUV, and they got out. Braden was already heading for the parsonage, with Trinity and Deacon following.

Both of them stopped at the same instant.

"Do you see—?" Trinity began.

Deacon said, "It wasn't red yesterday, was it?"

"No. It's never been red."

"It is now." He stared at the parsonage, which was not only red but decidedly odd in a way he couldn't really define. Maybe . . . distorted somehow. Maybe. But only when he moved his gaze from place to place, as if he saw it through a lens that was made up of different thicknesses. Or as if he saw it through very old glass, before machine polishing had made it all perfect.

Braden was waiting for them, paused on the steps, head turned as he waited.

The front door appeared to be open.

"Trinity?"

"Yeah?"

"When did it snow up here?"

"The question," she said, "is why the snow is only around the parsonage and graveyard."

Deacon drew a breath and continued walking. Following footprints in the snow. Braden's footprints.

"You know," he said absently, "for someone who claims to have no experience with the paranormal, you're handling all this very calmly."

"It's my nature."

"To take things calmly? Or to suppress everything you're feeling?"

"Are you trying to read my emotions?" She sounded very calm.

"No, I'm doing my best to keep my shields up," he said frankly. "Because everything about this feels—to me—wrong. The snow, the red parson-age, the fact that Reese and Hollis came up here, all of it. Wrong. Yesterday there was a murder victim not too many yards behind us in front of the church, and today there's a winter storm on the way—and I'm feeling pushed."

"As if we're going where we're supposed to be. Where someone wants us to be. Their wishes and timing, not ours."

Deacon noted she had not made it a question. "You feel that, too, huh?"

"Only since I saw the red parsonage."

"Braden doesn't seem bothered."

He didn't, just standing there waiting for them to join him on the steps.

"I don't know if I feel safer with him," Deacon said, "or if I should be even more worried."

"He's never led me into a dangerous situation," Trinity noted.

"Just to two dead bodies."

"There is that."

"Think there's another body in there?"

"If there is, it isn't one of the surviving members of The Group. We know where every one of them was as of an hour ago, at least if everybody stayed put or didn't break usual habits."

"Except the other ones," he noted. "The ones who were already dead before this started." Still a yard back from the steps, he stopped and looked at Trinity. "Dead."

She had stopped as well and frowned at him. "What are you thinking?"

"I'm thinking Hollis is a medium. A medium with a history of drawing spiritual energy to her. A medium who has a knack for handling all kinds of energies—in unexpected ways."

"And that's why we're seeing the parsonage red? Why we're seeing snow all around it? You think she's opened some kind of door?"

"It's as good an explanation as anything else I can think of." He looked at the parsonage. "Although . . . if that's what she's done, Bishop's going to have to add a whole new section to her file. We have another medium capable of pulling somebody into a spiritual realm she visits herself, but not in the flesh.

"You and I are wide awake and we're definitely

here. And I've never heard of anything like this before. My understanding is that there always has to be at least some kind of connection between the medium and whoever is also able to see and feel whatever comes through that open door."

"Connection?"

"Yeah. Physical, emotional, psychic—or blood, as in a sibling or child or parent."

"None of that seems to apply to us, unless you're connected to her psychically."

"I'm not," he said immediately. "The fact that I felt her headache was way more her than me, and whatever that was, it wasn't a connection. More like . . . a shock wave. Or several."

"Because she broadcasts."

"I guess. But my shields are up and as strong as I know how to make them."

"So you shouldn't be affected by her psychic abilities."

"No, not under normal circumstances. And you certainly shouldn't." He gestured with one hand toward the parsonage. "And yet."

After a moment, and still oddly calm, Trinity said, "Maybe Hollis opened more than a door. Maybe she opened a portal. One much larger than for just a single person, or even two, to step through."

"As in—a time portal?"

"Maybe. Or one into a different dimension. You'd know more about this stuff than I do."

"Oh, no, I don't," he objected. "I'm an empath. I feel things other people feel. In *this* time, in *this* dimension."

"You mean normal time and normal dimension. For us. Which I'm thinking is back there somewhere."

It took him a moment, but then he realized. "We're already in it. Whatever she did, whatever Hollis opened—we're inside."

"I'd say so. Inside—where the parsonage is red and just a little distorted, and where there's snow all around."

Deacon looked at the house, at the wide open door, at the dog waiting patiently on the steps. "And where we don't know the rules," he said slowly. "If it's a different dimension, the rules are going to be different. The way things work. The way things *are*."

"Still feeling pushed?" Trinity asked him.

"Or pulled. Hard to tell which. All I know is that I need to go inside."

"Then let's go," she said.

Yes, come. Come into my world. Let me show you what I can do here.

Both Deacon and Trinity were startled when, upon entering the weirdly red parsonage, they found Hollis and DeMarco standing calmly in the foyer, clearly waiting for them.

Holding hands, which seemed a bit odd.

"Took you long enough," Hollis said. "And we've decided it is."

Trinity frowned at her. "Is what?"

"Another dimension. Or time. Maybe both."

"But definitely," DeMarco said, "not in sync with our own dimension or time."

Deacon looked at Trinity and said, "You know, we're all a little too calm about this. Am I the only one bugged by that?"

"Apparently."

Before he could waste a glare, DeMarco gestured with his free hand toward a grandfather clock against the wall opposite the stairs. "Take a look at that."

At first, Deacon didn't know what he was supposed to be seeing. But then he realized. "No hands. No numbers. The face is blank."

Hollis was nodding. "It's like that in Diana's gray time. I mean, she *calls* it the gray time, but time isn't there. Or doesn't work the same. The clocks have no features, just like that grandfather clock has no features."

Trinity said, "So we're in some kind of spiritual realm?"

"I think so," Hollis said cautiously.

Still calm, Trinity said, "You're the only medium here, as I understand it. So how come all four of us—plus Braden—ended up in some kind of spiritual realm? In the flesh?"

With a sigh, Hollis said, "Our boss holds the

316

belief that the universe puts us where we need to be. He says if you find yourself in an unexpected place, by whatever route, chances are you're supposed to be there. After that, follow your nose."

"And since we're here?" Deacon ventured.

"Well, we're investigating two very unnatural deaths. When you think about it, that's what the four of us have in common. The universe put us here—wherever or whenever here is—presumably to continue investigating."

Trinity said, "But the parsonage doesn't have anything to do with our murders."

"Wish you hadn't put it quite like that," Deacon murmured.

"You know what I mean. The murders we're investigating have no connection with this parsonage."

"They must have," Hollis said, adding simply, "because we're here."

Deacon looked at DeMarco, who said only, "I'm a stranger in a strange land myself. Hollis said this feels like spiritual energy to her, and I believe her. She says we have to be here because we have a pretty good idea of *what* the killer is, if not who, and she's supposed to face him here. Somehow."

"Wait," Trinity said, absently shifting her jacket so as to be able to get to her gun as quickly as possible if need be. "Hollis knows *what* the killer is, but not who?"

DeMarco was wondering how to explain the inexplicable, when Hollis did it very simply.

"Remember the bogus preacher from Atlanta, the one you had to rescue Melanie from? Somebody killed him, but he's been after us pretty much ever since, the SCU and Bishop, from his grave, first by proxy and now, apparently, by hijacking himself another body. And I'm betting you'll recognize him before we do if he's still in that body, because whoever it is was born and raised here in Sociable and probably, at one time or another, was or could have been part of The Group."

Oddly enough, Trinity latched onto a single phrase in the whole explanation. "If he's still in that body?"

"He's burning it out, more or less. Too much energy, too much power. What he could harness and control in his previous incarnation, he can't handle in this new host. It's . . . spilling out. He can't control it all. Can't you feel it?"

"I can, as a matter of fact." Trinity drew her gun, looking around warily.

"If he burns it out, or believes he's going to, he'll be looking for another host. I'm betting one or all of us get nominated."

"Lovely," Trinity said.

"He's here," Hollis told them. "Somewhere. And we have to stop him here. Before he invades one of us, or manages to get away somehow

318

and . . . survive to fight another day. He's a monster, and he has to be stopped, this time for good."

"And you know how to do that?" Deacon asked.

"I hope I will. When the time comes."

Trinity eyed her. "You know, you sound very matter-of-fact about this, but I get the sense it's scaring the hell out of you."

"Good guess." Hollis drew a breath and let it out slowly. "See, I get the sense that either I opened a door into some kind of hell, or somebody—some *thing*—opened it for us. If I did it, I don't know how I did it. If it was opened for us—it's intended to be a trap. And I don't think we get out without destroying the monster."

Deacon drew his gun. "I'm guessing bullets can stop the body, even if we don't know yet what'll kill the monster."

DeMarco said calmly, "We have a few issues to deal with. Either because he knows he's burning out the body he has or because he wants a new toy to play with, Samuel has tried more than once to . . . possess . . . Hollis." He lifted their clasped hands briefly. "I've extended my own shield to offer her some protection, but we've never really tested the limits of that. I can feel whatever he's become, not all the time, just now and then, probing. Looking for a way in."

"I thought you could handle negative energy," Trinity said to Hollis.

"This stuff is . . . more than negative. I can't really explain it because I don't understand it. But I have the very strong feeling that I have to be the one in control if the only way to kill the monster is to . . . channel all that dark energy. If I can. If I let it in."

"No," DeMarco said.

She managed a shaky laugh. "I'm here, Reese. I'm one of only two people we know of who took a direct, unshielded hit from Samuel's dark energy before he died—and lived to tell the tale."

"Hollis—"

"And since then, I've channeled enough dark energy to build half a dozen monsters. What was that, if it wasn't the universe getting me ready for this?"

"I admire your fatalism," Trinity said. "I think."

"I just have to be able to control the energy," Hollis said.

"I'd call that an issue," Deacon said. "Do you know how to be in control?"

"Not yet. This kind of thing has always just sort of . . . come to me. In the past, I mean. Bishop calls them instincts awakened by circumstances. I'm really hoping he's right about that, and whatever I need to know will come to me when I need it to. Until then, my best guess is that we treat this house like it's a piece of the puzzle and just start studying it. Looking for the monster."

Trinity was looking at DeMarco. "There's something else."

He answered readily—though not very comfortingly. "We have absolutely no idea how long we'll be in this place. Or even how long we *can* be and still emerge safely."

Hollis said, "Any spirit realm is meant for spirit energy. Our spirit energy is encased in flesh. We don't belong in this place, in this form. We're like . . . an invading bacteria."

"Seriously?"

"I know how it sounds, believe me. But I'm absolutely certain that this very place will try to eject us. Right now, Samuel's dark energy is pretty focused on me, and it's . . . keeping the rest at a distance. There's other dark energy in this place, energy that's angry, that's suffering, that's . . . crazy.

"Too crazy even for Samuel, or . . . too much for him to control in his present host. Whatever that energy is, it isn't focused on me. It isn't focused at all. Yet. The good news is, everybody's shield seems to be holding. Your auras have that metallic outer edge I associate with repelling energy."

After a moment, Deacon looked at Trinity. "Which one of us said it was a good idea to come here?"

"I don't think it matters anymore. We're here." She looked down at the black dog sitting so calmly beside her. "I do wish I knew what he has to do with all this."

"Maybe we'll find out," Deacon suggested. "Want to flip a coin to determine who goes upstairs and who checks out this floor?"

He saw Hollis's mouth tighten, but her voice was as calm as ever when she said, "Reese and I will take the upstairs; you two take this floor. Stay within sight of each other if you can. And *don't* go into the basement."

TWENTY

"It looks so . . . normal," Hollis said slowly to her partner as they moved along the upstairs hallway from room to room. He was still holding her hand, and she had no desire to pull away.

He understood what she meant. "Not red, not . . . distorted. Perfectly ordinary rooms. As if the people who once lived here could reappear at any moment."

"I hope not," Hollis said.

"See any spirits?" He only knew that he saw none.

"No. And that's what's spooky."

"What do you mean?"

"They're all around us, Reese. I can feel them. It's almost like they're hiding."

"The negative energy?"

"Yeah. They may be too strong for Samuel to handle right now, but crazy as it is, as dark as they are, they're afraid. I can feel that. They must be afraid of him."

"Maybe not," DeMarco said calmly. "Maybe they're afraid of you."

"No, I—"

"Maybe Samuel can control energy, Hollis. But you can transform it. Dark into light, remember? Maybe whatever this dark energy is, whatever they are, they stopped wanting to be anything but dark a long, long time ago."

"Maybe." Her voice was thin.

DeMarco's fingers tightened around hers. He could feel the dark probing of his protective shield. And he could feel her hand shaking. "Hollis? Don't let go."

"I don't know if that's going to be enough." They had followed the landing around and were approaching the closed door of what both remembered was the room behind the left front window.

"You're strong enough, we both know that."

She stopped. "I don't want to open that door."

"Because the black energy is there?"

Hollis shook her head slowly, her gaze fixed on the door. "That's not what I'm afraid of. It's . . . done something. Something special, just for me."

All traces of humor or calm had left Hollis. She was tense, her eyes wide, her hands shaking. Breathing as though she couldn't quite get enough oxygen into her lungs.

"How do you know?"

"I can smell it," she whispered.

It took DeMarco only a moment to understand what she meant. Because he could smell it as well. It was something that jarred old memories inside him. Memories of war, of broken bodies.

Blood. A great deal of blood.

"He thinks he can get in that way. He thinks he can . . . hurt me enough . . . shock me enough . . . frighten me enough . . . so he can get in. That was the plan, Reese. All along."

"To get you?"

"Me first. Not just . . . because we beat him. Because he wants to prove . . . he isn't afraid of mediums, like we thought. He wants to prove . . . he can control one. Me. He wants . . . revenge. He wants . . . power. He wants . . . to make me suffer."

DeMarco's fingers tightened around hers. "Then I say we don't give him what he wants. We can leave, Hollis. Now. Come back later, when the odds are in our favor." He hesitated, then said, "We both know there's nothing alive in that room. No one we can save by opening that door."

"Except me," she whispered.

"Hollis—"

As strong as he was, she was still able to break the grip of his fingers, wrenching her own free and almost stumbling forward to open the bedroom door.

She made a soft, wordless sound DeMarco thought would haunt him until his dying day, standing in the open doorway, stiff, her hands braced on the door frame on either side of her.

He took a step, his hands lifting to her shoulders, looking past her to see.

A bare room with only a mattress on the floor.

A stained mattress. A soaked mattress.

And on it . . .

She had probably been pretty once. But now her naked body was horribly wounded, sliced and gashed. Her legs splayed open to reveal . . . display . . . the butchery done to her.

The blood was still wet, still dripping.

DeMarco had the sickening feeling that if he touched her, he would find her still warm.

It was only then that he looked at her face, and shock tumbled through him. Shock and pain and a sudden brutal realization of what this meant.

What this sacrifice meant.

Hollis was right, this was for her.

Because even though there wasn't so much as a smear of blood on Toby Gilmore's face, it was grievously mutilated.

Her eyes were gone.

Deacon really didn't know what to expect as he and Trinity—and Braden—moved slowly from room to room. He had searched this place, this floor—God, had it only been the day before?—so it was familiar. And it looked so normal.

He had no idea who they were looking for.

What they were looking for.

The old-fashioned house had one room running into another, so they could almost literally circle through. They had circled around to what had been used, clearly, as a front parlor, when Braden stopped, the low rumble of a growl eerie in the otherwise quiet house.

"Look," Trinity said, almost in a whisper.

He followed her gaze upward—and saw the blood seeping through the ceiling. It had been dropping on the rug below, the faded ruby-colored rug that now looked sickeningly fresh and bright just in spots. Large spots.

Where a lot of blood had fallen.

They heard a sound from upstairs, DeMarco calling Hollis's name, then hurried footsteps on the bare wood floors above, and from where they stood in the parlor, they could see Hollis coming down the stairs, one hand on the railing.

When she reached the ground floor, she turned immediately toward them, and they could see her face was white, her eyes wide and dark and unblinking, her mouth set. Her movements were stiff, as though every joint ached.

DeMarco was right behind her, his face not impassive as it had always been, as Hollis's was now, but twisted into an expression of pain so deep that Deacon wanted to look away.

"Who?" Trinity demanded hoarsely.

Hollis stopped just a step inside the doorway,

her gaze going to the bright red spots on the faded rug. She didn't look up at the ceiling.

"I . . . recognized her from . . . her picture . . . in the file." Her voice was deadened. "Toby Gilmore."

Trinity sucked in a breath, her own face whitening. "Son of a bitch. That sorry son of a bitch . . ."

"Too kind."

They all turned, even Braden, and then they froze. Even Braden.

He stood in the doorway that led to a dining room, an ordinary-looking man in his early thirties. Not too handsome, but not plain. Pleasant features. But his eyes . . .

They were insane.

And the contraption wrapped around him was insane. They could all see the explosives, enough to blow up the house, to destroy them, enough to put a hole in the side of the mountain. They could see in the hand he held up a dead man's switch.

"Sonny," Trinity said. "Sonny Lenox. I heard you were dead." Slowly, she raised her weapon, aiming it at him.

"I was." His voice was incongruously pleasant. If he even noticed her gun pointed at him, Deacon's, and DeMarco's big silver gun, he didn't appear to be the least bit disturbed. "Well, almost. Brain-dead, they said. If there'd been family to pull the plug, they probably would have pulled it. But then I woke up."

"You didn't wake up." Hollis's voice was still oddly deadened, flat, her eyes still very, very dark as she stared at him. "Samuel got you. Does he let you speak for yourself now and then?"

Sonny Lenox looked faintly troubled. "I have these blackouts," he said in a puzzled tone. "And when I wake up . . . I think I've done things. Bad things. And I'm tired. I've been tired a long time. So it's going to be over." He lifted the hand holding the dead man's switch a bit higher. "It's going to be over. I'm going to be able to rest."

"You killed Toby," Trinity said.

He blinked. "No. I loved Toby. I remember that. I loved her . . . and she broke up with me. So I left. But I still loved her."

Stark, Trinity said, "That's her blood dripping from the ceiling."

He looked up, frowned, then returned his gaze to her face. He looked at each one of them in turn, finally settling on Hollis. "You're the one," he said.

"Am I?" No expression on her face. No emotion in her voice.

"Yes. You're to leave now. Go outside. Go to the church. Wait there."

"What am I waiting for?"

"For him."

Hollis shook her head. "No. He'll come to me. Here."

"But I'm going to blow up here," Sonny Lenox

said reasonably. "And get rid of these others. He wants you, though. Maybe he'll let you sleep more than he let me sleep. You should ask him about that."

"No."

He blinked. "What?"

"No. I'm not going to the church. I'm not moving. If he wants me, he'll have to come get me."

Perhaps not surprisingly, Deacon felt it first, flinching as a wave of dark rage battered his shields.

Without looking at him, Hollis said, "Samuel was a psychic, Deacon. And he could project. Shore up your shields."

Deacon wondered how it could be Hollis giving him that advice, how she could look so calm, even if DeMarco's shield was still wrapped around her—

And then he recognized something bleak in DeMarco's expression, and he realized that not only was the other man no longer extending his shield to protect Hollis, but he no longer had to.

She was protecting herself. Whatever horrific things had been done to Toby Gilmore, something about her death had changed Hollis. It had given her a shield.

"Samuel," she said, her voice suddenly soft, singsong, like a child calling another to play. "Come out, come out, wherever you are."

"Hollis," DeMarco warned.

She didn't seem to hear him. "Come on, Samuel. Haven't we danced around each other long enough? Aren't you tired of it? I know I am."

Sonny Lenox opened his mouth to say something—and then his face twisted, his skin reddened, the mad eyes glittered with a savage new intensity.

"There he is," Hollis said softly. "There's the late, great Reverend Samuel."

"Bitch," he snarled. "You think I won't let this go? Won't blow this sorry excuse for a man all the way to hell? It won't hurt me. I'm energy. I'm *power.*"

Trinity said, "Maybe so. But that sorry excuse for a man isn't exactly in control of your little bomb."

The hand of Sonny Lenox lifted another inch—and then began to tremble. It shook as though a much greater force prevented it from doing its will.

Deacon looked at Trinity, saw something in her eyes, an intent focus he recognized, and murmured, "I'll be damned. You're telekinetic."

"Comes in handy sometimes," she said, clearly able to both prevent Samuel/Sonny Lenox from detonating the bomb and speak with no trace of strain in her voice. "Braden—truck."

The dog, who had been still and silent through it all, immediately obeyed his mistress, slipping from the room and the house to go and wait for her in the Jeep.

Samuel wasn't nearly so compliant.

"Whore," he muttered, rage building visibly in that once-human face. "Filthy bitch. I'll—"

"You'll what?" she taunted. "Invade me? Possess me? I know what evil looks like. I know *exactly* what it is. What you are. I told you so the other day in the church. When I first saw you."

Hollis said, "We all know what you are. You can't deceive us, and that means you can't possess us. Any of us." She smiled. "Especially not me. You couldn't handle me, Samuel. On your best day on earth—or in hell—you could never handle *me*."

It might not have worked. As Deacon said later with some feeling, there were so many forces and personalities pulling at Samuel in those few eternal moments, it was a sheer miracle both he *and* the bomb didn't blow off the top of the mountain.

Instead, startling at least two of the people in the room, Samuel let out a tremendous roar of frustrated rage—and what looked, literally, like a thousand black snakes shot from his body, reaching out for the four people before him.

Hollis moved only then, taking three quick steps, putting herself out in front of the others, her hands half lifted as though forming even more of a barrier. And even as his furious roar became one of pain, the many snakes writhed together and struck Hollis squarely in the middle of her body.

She never flinched.

It lasted only seconds, though to those watching it seemed much, much longer. A lifetime.

The blackness surged or was pulled into Hollis, and as the others watched, her aura became visible.

There were colors at first, bright and clear, a pulsing rainbow wrapping her body. And then the colors shifted, sparkled, and suddenly her aura was pure white and silver, extending out from her body at least two feet, an incredibly bright shimmer of clean, positive energy.

The last of the dark energy snaked out of the body of Sonny Lenox and into Hollis, and they could all hear the hissing and crackling and popping, smell the ozone as though lightning had struck too close for comfort.

For an endless moment longer, they were a frozen tableau, only Hollis's aura moving, gradually fading as it drifted outward from her body and vanished into nothing.

Hollis took a step back, shaky for the first time, and DeMarco was there, his gun holstered, his arms around her.

"You two got this?" he said to the others, nodding toward the apparently still frozen and now blank-eyed Sonny Lenox.

"We're good," Trinity said. "Take her out of here."

"Don't waste time," DeMarco told her. "There's other darkness here besides what he was, hiding for now. You don't want to be here when it all comes out to play."

DeMarco didn't hesitate a moment longer. He lifted Hollis into his arms, cradling her slight body easily, and got her out of there.

Deacon said to Trinity, "We've got this?"

"Yeah." She holstered her weapon, then walked over to the still man and carefully pried the dead man's switch from his hand. Holding it, she stepped behind him, and in no more than a couple of minutes was unfastening the explosive-laden vest from him and stepping into the dining room to lay it carefully on the table.

"Wait, the switch—"

"It's okay," Trinity told him calmly. "I worked the bomb squad in Atlanta. The only thing remotely fancy about his bomb was the dead man's switch, and they're actually pretty easy. It's safe now. Though I won't feel entirely comfortable until it's all dismantled and out of here, if Reese was right about that other dark energy."

She glanced toward the ceiling, and her face tightened as she watched the blood still dripping. Another friend dead. From Hollis's reaction and all the blood . . . A friend butchered.

I'm sorry, Toby. I should have kept you safe.

Deacon, unaware of her thoughts, was still warily eyeing Sonny Lenox. "What about him?"

333

"The only thing holding him up," she said, "is me." She turned her head, looked at Sonny Lenox—and he dropped like a stone to the wide plank floor.

"He's dead?"

"Arguable whether he's been alive, at least for a long time. But, yes, he's dead. And this time there's no EMS squad and trauma unit nearby to put his body on life support." She looked down at Lenox with a singular lack of remorse in her eyes. "This time, both Sonny Lenox and Samuel are dead for the last time."

It was cold outside, and a few flakes of snow were beginning to drift downward. DeMarco carried Hollis to their SUV. Instead of placing her in the front, he opened the back door and set her carefully on the seat so that she faced him as he stood in the open door.

"Hollis?"

Her gaze was looking past him, through him, miles away. And her eyes were still dark.

"Hollis, look at me."

Nothing changed. DeMarco reached out, surrounding her face with his hands. He felt her flinch back, as if she would have pulled away, but his hands were large, and though he made sure she wouldn't feel trapped, he also held her steadily.

Something flickered in her eyes, and she went still again.

DeMarco hesitated, then said quietly, "Now you know. Now you know how bad it had to be before your mind felt the need to build walls, a shield. Because you've got one, Hollis. But it's not for you to hide inside. It's not for you to use to shut out the people who care about you. It's only . . . to give you a private, safe place to be. Sometimes."

Again, something flickered in her dark, dark eyes.

"He tried to hurt you, and he did. But you won, Hollis. He's dead and you're alive. You won."

"You . . . don't understand," she whispered.

"Yes," he said. "I do. I understand that you've survived more horror and agony than any human being should ever have to bear. I wish I could take away the pain, at least. But, Hollis, everything that's happened to you has made you the woman you are today, right now. The bad as well as the good. You know that."

"I know . . . I didn't want to remember. I didn't want to think about the monster who took my eyes. But when I saw her—her face. When I saw her eyes were gone, I *remembered*." She drew a sudden, deep breath, and her eyes began to lighten.

And fill with tears.

DeMarco didn't hesitate. He stepped closer and pulled her into his arms. She was stiff for just a moment, resisting. And then her new walls . . . slowly came down, and her arms went around him.

And for the first time, Hollis Templeton cried for everything she had lost.

And everything she had gained.

EPILOGUE

"What I want to know," Deacon asked some time later as they all gathered in the conference room of the sheriff's department, "is when the parsonage stopped being red. Because it was red when we went in, and white when we came out."

"My guess would be that when Samuel finally died—really died this time—the red vanished," Hollis said, sounding tired but steady. "It was his bubble of energy we were in."

"Not another dimension?" Trinity asked.

"I don't think so. No way to be sure, of course, but I think he used some of his own energy, combined it with the weird natural energy up there, and . . . built himself a home. He was enough in control of it to open a door and let us in."

"That wasn't you?" Trinity asked.

"No. He'd already figured out he couldn't get to me outside his bubble, but he believed he could once he got me inside. Especially after I saw . . . her."

DeMarco's arms tightened around her. He was

actually sitting on a big, slate-topped desk that had been shoved into one corner of the conference room, and Hollis stood between his knees, leaning back against him.

She looked very comfortable.

"Maybe he thought the shock would do it," she continued steadily. "Seeing another woman dead the way I was supposed to have died years ago. Seeing what he did to her. But that didn't make me vulnerable to him. If anything, it made me stronger."

"I think we all saw evidence of that," Trinity said, her tone a little dry.

"You were the surprise," Deacon said to her. "A born telekinetic?"

"Umm. Runs in the family."

Somewhat indignant, he said, "And you didn't think we needed to know that?"

Smiling faintly but unapologetic, Trinity said, "It's always been an ace up my sleeve. I use it sparingly, to say the least."

Hollis looked at her. "Is that why Bishop hasn't recruited you?"

"I've tried, believe me." He came into the conference room along with Miranda, and it probably spoke volumes that no one was surprised to see him.

Mildly, Trinity said, "I like small-town life. Especially when there isn't a resurrected maniac killer murdering my friends."

Hollis looked at Miranda and asked, "Where are the others?"

"Tying up loose ends in the mountains. We found the last two girls before she could kill them."

"Ruth?" DeMarco guessed. "She was always his most devoted follower. I always thought she'd probably kill for him if he asked."

"I gather she was supposed to kill the last two while he was busy here in Sociable," Miranda replied. "To keep most of the heat off him here as long as possible. He'd killed the others, but not even Samuel could be two places at once. He needed to be here. He also needed those girls dead. What he didn't count on was that Ruth was convinced she could persuade the girls to become followers of Samuel."

"That doesn't surprise me," DeMarco said. "Though I do wonder . . . Did she recognize him despite his shiny new body or because he went looking for her and proved himself?"

"The latter," Bishop said. "She was still in North Carolina, so easy to find. And apparently all he had to do was touch her to cause her to remember everything."

"Yeah, that was his thing," DeMarco said with clear distaste.

Miranda was looking at Hollis steadily. "You aren't okay," she said.

"No," Hollis agreed, "but I will be. Now."

DeMarco's arms tightened around her, and Hollis smiled at Miranda. "I'll be fine."

"About damned time," Miranda responded solemnly.

"Yeah, now you can spend your time and energy worrying about some of the others. I'm sure there's enough to occupy your time."

"True enough."

"What I want to know," Deacon said, his voice a bit louder than, perhaps, he intended, "is what about Braden?"

Trinity looked at him, brows rising. "What about him?"

"Oh, come on. If he's an ordinary dog, I'm—I'm—" Apparently, he couldn't think of anything weird enough, and settled for a glare.

"Ask Bishop," Trinity suggested.

The SCU unit chief smiled faintly, the expression making his very handsome but scarred face look more dangerous than amused. "You figured that out, huh?" he asked Trinity.

"I know you're all kinds of subtle and Machiavellian," she told him gravely, "but a strange, beautifully trained, and eerily prescient dog shows up on my front porch just when I'm thinking about getting another one—something I had recently said to you—and I'm not supposed to guess he's here because of you?"

"He's here because of you," Bishop said firmly.

Deacon scowled at him. "What'd you do, ask him where he wanted to live?"

"Yeah," Bishop said.

Deacon blinked. "Didn't know you were telepathic with animals."

"Neither did I. Until I crossed paths with Braden."

Miranda spoke up then to say, "An old friend contacted me. He's a sheriff in a small Tennessee town. Braden turned up a stray, Alex recognized there was something . . . unusual . . . about him, and figured he should probably be with us."

"Why isn't he?" Deacon asked.

"I told you," Bishop said. "He wanted to live in a small town, and he wanted to be a sheriff's dog. Alex already has three; Braden is the sort who prefers to be an only dog. I thought of Trinity and her desire to get another dog and—"

Braden got out of his chair, walked across the conference table—neatly avoiding numerous files—and sat down, offering Bishop a paw.

Bishop accepted it. "And he did something like this. Clearly, he's happy here."

Braden's tail swept across the polished surface of the table, sending a file skidding toward the edge. Nobody minded.

"I'm not a telepath," Trinity reminded him.

"Actually, you're a latent telepath," Bishop told her. "And your energy signature is the closest to Callie Davis's I've ever come across. Since she can communicate with animals, dogs in particular, it only made sense to me that you might be able to as well. With time and practice."

She eyed him. "Like Braden, I prefer small-town life. Don't think you're going to rope either one of us into joining the team."

"It never crossed my mind."

Trinity made a rude noise, but all she said was, "Well, for Braden and for all the other help, I'm more than grateful. I have friends to bury and a town to soothe, but I know it could have been a hell of a lot worse than it was.

"Look, I know you all must be exhausted—and we've got a storm about to hit. You could try to make it to the air strip, but I have my doubts about that, and these roads are really mean when they're slippery. So why don't you all stay at the hotel for the duration. I'm sure you could use a few days off. Rest, good food, interesting people."

Her gaze returned to Bishop. "And we can talk a little more about just how much you really know about Braden."

Before Bishop could respond, the black dog sitting on the conference table did, startling them with two sharp barks.

"Two barks for *yes?*" Trinity asked politely.

Braden barked twice more.

Deacon stared at him. "I'm trying to think of a *no* question. One bark for *no,* Braden. Can we make it to the air strip before the storm hits?"

Braden barked.

Once.

"You're sure?"

Two barks.

To Bishop, Trinity said, "We *really* need to talk about him."

Braden barked. Twice.

AUTHOR'S NOTE

Please indulge me as I take a few pages to speak to you about my second vocation in this life: animal rescue, in particular dogs and cats. And about the inspiration for one of the main characters in *Haunted*.

The canine character of Braden in this story is based on a real shelter dog with that name and likeness who was handed a few lousy breaks in life—and then was granted a second chance.

No one can know, really, why Braden ended up where he did at a young age, not a puppy but barely an adult (most dogs in this country never live to see their third birthday). Sometimes a stray is brought in, with absolutely no one able to provide information on the animal. Quite often, dogs and cats are "surrendered" by owners; sometimes an owner-surrendered dog comes with a story, but more often than not, background information is at best incomplete, and human reasoning for the abandonment is, to some, inconceivable because we view our pets as lifelong companions.

But sometimes a reason is provided, and it rarely has anything to do with the dog's temperament or behavior. A gift puppy grew up and wasn't "cute" anymore. There was a divorce.

Someone went off to school. There was a marriage. Someone new came into a relationship with their own better-loved dog or medical issues, such as allergies, that made having a dog in the house a problem. There was a new baby. There was a move. A change of job. There was something that made the poor dog an inconvenience. And the bewildered, frightened dog is ripped from, probably, the only home he's ever known and abandoned by those he trusted, surrendered to a shelter or pound, often guiltily and with totally unrealistic "hopes" that he will somehow land in a better home instead of being euthanized, which is far, far more likely to be his fate today in twenty-first-century America.

Especially if he's a dog like Braden.

Braden had three strikes against him. He was a mix most commonly recognized and referred to as a pit bull, or pit bull terrier, the most misunderstood and mistreated dog "breed" in this country; he was black, the coat color most overlooked in shelter dogs *and* cats by potential adopters; and he was abandoned at a small, high-kill, county-run rural facility too often forced to kill healthy, adoptable animals simply for lack of room and funds.

His chances of making it out of that stressful, frightening, lonely place alive were virtually nil.

But this particular shelter had and still has a highly active group of volunteers (Clifford's

Army Rescue Extravaganza—CARE—in Shelby, NC; Facebook.com/Cliffords.Army) who work hard to see to it that as many dogs and cats as possible are rescued, or at least have a better shot. They take attractive photos of each animal and offer its story and information about its personality as observed by them. They work with rescues to help, sometimes providing temporary fosters until a rescue can make arrangements within its own group.

As part of a growing network of animal advocates and rescue groups using social media such as Facebook and Twitter, CARE posted Braden's picture and information online so that people all across the area and, indeed, the country, who would never walk into that facility, could see him and read his story. They urged friends, family, and other advocates to spread the word, share Braden and his story, and help whenever possible by pledging funds or donating to fund-raising accounts to help cash-strapped rescue organizations with the financial resources necessary to save him from certain death—to have him vetted, neutered, and living safely with a foster or the rescue until his Forever Home could be found.

In Braden's case, as with some other lucky shelter dogs and cats, a sponsor stepped forward with the offer to fully fund Braden's rescue. The sponsor committed to covering all costs associated with his rescue, from the fee to "pull" him from the shelter to vetting and, if necessary, boarding costs until he could be placed or fostered. Even with that guarantee, it doesn't always end happily with a successful rescue; some shelters simply lack the resources to keep dogs and cats very long, and most rescues are overwhelmed by the sheer volume of abandoned dogs and cats in both cities and rural areas. And there are never enough fosters stepping up to provide temporary homes for these pets while permanent homes for them are sought.

Braden was very lucky. He was rescued by Sassy Paws Angel Rescue out of Denver, North Carolina. (For more information on this rescue, contact them at:

Facebook.com/Sassypawsangelrescue
or Sassypawsangelrescue.com
or sassypawsrescue@yahoo.com.)

He was literally on death row, as dogs and cats are on death row at "shelters" across the country every single day. And without the tireless efforts of countless people who care about those shelter animals, Braden would have been led or dragged on that last walk to his execution—and still in many "shelters", today, that means a cruel and terrifying slow death in a gas chamber.

And there is nothing in the least humane about that. (Want to help stop this madness? Check out the American Humane site for the facts on euthanasia, or Google it. Go to Facebook.com/

TakeAction.BanAnimalGasChambers, or Google your own state to find out what the law is and what you can do to protest and help change inhumane practices; sometimes just signing a petition or sending an e-mail to one of your representatives in state or federal government can make a difference.)

As I said, Braden was one of the lucky ones, and because I've seen too many dogs like Braden become tragic statistics, I felt I had to speak out in a positive way about both pit bulls as a "breed" (I have one myself) and shelter rescues (which all three of my dogs are), and to encourage responsible pet ownership. If you check out the pages on my website (KayHooper.com) devoted to my pets, you'll see several reminders and pleas to have your pets spayed and neutered and to adopt from rescues and shelters rather than buying from pet stores (which supports the horrific business of puppy mills unless you're *certain* the store offers only rescue animals for adoption, not purchase). You'll see on my personal Facebook page (Facebook.com/kay.hooper.5) that I advocate and network continually for shelter animals from facilities both local and across the country. (My author Facebook page can be found at Facebook.com/BishopPage if you prefer to have information only about my books and writing career and news of upcoming projects.)

You should know that in all the decades I've

been writing, this is the first time I have asked my publisher for these extra few pages to advocate for a cause I feel deeply about; the first time I've sent photos of a dog (provided by Sassy Paws; thank you, ladies!) to my publisher and asked that he be included in the cover design.

The dog Braden in *Haunted* is the character he needed to be in this story, as all my characters are who they need to be. The shelter rescue Braden, who passed a temperament test with flying colors and, as I write this, is living happily with his foster while the rescue searches for his Forever Home, is as most shelter dogs tend to be—a nice dog and a grateful one.

He is, in the words of his foster, a "precious soul." He loves to hug, cuddle, and give kisses (common pit bull traits), and plays happily with his foster's family members, especially shepherd mix Sissy and puppies. He loves puppies. He loves just about everyone he meets. He also loves being with his humans, observing all intently with great interest, and dearly loves his food. And his treats.

Braden is still young, still learning, and off to a very promising second chance in life.

Because Braden is safe. A group of people, most of them strangers to each other, cared enough to work on his behalf, and because of that, Braden has a happy life in store for him.

And doesn't every dog and cat deserve that?

Special Crimes Unit Agent Bios
(in order of appearance)

HOLLIS TEMPLETON—FBI SPECIAL CRIMES UNIT

Job: Special Agent, profiler

Adept: Medium—with "bells and whistles." Perhaps because of the extreme trauma of Hollis's psychic awakening (see *Touching Evil*), her abilities tend to evolve and change much more rapidly than those of many other agents and operatives, with some entirely new abilities triggered by the stresses and/or events of an investigation. Even as she struggles to cope with her mediumistic abilities, each investigation in which she's involved seems to bring about another "fun new toy" for the agent, though the events of *Hostage* may have stabilized her abilities.

Appearances: *Touching Evil, Sense of Evil, Blood Dreams, Blood Sins, Blood Ties, Haven, Hostage, Haunted*

REESE DEMARCO—FBI SPECIAL CRIMES UNIT

Job: Special Agent, pilot, military-trained sniper; has specialized in the past in deep-cover assignments, some long term

Adept: An "open" telepath, he is able to read a wide range of people. He possesses an apparently unique double shield, which sometimes contains the unusually high amount of sheer energy he produces. He also possesses something Bishop has dubbed a "primal ability": He always knows when a gun is pointed at or near him, or if other imminent danger threatens.

Appearances: *Blood Sins, Blood Ties, Haven, Hostage, Haunted*

MIRANDA BISHOP—FBI SPECIAL CRIMES UNIT

Job: Special Agent, investigator, profiler, black belt in karate, and a sharpshooter

Adept: Touch-telepath, seer, remarkably powerful and possesses unusual control, particularly in a highly developed shield capable of protecting herself psychically, a shield she's able to extend beyond herself to protect others. Shares abilities with her husband, due to their intense emotional connection, and together they far exceed the scale developed by the SCU to measure psychic abilities.

Appearances: *Out of the Shadows, Touching Evil, Whisper of Evil, Sense of Evil, Hunting Fear, Chill of Fear, Blood Dreams, Blood Sins, Blood Ties, Hostage, Haunted*

DEACON JAMES—FBI SPECIAL CRIMES UNIT

Job: Special Agent

Adept: Empath. A rare male empathy, Deacon has a solid shield and is seldom blindsided by the emotions of others; even when he "tunes in," he is able to tap into less than half of the people he encounters. His is an ability he was born with, not one triggered later in life, so he has fair control.

Appearances: *Haunted*

NOAH BISHOP—FBI SPECIAL CRIMES UNIT

Job: Unit Chief, profiler, pilot, sharpshooter, and trained in martial arts

Adept: An exceptionally powerful touch-telepath, he also shares with his wife a strong precognitive ability, the deep emotional link between them making them, together, far exceed the limits of the scale developed by the FBI to measure psychic talents. Also possesses an "ancillary" ability of enhanced senses (hearing, sight, scent), which he has trained other agents to use as well. Whether present in the flesh or not, Bishop always knows what's going on with his agents in the field. Always.

Appearances: *Stealing Shadows, Hiding in the Shadows, Out of the Shadows, Touching Evil, Whisper of Evil, Sense of Evil, Hunting Fear, Chill of Fear, Sleeping with Fear, Blood Dreams, Blood Sins, Blood Ties, Haven, Hostage, Haunted*

TONY HARTE—FBI SPECIAL CRIMES UNIT

Job: Special Agent, profiler

Adept: Telepath. Not especially strong, but able to pick up vibes from people, particularly emotions.

Appearances: *Out of the Shadows, Touching Evil, Whisper of Evil, Sense of Evil, Hunting Fear, Chill of Fear, Sleeping with Fear, Blood Dreams, Blood Sins, Blood Ties, Haven, Hostage, Haunted*

PSYCHIC TERMS AND ABILITIES

(as Classified/Defined by Bishop's Team and by Haven)

Adept: The general term used to label any functional psychic; the specific ability is much more specialized.

Clairvoyance: The ability to know things, to pick up bits of information seemingly out of thin air.

Dream-projecting: The ability to enter another's dreams.

Dream-walking: The ability to invite/draw others into one's own dreams.

Empath: An empath experiences the emotions of others, often up to and including physical pain and injuries.

Healing: The ability to heal injuries to self or others, often but not always ancillary to mediumistic abilities.

Healing empathy: An empath/healer has the ability to not only feel but also heal the pain/injury of another.

Latent: The term used to describe unawakened or inactive abilities, as well as to describe a psychic not yet aware of being psychic.

Mediumistic: Having the medium's ability to communicate with the dead.

Precognition: A seer or precog has the ability to correctly predict future events.

Psychometric: The ability to pick up impressions or information from touching objects.

Regenerative: The ability to heal one's own injuries/illnesses, even those considered by medical experts to be lethal or fatal. (A classification unique to one SCU operative and considered separate from a healer's abilities.)

Spider sense: The ability to enhance one's normal senses (sight, hearing, smell, etc.) through concentration and the focusing of one's own mental and physical energy.

Telekinesis: The ability to move objects with the mind.

Telepathic mind control: The ability to influence/control others through mental focus and effort; an extremely rare ability.

Telepathy (touch and non-touch or open): The ability to pick up thoughts from others. Some telepaths only receive, while others have the ability to send thoughts. A few are capable of both, usually due to an emotional connection with the other person.

UNNAMED ABILITIES INCLUDE:

The ability to see into time, to view events in the past, present, and future without being or having been there physically while the events transpired.

The ability to see another person's aura, or energy field.

The ability to channel energy usefully as either a defensive or an offensive tool or weapon.

BISHOP/SPECIAL CRIMES UNIT TIMELINE

For those readers who wish to "place" each of these stories in time, I should explain that—in order to not age my characters too quickly—I have not set these books in real time, but in "story" time. Roughly speaking, each trilogy within the series takes place within the space of a year or a bit less.

In simple terms, if you look at the information offered below, you'll see that from the time the Special Crimes Unit was formally introduced in *Out of the Shadows* until the events in this story, *Haunted*, only about four years have passed *within the series*. (The Special Crimes Unit was being built and developed by Bishop for about three or four years prior to that, but in *Out of the Shadows*, the story of the unit, of Bishop and his team, really begins.)

Stealing Shadows—February

Hiding in the Shadows—October/November

YEAR ONE:
Out of the Shadows—January (SCU formally introduced)
Touching Evil—November

YEAR TWO:
Whisper of Evil—March
Sense of Evil—June
Hunting Fear—September

YEAR THREE:
Chill of Fear—April
Sleeping with Fear—July
Blood Dreams—October

YEAR FOUR:
Blood Sins—January
Blood Ties—April
Haven—July
Hostage—October

YEAR FIVE:
Haunted—February

Center Point Large Print
600 Brooks Road / PO Box 1
Thorndike, ME 04986-0001 USA

(207) 568-3717

US & Canada:
1 800 929-9108
www.centerpointlargeprint.com

DATE DUE

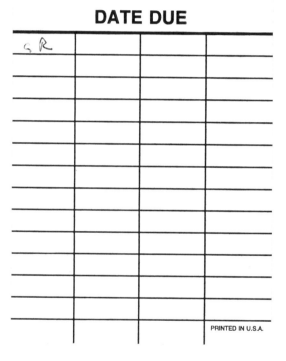

G R			
			PRINTED IN U.S.A.